BACKSPIN

ALLISON RAYNE

Cover design by Allison Rayne
Edited by Emilie Mortati

This novel is a work of fiction. Names, characters, businesses, places, and incidents in this book are either the product of the author's imagination or used in a fictitious manner. Any resemblance to actual persons, living or dead, is purely coincidental.

ISBN (paperback) : 979-8-9902897-4-1
ISBN (ebook) : 979-8-9902897-5-8

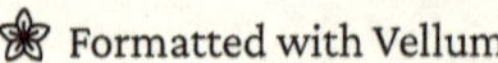

For the nostalgic ones.

May you find the strength to let go of what no longer serves you, so what's meant for you can find its way.

AUTHOR'S NOTE

Backspin is the second book in the West Brook series, but can be read as a standalone. The first is called Getting Pickled.

If this is your first time reading one of my books, hello! I truly hope you enjoy. If you did read Getting Pickled and have been waiting on the edge of your seat for Angie and Asher's story, thank you and welcome back!

(Love you, miss you!)

For timeline purposes, Backspin begins around the final chapter (pre-epilogue) of Getting Pickled, when the characters are together in London.

CONTENT WARNINGS

Backspin is a spicy, romantic story, and includes some heavy, complex themes that I want readers to be aware of.

- Explicit language
- Explicit (and consensual) sex scenes
- Childhood emotional neglect
- Parental death (heart attack) and grief
- Discussion of car accident death
- Toxic relationships
- Mention of marriage separation, infidelity, and divorce (<u>not</u> main characters)
- Alcohol and marijuana consumption

All dogs in this story remain alive and happy at the end, as always!

1

ANGIE

You can't hurt me. I was once broken up with over text by a guy named Chad, who said things like "supposebly" and "you remind me of my sister."

He did have the most perfectly proportioned penis I've ever encountered, however. His PPP was his one redeeming quality.

I've always believed in getting my happily ever after, but each year it gets harder and harder. I'm pretty sure you only get so many chances for love in one lifetime, and I hope to god at twenty-six, I haven't used mine all up. If it's meant to happen, it will, so I try to focus on living in the moment and having fun with no strings attached.

I'm a sucker for a good love story, and can't help but get excited when others find their happy ending. I'm watching it play out right now for my best friend, Willow, and her boyfriend, Luca, who flew out here to London to surprise her and confess his undying love.

The three of us live back in the States, but Willow and I came out here a few weeks ago for a fun getaway after their unfortunate and dramatic breakup. Before he arrived, we had been filling our days traveling around the UK exploring and meeting new people. It's the most fun I've had in a long time, but unfortunately, it's about time to get back to reality.

"Can't believe you're leaving me for some guy," I say with a pout, looking around the hotel room we had been sharing.

"Well, I can't believe how much has changed since we got here," Willow says, stepping closer. Her tone uncharacteristically gentle. "I haven't had a chance to thank you for everything you've done for me. Getting me to come out here, conspiring with Luca."

"Aw, don't get all sappy now. You would've done the same for me."

She pulls me in for a tight hug, resting her chin on the top of my head as I wrap my arms around her torso. I cherish these moments with her because I know how guarded she is, only letting a select few people see her vulnerable like this.

"Love you, Angie," she says, her cheek smushed into my hair.

"Love you more."

Just then, my phone buzzes in my back pocket, and I pull away with a smile as I answer my phone.

"Hi, Mom!"

"Hey, baby!" The sound of her voice is like being wrapped in a warm blanket.

"Just checking in. How is everyone out there?"

"We're good. Having our farewell dinner tonight to see off Willow and Luca."

"Oh, wonderful. Those two are so good for each other, I'm so happy for them."

"Yeah, me too," I say softly, mindlessly picking a piece of lint off my pants.

"You okay?" she asks after a beat of silence. I swear this woman misses nothing.

"I'm good, Mom. Promise. I love you."

"I love you too, honey. And tell Willow she can come get the dog whenever she wants. I'll be around." I smile. What would we do without her?

Dropping my phone back in my purse, I remember how grateful I am for the people in my life. I know I don't *need* a man to be happy, but it sure is lonely coming home to an empty townhouse every night.

"Ready to go meet Wesley?" I ask. "He told me about this cute little Italian place he wants to take us to."

"Yeah, let me grab Luca and we'll meet you downstairs."

The hotel lobby is enormous. Ultra modern and sleek, with sharp geometric shapes and bright pops of blue and gold. After staying here for a few weeks, I've really come to love this place. At first it felt too trendy, like I didn't belong here, but soon I found it to be rather cheerful and lively.

I immediately spot my brother, Wesley, at the hotel bar. Dirty blond hair, dressed in fitted black slacks, a trim Kelly green button-up with the sleeves rolled up his forearms, and talking with some beautiful woman with long brown hair. I can't help but laugh to myself. Of course, everyone I know is getting lucky except me. Unless I want to have a one-night stand with some hot British dude I'll never see again.

Which...honestly, wouldn't be the worst thing. But I'm not sure I'm up for it right now. The flings and the one-night stands are not as fun as they used to be. Maybe I'm getting too old for all that.

When Wesley spots me at the entrance, he turns to whisper something to the hot brunette, who could easily be a supermodel, and she walks away with a sly grin. I feel a tiny pang of guilt for cock-blocking him, but it's short-lived. He'll get over it.

"Hey, sis!" he says brightly, opening his arms for a hug. "Long time no see!"

I let him wrap me in a tight hug, my arms finding his back. He has always been a kind and affectionate older brother. I know I lucked out with my family, despite everything we've been through.

"I saw you two hours ago, you freak."

Wesley is the whole reason we were even able to do this vacation. He oversees management for this hotel—one of many out here—and his company has been opening up several new resorts around the world. He's doing pretty well for himself. Thankfully, he has wielded that power to hook us up with all the best places to stay.

He pulls away and hands me a glass of white wine as I take a seat at the bar. "Here you go, m'lady."

I nod my thanks as I take it from him. "Hey, who was that woman you were talking to? She's gorgeous. You didn't have to turn her away just for me." I take a sip.

"Oh, that's just Nelle, my secretary."

I choke on the liquid and immediately start coughing. It takes me a full minute to recover, but when I do, I level him with a searing glare.

"What?" he says with feigned innocence.

"Please. Your secretary? You're obviously sleeping with her."

"No! We have a very...professional relationship." He brings his glass of beer to his lips to hide his growing smile as he leans an elbow on the bar.

"Yeah, I bet."

As more and more people squeeze into the bar area, I

glance at my watch, wondering when Willow and Luca will show up. Hopefully they're not fucking...again.

Wesley tips his drink at me. "At least you're not still dating choad—I mean Chad. What's it been, like two months now? Seeing anyone else lately?"

My eyes dart away, and I take another sip of my wine, slowly shaking my head. I aim for indifference, but Wesley isn't buying it, of course. He's just like Mom, always observing. I shift on the bar stool.

"I'm sorry, Ang. You're not still hung up on him though, are you?"

I snort. "Oh god no, he was the worst."

He nods, raising an eyebrow. "So you're good?"

"I'm good, I swear. I've got great friends and a great life. What more could I ask for? I just want to be around people I can have fun with, you know?"

He clinks his glass with mine. "One hundred percent. How about this...tonight after dinner, I'll take you out on the town. And if you happen to see someone you 'just want to have fun with,' I'll be your wingman, just like old times."

My chest warms, and I can't help but smile. He always knows how to cheer me up, and he is a notoriously good wingman.

"Sounds perfect."

2

ASHER

Sitting at an outdoor cafe in London, I sip on my cappuccino and catch up on work emails. Bright street lamps and strings of market lights illuminate the sidewalk as throngs of people pass by.

It's unseasonably warm for a mid-November evening, so I left my trenchcoat back at the hotel to enjoy this weather while I'm still here. I only have a few more days before this trip finally ends and I can go back home to Indiana.

Part of my job as a travel agent is to scour the world for the best places to recommend to our clients, put together itineraries of hot spots and hidden gems people might want to visit, and sample as much of the local cuisine as I possibly can.

This particular cafe I've come back to many times. It's comforting.

For the past five years, this job has been something I loved and was actually good at. Even if this is somewhat of a dying industry. But for whatever reason, I just haven't been enjoying it as much as I used to. Traveling used to be my favorite pastime, allowing me to reconnect with myself and explore different countries and cultures. I've always been fascinated with how other people live, and could listen to someone tell their life story all day. There's something so powerful in connecting with someone with completely different experiences and views from your own.

Anthony Bourdain's *Parts Unknown* is still one of my favorite shows of all time.

Sarah rarely came on these trips with me because she hated flying, and her ideal vacation was sitting on a beach with a good book. Not that I don't enjoy that once in a while, but she always said I could never sit still. I want to be out trying something new, like eating at some hole-in-the-wall in Italy, and learning about someone's great-great-grandfather's winery.

So I would often go alone.

Just like in two days I'll be traveling alone...on my birthday.

As I scroll my phone, a meeting invite from my boss pops up, titled "Check In" for after Thanksgiving. Well that's not vague at all. Bryn is probably looking at my numbers for this past year and wondering if she should let me go from the agency. I wouldn't blame her.

The agency I work for is a small team, and I love all the people I work with. My clientele is split between corporate or business trips and young, single people. I'm great at putting together big adventure packages; however, I know I'm missing out on a lot of opportunities to work with families and couples. Mostly because the vacations I always take have only been me. It's all I really know.

I shoot her a quick email, detailing all the great stuff I put together from this trip, hoping it will deter any thoughts from firing me just yet.

Or should I let her? Do I even still want to do this?

Traveling lets me immerse myself somewhere completely

new and puts everything in perspective. It helps me find a moment of peace. But I've lost any interest in imagining honeymoons and big family vacations.

That kind of life is never going to be mine.

Though it may seem contradictory as someone who likes to travel and go on adventures, I've always had trouble opening up and trusting people when it came to anything real. And it only became worse after Sarah.

My parents certainly didn't model great behavior when it came to relationships. It was one of the reasons I was always at my next-door neighbors' house growing up. Wes quickly became my best friend, and we spent every day together. His sister, Angie, would tag along sometimes, and the three of us would have the most fun together, calling ourselves the "trio."

Wes and I were closer than brothers, but things changed as they tend to do when you get older.

I hate how I left things with the two of them.

Just as my thoughts drift to my old friends, I feel the back of my neck prickle. Looking around, I don't see anything out of the ordinary, so I go back to looking at my phone. Until I hear it.

Those voices. Voices so familiar, like a melody you know by heart or a song that takes you back in time.

I stand from my chair and drain the last of my cappuccino, grabbing my laptop bag and hoisting it over my shoulder. I search desperately for the sound. Did I imagine it? Am I so starved for human interaction that my brain replayed their voices like an old recording?

But when I turn the corner, I stop in my tracks. A quaint little Italian restaurant with the door and the windows wide open. And just inside at a small table are four people talking and laughing. Two of the people I don't recognize, but with them, sure enough...are Wes and Angie. Two of my favorite people in this world. We knew each other so well once, and they're still a part of me.

What are they doing here?

My heart pounds as I force a few deep, calming breaths. Would they even remember me? Would they even care?

Why am I suddenly so nervous? They are my oldest friends, even if I haven't seen them in almost a decade. But I know what's really happening. My insides are going crazy at the sight of *her*, like no time has passed at all. All those feelings I had as a teenager come roaring back like they never left, and it's almost too much to bear.

Because we're not kids anymore.

She's grown into the most stunning woman I've seen in my life. Same wavy blonde hair and cute round face...and then she laughs. Hearing it again makes my breath catch. She's still the Angie I remember, but she's lived a whole other life that I was never a part of. I suddenly want to go to her and learn every detail I've missed out on.

Maybe the universe is giving me another chance. A chance to course correct and make up for what happened.

3

ANGIE

I knew it the moment I heard his voice.

I never forgot that voice.

Three words: "There he is!" and I knew he was here.

Or maybe this is all a dream.

I turn slowly in my chair, my eyes focusing solely on his shirt as I allow myself a moment to let this all sink in. A royal blue Henley that looks buttery soft. Sleeves pushed up to his elbows, showing off several intricate, swirling tattoos on his pale, muscular forearms. My eyes slowly aim higher and higher, but I pause at the collar of his shirt, because I'm not quite sure I can handle seeing his face yet after all this time.

Is this really happening?

Images flash through my mind of the last time we saw each other. Him getting in his beat-up maroon Oldsmobile Cutlass Ciera. Swearing his eyes caught on mine for a few agonizing seconds before he shut the door at his side and drove away to college, and out of my life for good.

His short, manicured beard is a mosaic of red, shiny blond, and dark brown. He's never had a beard before.

Auburn red hair sits atop his head, styled on top and cut short in the back and the sides. A few light freckles dance across his face.

My gaze finally meets his, just as Wesley knocks into him with a crushing hug. But his emerald green eyes never leave mine. Not until Wesley says, “Asher! Oh my god, what are you doing here?”

They pull apart, and Wesley’s smile overtakes his face as Asher claps him on the shoulder.

“In town for work. What about you? I can’t believe I’m running into you here.” Asher looks sheepishly around our table and raises his hand. “Hello, sorry to interrupt.”

I can’t move.

Can’t breathe.

From the corner of my eye, I see Luca stand up to shake his hand, then Willow, as Wesley makes the proper introductions.

“...and of course you remember Angie.”

For a moment, it’s deathly quiet, and I know everyone is staring at me, waiting for any kind of reaction. But I’m not sure I’m even in control of my body right now.

Asher’s eyes find mine again. Soft and searching. “Of course. Hello, Angie. It’s good to see you again.”

A tidal wave has snatched me from the shore and pulled me under the surface, and I have to force my lungs to intake oxygen. “Asher. Wow, it’s been a while. You look great—I mean...how are you?” My face flushes with heat.

His smile is small but charming, and suddenly I’m fifteen again. Teasing him in our kitchen, desperately trying to be funny enough to earn one of those deep dimples that would send my stomach fluttering. Silently begging him to finally notice me as more than his best friend’s little sister. Wishing he would make some sort of move so I would know this wasn’t all in my head.

Wesley squeezes a chair between ours for Asher to sit down. "Join us, please. I want to hear everything."

"I'd love to," Asher says, pulling off the strap of his bag and hanging it on the chair, as he and Wesley take their seats. With all of us crammed in so tightly, I try to make some room, just as a sharp pain in my shin has me wincing. I look across the table at Willow, and she's giving me the *what the fuck* look. I shoot one right back as we engage in silent conversation.

She tilts her head. *What's the deal with this guy?*

I shake my head. *Not here.*

She raises one eyebrow. *Old boyfriend?*

I shake my head, slower this time. *Not quite.*

She pouts. *Are you keeping secrets from me?*

My eyes go wide as I press my lips together. *I'll tell you later!*

She rolls her eyes, effectively ending the conversation.

Willow knows next to nothing about Asher. It's one of the only things I've really kept from my best friend.

The feelings I had for him felt so real at the time, but I couldn't let anyone else know. Eventually, I convinced myself it was all a silly crush and that I was young and stupid. That I didn't really know what love was. I took all those memories of him and locked them away so no one would ever find them, and I could convince myself it didn't hurt so much.

Willow was there for me in college, when my boyfriend of three years ended things out of the blue. I thought John and I would get married and have kids together, but in the end, he wasn't so sure I was "the one." She is my best friend in the whole world, my ride-or-die. I'll tell her everything tonight.

Asher shifts in his chair, and I swallow a gasp when his knee lightly brushes mine. He continues talking to Wesley as if nothing happened, but he must have felt it; the intense wave of heat concentrated in the half inch of space where our bodies had just touched.

I beg my heart to slow down. I can't be taken out by a passing, featherlight touch. It's embarrassing.

The waitress arrives to take our order, but I can't possibly think about eating right now. The butterflies in my stomach won't settle, and I can feel a drop of sweat gliding down my spine. I realize too late that I've been picking my nails raw, an old habit I haven't done in ages.

This is all too much. I need some air.

And I need to breathe.

Why am I not breathing?

Why is it the moment you think about breathing, your body can't do it automatically?

Willow looks over at me with concern, but I shake my head and put on my best smile as I stand from my chair.

"Order me whatever you're getting," I say quickly, already walking toward the back of the restaurant.

I enter the washroom and stand in front of the mirror, gripping the sink tightly. Every possible emotion threatens to erupt as I squeeze my eyes shut, holding them at bay.

Not here, I tell myself.

The first time I met Asher Hayes was the year I turned ten. Just months after my dad passed away from a sudden heart attack. Asher was eleven and had recently moved in next door. He and Wesley were the same age and instantly became best friends. Inseparable from that point forward.

Things at his own house weren't great, so he always found an excuse to come over. He would help Mom out whenever he could, cooking and baking with her, helping pick up the house. I found myself smiling more when he was around. He helped pull us all out of a dark time.

When he moved away to college, it felt like a piece of my heart went with him.

The door opens behind me, and Willow puts a gentle hand on my shoulder. "Hey, you okay?"

I plaster on a smile. "Yeah, fine. I was just...I wasn't expecting to see him, is all."

"You sure? Do I need to make him leave?"

I huff a laugh. She wouldn't hesitate if I said yes. "No. Not at all. I'm good, I swear. I just need a minute."

She steps to my side and raises her eyebrow. "He is awfully cute."

"Cute? Since when do you say things like that? What have you done with my best friend?"

She rolls her eyes, waiting for my reaction.

"Let's get back out there," I say, wrapping an arm around her waist.

"Okay. But I'm going to need serious details later."

"Obviously."

She gives my side a quick squeeze before we walk through the door, weaving through the tight space between tables, until we reach our seats.

I grab my glass of wine and take a long sip, needing something to do with my hands.

My heart kicks up a notch when Asher glances at me, still talking with Wesley.

I want to ask *Why did you leave?*

Why didn't you ever reach out?

Did you ever feel the way I felt about you?

Instead, I straighten my spine and take a deep breath, determined to make the most of whatever time I have with him.

Asher Hayes. Here again after all these years.

Now that the initial shock of seeing him is starting to wear off, I realize there's nothing stopping us from having a little fun. Though I'm not sure that's what Wesley had in mind when he promised to be my wingman.

4

ASHER

"Good morning," Wes says as I walk into his hotel's sleek restaurant. The aroma of cheesy eggs, hashbrowns, bacon, sausage, and coffee hits me all at once, and suddenly my mouth is watering.

"Morning. Gotta say, this place is amazing. I'm impressed."

"Thanks, man. Come on." He claps my shoulder, leading me to a cozy table on the opposite side of the dining room, tucked away from the rest of the morning crowd. "I got coffee for the table, and there's an awesome breakfast buffet over there. Anything off the menu is great too. My treat, of course."

We sit down, and I pour myself a steaming cup of coffee, still a little groggy. I've never been much of a morning person, but Wes said he had a meeting he couldn't get out of and asked if we could grab breakfast together. And I didn't want to miss the chance to spend time with my oldest friend before I leave.

I had initially been dreading the rest of my stay in London, but now I'm practically buzzing at the idea of spending more time with him and Angie. It'll be like old times.

“Sorry I have to head out in a little bit. Hopefully this meeting doesn’t take too long, and we can meet back up this afternoon.”

“Hey, no worries. I’m just glad we’re getting the chance to catch up. Plus, I’m used to wandering around places and getting lost. It’s one of the best parts of traveling.”

“I can’t believe you’re leaving tomorrow,” he says, frowning.

“I know.”

On my birthday, no less.

“So what else have you been up to? I want to know everything,” he says before taking a sip of coffee.

I tell him about the trips I’ve taken, my job, what college was like when I moved away. Stopping only to go fill up plates of food at the buffet when my stomach starts growling.

Wes tells me all about the hotel business and his company, and how he’s been busy opening their newest resort in Antigua.

I’m about to ask him if he’s seeing anyone when Angie appears at the entrance of the restaurant. Wes and I both stand as I take in the sight of her, my heart immediately kicking into overdrive. An oversized cream sweater hangs off one shoulder, paired with black leggings and ankle boots. Her long blonde hair cascades in waves down one side, and her ocean blue eyes are wide.

Utterly breathtaking.

I still can’t believe she’s really here.

Wes opens his arms and pulls her into a hug, swaying back and forth, while I take slow, measured breaths to bring my heart rate down. When they break apart, she looks to me. Her face is kind, and her eyes are striking, just as I remember from so many years ago. Except she’s all grown up now.

I wrap my arms around her, and her hands come to rest on my back. I lean into her warmth and take a deep breath of her hair. The familiar scent of coconut and lavender infiltrates my senses, and my entire body relaxes.

"It's so good to see you guys again," I say as she pulls back from me, our hands still resting on each other's forearms. "I've missed you both."

"You too," she says a little breathlessly. "I mean...it's good to see you again. And I've missed you too. Both things." Her cheeks take on a tinge of pink as I fight back a smile.

Wes clears his throat, causing us to break apart completely. His eyes narrow as he says, "Ang, I was just telling him I have that meeting this morning for the new resort, so I'm going to have to bail on you guys for a few hours."

"Oh, okay," she says as we all sit at the table, Angie taking the chair next to mine. "You know I don't mind wandering around and getting lost for a while."

The corner of my mouth twitches. "I just said the exact same thing. Maybe I could tag along and we could get lost together."

Her growing smile makes my heart skip a beat.

Wes adds, "Just for a few hours, then I could meet up with you all later."

She nods, avoiding my stare as she reaches for the carafe of coffee. "I think we can manage just fine without you, big brother. Like all those times you ditched us for your girlfriend back in the day." Angie shoots me a glance and then winks before blowing on her mug.

My cock twitches as I raise my own cup to my mouth, desperate for a distraction. I am so far gone it's pathetic.

Wes rolls his eyes, unaware of the war waging between my dick and my brain. "Here, I'll text you both when I'm done." He types out something on his phone, and soon both Angie and I are looking at ours.

GROUP CHAT

WES

THE TRIO IS BACK BABY!

Then a GIF of Luke, Leia, and Han Solo from *Star Wars* pops up.

We always used to joke about being the trio, and I prayed that Angie and I would end up like Leia and Han. At least before *Episode VII* came out.

Nothing happened between us growing up, but I wanted it to. God, did I want it to. The three of us hung out all the time. Angie was so fun to be around. Blonde hair and peppy, always smiling and laughing. Lighting up every room like the sun.

Sunshine.

I rub my chest at the memory, and that familiar longing settles in.

There's a certain kind of ache that comes with being around someone you can't have. Like some force is pulling your body in opposite directions. You want to be near them—you crave it—but their presence also reminds you that you can't have them. It's torture. And I already lived with that feeling in high school after Wes made it clear she was off limits.

I thought I had moved on, but clearly, I was fooling myself.

"Now you have my new number," I say to Angie, elbowing her side.

And now I have hers again.

"Awesome. I'll save it now," she says with a smile.

I shouldn't save hers. Instant access to Angie Harris twenty-four seven? All it would take is one drunken night to confess to her every dark secret I've ever held.

Wasn't that the whole reason I changed my number in the first place?

This is a very bad idea.

5

ANGIE

Asher and I say our goodbyes to Wesley and begin walking down the quiet cobblestone street together. The fall colors are starting to fade a bit, but the bright yellow trees lining the sidewalk add warmth to this chilly, overcast day. I curse myself for not wearing a coat as I rub my arms.

A silence stretches between us that I don't quite know what to do with. It's the first time we've been alone together in ages. What do we even talk about?

Willow and Luca are on their way back to the States today, so I had planned on spending the next few days catching up with Wesley. I never dreamed I would be catching up with Asher, too. How can it feel like a lifetime since I've seen him, but also like it was just yesterday?

I told Willow everything last night after dinner. Explained how I met John just months after Asher left, and how it felt like I could've made the whole thing up with how quickly Asher had vanished.

She was understandably shocked that I had never told her any of this before, and now she's completely invested and wants constant updates. I had to remind her that he never felt that way about me, and that there would be no updates to speak of.

Falling in love has turned my cynical friend into a dreamy-eyed optimist. It's unsettling.

I quietly observe Asher as we walk side by side. He hasn't lost that boyish charm I loved so much, but...he's a man now. Wider chest, more muscular, and the beard definitely ages him up a bit. I can't stop looking at him.

Earlier when we hugged, it was the first time we had touched in a decade. I accidentally caught a whiff of his familiar scent, and it sent me into a spiral. That smell. Like fresh soap and the outdoors. I loved the way he smelled so much that I would regularly steal his hoodies and "forget" to give them back.

"So..." he says, shoving his hands in the pockets of his trenchcoat. "What have you been up to, Sunshine?"

I nearly trip over my own feet, my face flushing with heat at his old nickname for me. But only whenever Wesley wasn't around. It was just for me, like our own little inside joke.

"I don't even know where to begin, honestly," I say, looking up at him, crossing my arms.

He nudges me with his elbow again, not knowing the slightest contact from him sends sparks across my skin. "Come on, tell me everything."

"Ha! Everything could take a while."

"I've got time," he says. "Hell, we have all day."

Where should I start?

Hi, apparently I'm still in love with you, I'm also unemployed and have no idea what I'm doing with my life and will probably die alone. And you?

A double-decker bus passes by, whipping my hair across

my face, and I do my best to smooth it back out and tuck the strands behind my ear.

"Okay. Well, right now I'm living in Athens, Illinois. I—"

"Wait," he cuts me off, putting a hand on my arm to stop me. A shiver erupts at the point of contact. "Athens?"

"Yeah, why?"

He pulls his hand away, placing it over his heart. "I'm in Indy."

I blink several times. "Indianapolis? Really? That's not too far, like three hours?"

He nods as we start walking again, dodging pedestrians and street performers. "Crazy. This whole time we could've been staying in touch."

Why didn't we? I want to shout. *Why did it have to end the way it did?*

"Did you not like California?" I ask.

He shrugs. "It was fine. College was okay, but I just...didn't feel like I fit in out there. Got a job opportunity out of Indy and knew I wanted to come back to the Midwest."

"You missed the corn, admit it."

"Who wouldn't?"

I huff a laugh. "Yeah, I always thought Cali was overrated, what with all the beaches and sunny, seventy-two-degree weather. Disgusting."

"Right? Christmas felt all wrong out there."

"I bet." I rub my arms again, about to ask if we can go back to the hotel when he turns to me.

"Are you cold? Here," he says, stopping us again as he takes off his coat.

"No, I'm fine," I lie.

"Bullshit."

Warmth envelops me as he wraps me in wool. The trenchcoat is comically oversized on me, but all I can focus on is the smell of Irish Spring soap.

His hands linger on the lapels of the coat. “Better?”

I fight a smile as we continue our trek. “Yes, thank you.”

“So what do you do in Athens?” he asks, sounding genuinely curious.

“Mostly hang out with my best friend, Willow, and her boyfriend, Luca, who you met yesterday. We play a lot of pickleball. Spending time with our other friends, Simon and Faris. Faris used to play pickleball with us, but he tore his Achilles a few months ago. It’s a whole thing.” I wave my hand around.

“I don’t know the first thing about pickleball. You’ll have to teach me sometime.”

I smile at that. Making plans to see each other again already? My stomach flips at the thought. Unless he’s just making small talk. But it’s not outside the realm of possibility, now that I know he’s only a few hours away.

“So, what else? Where’s your...husband? Boyfriend?” He avoids my gaze, and I can’t help but chuckle at the sudden shift in topic.

“Nope. Neither. What about you, are you...married?” I didn’t see a ring on his finger, but that’s never a reliable indicator.

He goes quiet, twisting his lips to one side, and I wonder if I said something wrong. But he’s the one who brought it up first, so I figured it was safe to ask.

“No, *definitely* not married. Had a serious girlfriend a while back, but...” He trails off, shaking his head. I get the distinct feeling he doesn’t want to elaborate. But that only makes me more curious.

“‘Definitely not?’ What does that mean?”

He shrugs. “I don’t really believe in marriage, you know?”

The words sting more than they should. Asher was never an option for me, so it shouldn't really matter.

"You *never* want to get married? Why not?"

"Come on, you remember what my parents were like." He digs his hands in the pockets of his jeans, his shoulders practically up by his ears. "I guess seeing that side of marriage really ruined the whole idea for me."

I do remember. His parents fought all the time, sometimes getting violent, and instead of separating, they insisted they stay together for their kid. Their extreme religious views taught them that divorce was never an option, but it was so much worse for everyone that way.

Asher was an only child, and I know he felt so alone in that house. Never having reliable, loving parents. Never getting to see two people in a relationship who love and respect each other, like mine.

I almost ask if he still talks to his parents, but decide to change the subject again. "So, what do you do for work?"

"I'm a travel agent."

My head rears back. "Really? Do people still use travel agents?" I laugh, and the corner of his lips pulls up.

"They do actually, thank you very much." He tips his head in a mock bow. "Not as much as they used to, though. It's kind of a tough business right now."

"Do you like it?"

"Honestly? I used to. It's lost a bit of the excitement for me lately." He looks over at me, and for the first time, I'm noticing how tired he looks. "Not really sure why."

"Seriously? Want to trade lives? I'd love to travel the world. I mean, look around." I gesture to our surroundings, to Big Ben off in the distance. "It's like magic being somewhere new, somewhere different. Meeting new people everywhere you go. Sounds like a dream."

"So what do *you* do for work?"

"I actually just quit my job before coming out here." He looks at me with wide eyes. "Yeah, I was a consultant for some big businesses out in the States, but they weren't going to give me the time off for this. Not enough PTO, blah blah blah. I actually didn't tell Willow, because I didn't want her backing out of this trip. I was growing bored of that job anyway, and I really wanted to come out here for an adventure, so I just... quit."

"Wow. Any plans for what you want to do next?"

I huff a laugh as I pick my nails. "Not really. I'm actually sort of low-key panicking because I hadn't thought that far ahead, and it's finally hitting me that I won't have any more paychecks when I get home. You know, to survive and all. But... I knew I would regret not coming out here. Something in me said this was what I needed to do."

Where I needed to be.

I do feel bad about lying to Willow. But I know her, and she wouldn't have agreed to this trip if she knew I was tanking my career over it. She needed this. We both did.

Asher and I stop at a little stone bridge overlooking a sprawling, serene pond surrounded by more vibrant yellow trees. A few birds chirp nearby as children throw pieces of bread at the passing ducks. He rests his arms on the ledge and leans forward. Turning his head to me, he says, "Well, I'm glad you did come. Otherwise we never would have reunited."

Something scratches at my brain when he says that. I take the spot next to him, mirroring his stance. Then it hits me. "Oh my god, do you remember that song my mom always used to play after we would come home from a vacation? And you would come over and hug Wesley like you'd been apart for years?"

His eyes light up, and at the same time, we both sing, "Reunited, and it feels so good!"

"Yes!" I squeal. "Peaches & Herb!"

"Oh wow, forgot about that one." His beaming smile makes my heart flutter, and those dimples nearly take me out at the knees. "How is your mom, by the way?"

I look back out over the water. "She's great. Living out on a couple acres of land. Just like she always wanted."

"That's awesome. She was always so nice to me growing up. Will you tell her I said hi?"

"Of course." I know she would love to hear about him. He was practically an adopted son to her.

My eyes find his again, and before I can stop myself, my hand comes to rest on his face, his beard rough under my palm. "Still not used to seeing you with this thing." I don't know what on earth possessed me to do that, so I quickly pull my hand away.

He smiles sheepishly, rubbing at the spot where I was inexplicably touching him. "You don't think it makes me look like a low-budget Prince Harry?"

A laugh bubbles out of me. "Is that why you're in London? Do you get special treatment out here?"

"Hardly. Mostly just weird looks."

"Well, I like it," I say with a smile, still unable to control myself around him.

"Hey, we should commemorate this moment." He pulls out his phone.

"Yeah?" I say with a tilt of my head.

He turns me so my back is to the water and drapes a strong arm over my shoulder, pulling me in close to his side, and I wonder if he can hear the thunderous beats of my heart. The smile that overtakes my face comes naturally as he holds up his phone in front of us to snap a picture. Wrapped in his embrace, I feel lightheaded and wish this moment could last forever.

After taking a few quick photos, he pulls his arm back, and I instantly miss the warmth.

"Will you send that to me?" I ask. "Or...are you on Instagram or anything?"

"Eh, I have an account that I never really post on. I'll just text it to you." His expression is unreadable when he adds, "Now that we have each other's numbers again."

"You know, as a travel agent, you really should be posting all your travel pics online. Could help boost your business. People love living vicariously through other people doing cool shit."

He slips his phone back in his pocket. "Maybe you should be a travel agent. You could probably teach me a thing or two."

My face flushes hot as my immature mind twists his words. "I probably could."

6

ASHER

I resist the urge to make this new photo of me and Angie my phone's background. That would be too much, and a bit creepy. No need to scare her off, not when she just came back into my life. This still feels like a dream, and if I do something wrong or question it, I'm going to wake up and she'll slip through my fingers. Only to be left with the memory of her. Again.

But she lives in Athens. Just a few hours away from me.

What have I been doing all these years? Did I really think I couldn't reach out to my oldest friends after everything we'd been through? I didn't even try.

I know things were tense between Wes and me when I left, but I should've been the bigger person and called them. I forgot how much I missed this. Needed this.

It's crazy how quickly Angie and I have fallen back into our old comfortable rhythm. We continue walking the streets of London, catching each other up on the highlights of the past ten years, occasionally pointing out landmarks or places we like, and reminiscing about the past. She was a little quiet at first, but now she is doing most of the talking, and I'm content to listen to the sound of her voice all day.

After a while, we decide to stop for a late lunch at a nearby shop tucked away from the busy streets. The place is cozy and dark and smells incredible.

We find a small corner table and continue our conversation right where we left off while splitting a plate of fish and chips and eventually ordering some drinks. I take note of the Chardonnay she ordered, because she's mentioned several times how good it is.

I still couldn't believe it when she said she wasn't married or involved with anyone. How that's even possible is beyond me. What could things have been like if I had never left? If Wes hadn't told me to stay away from her, or if I was brave enough to stand up and fight for what I wanted?

There's no point in questioning the past. What's done is done, and the universe seems to have given me a second chance to be in her life again. I'm not going to waste any more time thinking about what might have been.

"So...pickleball, huh?" I say after she insisted I take the last bite of fish. "How'd you get into that?"

She grabs a chip off the plate and pops it in her mouth. "Willow and I started playing after she accepted a graphic design job for a guy opening an indoor pickleball facility in Athens. We became obsessed right away. Now it's our favorite pastime and our favorite hangout spot."

I rear my head back. "An indoor pickleball facility? That's really a thing?"

She levels me with a serious expression. "Pickleball is the fastest-growing sport in America. It's insanely popular. I really need to get you out on the court sometime."

"Sounds good to me."

She takes a long sip of her wine, and I have to tear my gaze away from those pink lips.

"So what are *you* going to teach *me*?" she asks, and I nearly choke on my own drink.

"What?" I sputter.

"Well, if I'm teaching you how to be a better travel agent *and* how to play pickleball, what's in it for me?" A devilish smile plays on her lips, and my eyes dart away when I realize I'm staring at her mouth again.

God, I could think of a dozen things off the top of my head that I want to teach her, but I absolutely cannot say a single one of them. I shift in my chair as I clear my throat. "Uh, let's see...I did learn how to surf out in California. Is that something that interests you?"

She shrugs. "Meh, we'll see. If we find ourselves at a beach together, you're on."

I make a show of looking around. "Not today, I guess."

Just then, we're interrupted by a text from Wes.

GROUP CHAT

WES

Hey where are you guys?

Just finished my meeting

I look at the time, and holy shit, I didn't realize so much time had passed. Angie and I have been hanging out for hours, and it went by in an instant.

A part of me wishes he would keep himself busy so I could keep her all to myself for a little longer. But I realize there's no reason we couldn't get together back home now. Even if Wes lives out here, he probably goes back to visit Angie and their mom in the States. The thought of seeing them again fills a part of me that I've let stay empty for far too long.

Angie beats me to a response.

ANGIE

Want to meet back at the hotel in an hour?

WES

copy that

see you soon

I look over at her and shrug. "Guess we should head back, we've got a decent walk ahead of us."

She smiles brightly. "No rush. This was fun. How much longer are you in London?"

"Leaving tomorrow. You?" I wipe my hand on my napkin and add it to the neat pile of plates and silverware.

"Two more days."

"Seeing your mom next week for Thanksgiving?" I ask.

"Yep. Plus I need to relieve her of dog duty. What about you? Any plans?"

"Yeah, totally," I lie, saving her from feeling obligated to invite my lonely ass over out of pity. "Big gathering with some friends."

"Nice! I love a Friendsgiving. We all get together around the holidays back in Athens, too. If you ever find yourself without a place to go, you're always welcome to join us."

My heart soars. "That's very kind, thank you." Now I almost want to come, but I already told her I'm busy. Way to go.

We both stand from our table, and she offers to give me back my trenchcoat, but I take it and place it over her shoulders before she can stop me. No way am I going to let her walk all the way back to the hotel shivering.

I hold open the door for her as she tucks a strand of hair behind her ear and walks past me with a shy smile, her arm lightly brushing mine.

When we arrive at the hotel, Wes is waiting for us in the lobby with a huge grin. I'm instantly suspicious. We may have spent the last decade apart, but I still know when he's up to something.

"Why are you being weird?" I ask.

"I'm not being weird, you're weird," he shoots back. Before I can ask what the hell that means, he adds, "Come on, follow me."

Angie and I both glance at each other before following Wes through the lobby and into the hotel's restaurant. In the back corner, I spy a table with a flowing gold tablecloth underneath a balloon arch of various metallic colors.

In the center of the table is a two-tiered cake with the words "Happy Birthday" written on it in cursive.

My chest tightens.

"Happy birthday!" Wes and Angie both shout in unison. Their arms stretched out wide.

They remembered.

I fight back tears as my eyes dart between my two best friends. I don't deserve them, but god, how I've missed them.

Wes claps me on the shoulder. "I know it's tomorrow, but you're leaving, so I wanted to make sure we all got a chance to celebrate together."

I whoosh out a breath. "Wow, I don't know what to say. I mean...I can't believe you remembered."

"Come on, are you kidding?" Angie says. "We'd always celebrate with you before we left for Thanksgiving break."

I remember. Their family was always so good to me. They traveled to see extended family around Thanksgiving, but would make sure to celebrate me first. Making the holidays apart less lonely, knowing they took the time to make me feel special. Then we'd play "Reunited" and hug as soon as they got back in town.

Angie puts a gentle hand on my back, as if she can read my thoughts and knows I'm seconds away from falling apart. She is warm and soft when I pull her into my side. "You didn't have to do all this."

Wes crushes me with a hug. "Just shut the fuck up and let us spoil you, please."

That draws a laugh from me. "Okay, you win."

I look at them both again and commit this moment to memory.

"Thank you for this. I know I've said it more than once already, but I've really missed you guys."

We sit down at the table and enjoy cake and dinner, talking about the good old days.

I go to sleep that night with a full belly and an even fuller heart.

7

ANGIE

"Hey, Mom!"

I drop my bags in the large foyer as my mom approaches from the living room.

"Honey, you're back!" she says brightly, holding her arms out wide. She wraps me in a hug as I lean into her warmth.

"How did the kids do?"

"They were perfect, of course. Cally is out back, come on," she says, leading me through the house to the back door.

My mom watched my dog, Cally, and Willow's dog, Henry—Black Labradors from the same litter—while we were out of the country. They've been inseparable since we brought them home as puppies a few years ago, and now they're enormous. Willow already came to get Henry the morning after she got home.

I look around the familiar space. The tall, open living room blends into the kitchen, with long wood beams running along the ceiling. Couches with colorful quilts draped over them, and a basket of knitting stuff next to a worn recliner by the fireplace. It's a gorgeous modern, but cozy, farmhouse. With no neighbors around for miles.

My mom and I are best friends, but we are very different. We share the same blue eyes, but that's about it. Her hair is light brown and cut short, while mine is long, golden blonde. I'm more outgoing and like to be where the action is, and Mom prefers the solitude and quiet. She deserves this peace after everything she's been through in her life.

After Dad died, it was painful to watch her try to pick up the pieces. They were soulmates, I just know it. To have him taken away so soon was cruel and unfair. Wesley and I did everything we could to help her out back then, the three of us sticking together, getting each other through the worst of our grief.

I know Dad was still looking out for us even after he passed. We would notice these crazy signs that could've only been from him. Like the outside lamplight that Mom tried to get him to fix for so long it became a running joke. Then a few months after he passed, it magically started working again. He was always the handyman of the house, so when other things stopped working and then would somehow get fixed before me or Wesley could get around to it, we knew it was him still taking care of us. And we never questioned it.

To see my mom content is all I could ask for. She deserves it.

Mom opens the sliding glass doors to the back yard, which is just acres of open farmland. Cally freezes off in the distance, her head perked up at the sound of the door. When she sees me, she breaks into a sprint to greet me, tongue flapping out of the side of her mouth. Soon, I'm dripping with wet dog kisses as she paws at me relentlessly.

"Okay, okay! I missed you too, you big monster."

I grab a tennis ball from the porch and throw it into the

yard. Cally runs after it as my mom and I take a seat on the steps.

"Still playing pickleball?" she asks. "Some of my friends have started getting into it and told me I should join."

"You should! It's so fun. I've already agreed to teach Asher someday; I could teach you, too."

"I still can't believe you ran into Asher Hayes out there! How's he doing? You were annoyingly sparse on details over the phone."

Of course I was. What could I even say to her? I never told her about my true feelings for him, although there's no way she didn't know. She sees everything, reads everyone with scary precision. I wasn't even remotely ready to have that conversation with myself about Asher, let alone with my mom.

Cally returns with the tennis ball, and I throw it again. "We only got to spend a few hours together. He's Wesley's friend anyway," I add, trying to shift the focus off me. I don't dare look her in the eye.

"Yeah, Wes told me Asher's travel agency might be interested in some kind of partnership. He was a good kid. Glad everything turned out okay for him. I know his family life was pretty rough. Actually..." She snaps her fingers. "I think we might still have some of his things in the garage."

Wouldn't surprise me. She kept everything from our childhood. I could bring his stuff back with me and have an excuse to see him again. Then an idea hits me.

"Hey, do you still have my old journals?"

She tilts her head in contemplation. "Probably. They would be out there with everything else. You want some help looking?"

"Nah, I got it. You relax."

She squeezes my hand and offers a warm, genuine smile. I can't help but return it as I stand. God, I really hit the jackpot with my mom. I couldn't have asked for a better mother or friend.

Mom continues to throw the ball for Cally as I go back into the house. I open the door to the garage and flick on the light, illuminating the large, musty space. It can fit three cars, but she just has the one. The rest of the area is taken up with bins and boxes, crafts, tools, and various home projects. The far wall houses rows and rows of shelving units, holding even more bins. Thank goodness everything is meticulously labeled. At least she's an organized hoarder.

I scan the section of bins for each major holiday, home decor, and old clothes, until I get to the ones labeled "Wesley" and "Angie." And above them...

"Robert."

Rows and rows of them.

The backs of my eyes sting. What is all this? Mom said she got rid of his stuff years ago when she moved out here. I remember it clearly because it was a whole ordeal, and she was having a really hard time parting with everything, even though he had been gone for nearly a decade by then. But she was the one who insisted that holding on to his clothes and belongings was keeping her from moving on.

I don't understand.

I wish we talked about him more. We were always there for each other after he passed, and I'm so grateful for that. But we always avoided talking about him. I guess it was just too painful for everyone.

She must have her reasons, so I won't push.

Jumping back to my absurd mission of obsessing over my childhood crush, I find further subcategories for toys, art projects, report cards, and one labeled "keepsakes." Bingo.

I pull down the "Angie Keepsakes" bin, thanking my good luck that it's at shoulder height and I don't need to bust out her enormous rickety ladder. Popping off the lid, I see a bunch of old things I haven't thought about in years. School awards and trophies, concert tickets, random trinkets...and there they are. Lining the bottom are stacks of journals. Each one filled up and labeled on the front with specific dates.

I smile, knowing exactly which one I want to read. I'm dying to remember those words. It was the year I realized my full-blown obsession with Asher.

Pulling out the journal from eighth grade, I run a hand over the worn cover. Do I really want to read this? Do I want to reopen those wounds and subject myself to the story of Asher and me? The one where I spent years pining and obsessing over my brother's best friend, only to be left broken-hearted when he left?

On the other hand, maybe it will give me some much-needed closure. To see for myself how far I've come in life, and that maybe what I've kept locked up tight within my heart, is not my real story anymore. That what I've built up in my head no longer aligns with who I am or what I want.

I flip a few pages in, and it's like I'm transported back in time. I still remember these words and how they felt when I wrote them. In the margins, I spot messy scribbles. "Angela Harris-Hayes" and "Mr. And Mrs. Asher Hayes" and "A.H. + A.H. 4EVER."

Yikes is an understatement.

February 14

It's Valentine's Day, and I have a crush...on Asher! But I can't tell anyone. I'm not even sure how this happened. I've always thought of him like a friend...until sometime recently.

Actually, I take it back. I know exactly when and how it happened.

A few days ago, he slept over. The three of us were playing Mario Kart in the basement until like 1 a.m. At some point, I woke up, realizing I had fallen asleep... leaning on Asher! He and Wesley were still playing, but there was a blanket draped over me. And I know my brother wouldn't have done something like that. I pulled myself off him and said sorry. He had this adorable, sleepy grin as he said softly, "Don't be sorry."

It was like butterflies exploded in my belly!!!

I got so nervous I bolted upstairs and shut myself in my room. Unable to think or breathe.

What the heck was that???

Now I can't stop thinking about him. How am I supposed to deal with this? He comes over to our house every day! I can't avoid him, and I'm not sure I trust myself to act normally around him. I'll just have to try and play it cool. Pretend that never happened and just go back to having fun. It's not a big deal. Just a crush. I'm sure I'll be over it soon anyway. Because it would never work.

I can't have a crush on my brother's best friend!

Oh god, it's worse than I remember. But I was so innocent. To be so young and naive, I almost wish I could go back. Then I realize, I still feel the same way I did then. I got that same flutter in London. Even with a decade apart, I thought those feelings would have finally gone away, but they were just sleeping below the surface. Waiting for him to reappear in my life and remind me that I've been fooling myself into believing I was over him.

But maybe it's just that I never got proper closure. He's not interested in me that way, and probably never will be. Maybe this is my chance to finally face reality and put those feelings behind me.

It's time to grow up.

8

ASHER

I typically split my time evenly between working at home and in the office. In a sense, I am building my own business, but I work under a host agency. They help with making bigger connections and dealing with logistics and all that, but I control my own clients and bookings.

I roll out of bed and begrudgingly start my morning routine. Bryn, the agency's owner, asked me to come in today for a check-in meeting, which is unusual. We are allowed to work from home as little or as much as we want, and she usually only asks people to come in to the office if something major is going on.

Hopefully it's just to ask how my Thanksgiving was.

Lonely, of course. Like every year.

But what if she is cutting me loose? I know I'm not pulling my weight around here like I used to, and she probably thinks I'm dragging the company down. I wouldn't blame her. My performance and sales have been shitty lately. I really need to step up my game if I want to stay employed.

But how am I going to get more experience booking vacations for families and couples if it's only me on these trips? *Just me*, like it's always been. And always will be, apparently.

I've been home in Indiana for a week and a half now, and I still can't stop thinking about that day in London with Angie. Catching up with an old friend who knows me and my past filled something in me I forgot I was even missing. I guess I didn't realize how lonely I've been.

As I brush my teeth, I pull up the photo of us together on my phone and decide to post it on my barely existing Instagram account. I had sent her the photo before we left, but a part of me selfishly wants the whole world to see me with her. We added each other as friends on there too, and I only spent about two hours scrolling through all her pictures, due to my lack of willpower.

After typing out the caption "Reunited and it feels so good," a nod to our inside joke, and tagging her in the photo, I hit Post.

It's eight forty-five a.m. when I walk into our office. The space is open and bright. Tons of tall windows line the far wall, letting in a flood of natural light. Bryn spent a lot of time making this place feel warm and inviting, rather than bland and sterile. Placing my bag down on my desk, I fire up my computer for the day before heading into the break room for a fresh cup of coffee. My second of the morning.

When I get back to my desk, the reminder for my meeting with Bryn pops up, and I mentally prepare for what's to come.

At this point, I'm convinced she's letting me go. It's the only logical explanation. I suck at this job, and she no longer wants me tarnishing her brand. Which is totally fair. Maybe this job isn't for me. But what else would I do?

I take a deep breath as I get ready to face her. Maybe it won't be as bad as I'm imagining. Bryn is an amazing boss, and I wouldn't blame her for wanting me out of the agency, but maybe I can convince her to take pity on me and give me one last chance.

I approach her open door and poke my head in, rapping my knuckles on the frame. "Hello?"

Sitting behind her desk, her head pops up and she gives me a warm smile. "Asher! Good morning, come in, come in."

I start to walk in when she adds, "You wanna go ahead and close the door behind you?"

Fuck. I was right. This is it.

I plaster on a smile to hide how nervous I am. "Of course."

Her rich brown skin practically glows from the sunlight streaming into her large office, making her look closer to twenty than her real age of thirty-five. The fuzzy teal rug on the floor next to a soft loveseat gives off such cozy vibes. On a round glass table, a diffuser spouts a cloud of citrus. Behind her, framed diplomas, awards, and magazine articles decorate her wall. Photos of her husband and her dogs line her L-shaped desk.

The very definition of accomplished yet approachable.

Taking the seat across from her desk, I lean forward with my elbows on my knees, then sit back again, suddenly unsure of how to act.

"So," she says, scooting her chair forward and interlacing her hands on the desk in front of her. "Tell me about London."

I shift in the chair, rubbing the back of my neck. "It was...I don't know. It was fine. Good."

She stares at me unblinking, letting me sit in my awkwardness, knowing the silence will eventually force me to say what's really on my mind.

"Look, Bryn, I know I haven't been performing well lately.

If you want to let me go, just say so and end my suffering. I'll figure something out."

Her head snaps back. "Let you go? Is that what you think this is about?"

"Well...yeah. And I don't blame you either. I—"

She holds up a beautifully manicured hand to cut me off. "I'm going to stop you right there, Asher. I'm not letting you go."

I let out a long breath, relaxing my shoulders.

"...but I am concerned. Do you still enjoy doing this?"

My pause is much too long to be convincing. "I do."

"Okay. Then let's talk about some new ideas. What can we offer clients to get them on board here? What are *you* interested in that others might be excited about?"

What am I interested in?

My mind goes blank.

I don't even have any real hobbies. The only time I've been excited about anything in the last few weeks was seeing Angie.

So I say the first thing that pops into my head.

"Pickleball."

She tilts her head. "Pickleball...?" She says it slowly, like she's trying to understand its meaning, coming from me. I've never given any indication that I'm into pickleball, or any sport for that matter, before this very moment.

I clear my throat. "Yes. Uh...an all-inclusive vacation package for pickleball enthusiasts. Itinerary would include play time every day. I've already got one all planned out, actually." I cringe internally.

Stop talking.

"Really?" she says, sitting back in her chair. "Tell me about it."

Oh fuck, here we go.

One lie only leads to more lies, I hear my dad say. One of the only things he ever taught me.

"Oh...well, first of all, did you know..." I think back to my conversation with Angie, "...that pickleball is the fastest-growing sport in America? It's insane."

"So you play." Not a question. A statement. Because who in their right mind would lie about this?

"Yeah, of course."

What am I doing?

Stop talking. There's still time to take it all back.

But instead, I continue on. "Pickleball vacations are huge right now. We'd be crazy not to get in on the action."

She rubs her chin. "Wow. I have to say, Asher, I'm impressed."

"Thank you."

"So where's the destination?"

Where, indeed? I did say I had it all planned out already. Think. Someplace warm. Beaches. Where did Wes say they opened a new resort?

I blurt, "Antigua."

Her eyes go wide. "Interesting. You've really surprised me. Here I was thinking you were already one foot out the door, and instead you've been working on a brilliant new idea. I think you might have something here. How close is the package to being complete?"

"Oh, uh, it's pretty much done, just have to finalize all the agreements with the resort, get the contracts signed and all."

She sits forward, and her face is lit up like I just handed her a puppy. "Wonderful! When will you go?"

I freeze. "Go...?"

"Yes, obviously you'll need to go on the trip yourself, make sure the itinerary works, and meet with your contacts at the resort. We should do it as soon as possible, so we can start selling the package for the spring. What do you think?"

I laugh, shaking my head and contorting my face in my best *well, obviously* expression.

"And take your girlfriend, of course. I'd love to get her perspective on the vacation as well. Does she play pickleball too?"

My head tilts to the side. What is happening right now? "My...girlfriend?"

"I saw your post this morning, and I've been dying to get the details."

When I don't say anything, she tsks. "Come on. The girl in London? Reunited?" A growing smile overtakes her face. "Why didn't you tell me you were seeing someone? I thought we were friends."

I stop breathing.

The post with Angie. Shit. Did I make it look like we were together-together?

I can feel my face getting hot, a flop sweat forming between my shoulder blades.

Shut it down. Now.

"Oh, we're not—"

"Look at you, you're blushing! I've honestly never seen you look so happy."

I let out a harsh breath. I can't deny I *was* happy there with her. The happiest I've been in ages. It felt like we were teenagers again, laughing over stupid shit and staying up late talking. I already miss her. It's the same feeling I had when I left for college.

I realize I haven't said anything in a while when Bryn laughs. "Okay, I get it. You don't want to tell me about her yet; that's fair. I just want you to know I'm happy for you. We all are."

Oh great, so the whole office saw it too. Cool. I rub the back of my damp neck and give her a small smile. "Thanks, Bryn. That means a lot."

She stares at me for a few seconds before adding, "I think this will be really good for you. You've been so in your head about the work lately, you haven't taken any time to have fun. What does your girl do for work?"

My girl...

"She's...uh...in between jobs, actually. She was a consultant, but she is still trying to figure out what she wants to do. But yes, she loves pickleball even more than I do." The first true thing I've said this whole meeting.

"Then it's perfect! The universe always has a plan, and you now have a gorgeous girlfriend to share this experience with."

God, this got out of hand quickly. I should at least tell her the truth about Angie. Well, maybe not the whole truth. Leave out the part where I've been wishing she was my girlfriend since I was thirteen years old. How I've tried and failed to make any relationship in my life work. How when I saw Angie in London, my entire life became perfectly clear, and I knew that no one would ever compare to her, because I've been in love with her and denying it for literally half my life.

I should've corrected Bryn from the start.

"Bryn, I need to—"

Her phone rings, interrupting me. When she sees the caller ID, she motions that she needs to take it.

But before she answers, she adds, "And hey, get that girlfriend to help you post more on Instagram. It's a good look for you. And this trip will be a great chance to build your social media following."

I simply nod as I stand from the chair. My head is swimming with dizzying thoughts. When I get back to my desk, I try to make sense of everything that just happened.

Bryn thinks Angie is my girlfriend.

I didn't correct her.

We're going on an all-inclusive vacation together in the Caribbean, based around a sport I know nothing about, with no contracts or plan whatsoever.

I'm fine.

This is fine.

9

ANGIE

"You guys ready?" Willow calls out to our opponents, Max and Gary, two guys from our regular pickleball group. On Wednesdays, we typically play down the street at the neighborhood courts as long as the weather is warm enough. Max is Luca's best friend, and we've gotten to know each other pretty well, especially after this past summer when he and I were paired up for Dink Shot's big annual pickleball tournament. He also owns his own vet clinic, where Willow and I recently started taking our dogs.

"Ten seven on two," she says, before the bright yellow ball bounces in the diagonal square, where Max easily returns it, landing back in front of her. She steps up to hit it, and we both take the opportunity to run up to the line at the kitchen. The ball goes back and forth, our speed picking up until eventually Gary gets a shot past us.

"Fuck," Willow whisper-yells. "That would've been game."

"You know, I was hoping that getting laid on the regular would have loosened you up a bit so you wouldn't take these matches so seriously." I spin the paddle in my hand a few times. "But I guess that's not the case, huh."

She shakes her head. "I will never let a man change who I am, Ang."

"And thank god for that." We tap paddles and take our places, Willow up at the kitchen and me at the baseline.

Gary serves, and Willow and I lock in, ready to end this. It's gotten pretty chilly out since we got here, but we've been moving nonstop for the past three hours, so it actually feels nice. We ultimately beat them 11-8 and decide to end the night with that victory, because we are exhausted.

"Tell Kayla and the kids I said hi," I say to Max as we gather our stuff.

He tugs at his earlobe, and a flash of something passes over his face I can't quite read. "Will do. And Willow, tell your boy I'll be there tomorrow to help set up."

"Thanks, Max," she says. "Have a good night."

I zip up my sweatshirt as Willow and I walk home from another full evening of pickleball. With how cold it's been getting lately, I'm thinking this may have been our last outdoor session. We'll have to head over to Dink Shot until spring, which I don't mind. We love playing there, it just takes more time and gets pretty crowded in the winter.

Luca didn't come out tonight because he's been busy setting up a youth pickleball camp over there, and it's finally happening this weekend. He's put a lot of work into it, and I can't wait to see how it goes. I do take a decent amount of credit for getting him back together with Willow and forcing them to work through their issues.

If only I could do the same for myself.

"Lunch tomorrow?" Willow asks me as we turn onto our street. "Or do you have meetings?"

Heaviness settles in my gut.

I still haven't told her I quit my job. Time to rip off the Band-Aid. No time like the present.

"So, funny story," I say, adjusting the bag on my shoulder. "Like, so funny you're not even going to believe it."

She shoots me a confused glance. "Okay...?"

"Remember how I said my boss was totally fine with me traveling, and that I could work remotely on our trip, no problem?"

Her eyes narrow into slits. "Yeah."

All in one breath I say, "Well it turns out I made that all up because I knew you wouldn't go on the trip if I told you he was actually not okay with it, and so I quit instead because we needed to go and I would've never forgiven myself, and plus I hated my job anyway." I inhale deeply several times, avoiding her hardening stare.

"*You quit?*" she yells as she grabs my arm, halting us both. "How could you not tell me that?"

I take her hand in mine.

"Will, we needed that trip. You needed to get away from everything to sort out all your stuff with Luca. And we've been wanting to travel together forever. It was the perfect excuse for me to finally get out of there. This is a good thing."

Eyebrows furrowed, she says softly, "You really are a good friend. But...I still wish you had told me. I feel like you've been keeping things from me lately."

My gut twists. "I'm sorry. I didn't want you to worry about me." I wrap an arm around her waist, guiding us back down the sidewalk toward our townhouses.

"So what are you going to do?" she asks.

"Honestly, I don't know yet. Keeping my options open, you know? Maybe go back to selling feet pics?"

She scoffs. "But you hated doing that."

"Yeah, but the money was good. People pay a lot for some freaky shit."

"Your feet are not freaky."

"A few hundred subscribers would beg to differ." I shoot her a wink. "I wonder if I can reactivate my Ten Toes Down account."

"You do you, babe. But maybe take some time to think about what you really want to do. Like, long term."

I shove my hands in the pockets of my sweatshirt, letting out a breath that comes out in a white puff. "I know. I'm set for a little while, but I may just need a bit of extra money as I figure it all out. I don't want to rush into another job I hate."

"What would you do if money weren't an issue?"

I look over at her and smile. "Honestly? Traveling with you was the highlight of my year. Hell, maybe even the past decade. I wanted to stay and see everything."

Her smile matches mine. "Me too. Maybe you should talk to your childhood crush about getting into the travel business."

Obviously I've thought about it. It's not a bad idea. And he did say he'd be willing to help me get started if it's something I was interested in. I'd also love to have an excuse to keep talking to him again, even if it's just as friends.

I keep telling myself I'm ready to get over him, but I still brought home all my old journals from Mom's house. I've decided to read through them one last time before I put this ridiculous crush behind me.

"Yeah, maybe."

The once-colorful trees along our street are almost completely bare. I guess fall is really over. A long, cold winter ahead.

As we approach our townhomes, my phone buzzes in my pocket.

"See you tomorrow?" I ask.

"Yep! Love you, miss you!"

"Love you more," I reply with a smile as I pull out my phone.

Willow unlocks her front door and walks inside as I continue to my own a few units down. But I stop in my tracks when I see the text on my screen.

ASHER

Hey

Hey?

Hey???

There's so much to unpack in that one little word. Why is he texting me? What does he want?

My heart picks up as I type back:

ME

Hey! What's up?

Was that casual enough?

I'm still not used to the idea of him being back in my life. Are we friends again? Is this going to be a regular occurrence? Not that I would mind.

Once I'm inside my house, I flip on the lights, dropping my bag on the floor, and curl up on the couch with Cally, scratching her fur as I stare at the bubble with three dots dancing on my phone screen.

ASHER

This is going to sound really strange and out of the blue, but would you mind if I came out to Athens to see you? I have something I need to talk to you about.

What in the actual fuckery is this?

I haven't seen him in almost a decade, and now suddenly he wants to come see me? What is he up to? This is weird, right? But my traitorous heart flutters in response.

ME

You're right, that does sound strange...

But of course you can come out. I'd love to see you! 😊

I'm definitely intrigued, and I could never say no to seeing him again. Catching up with him in London was more fun than I could have imagined. I almost forgot how much fun we had together, how well we got along. How easy it was.

I didn't realize how much I missed him until he came storming back into my life like a big red hurricane.

ASHER

You have no idea how glad I am to hear you say that.

ME

haha why?

I hold my breath as I wait for him to respond. When he does, I drop my phone.

10

ASHER

This was reckless. This was stupid. I should've waited for her to say yes, or given any form of heads up before driving down here. I just left work and found myself getting on the highway instead of going back home. But this really couldn't wait. Bryn wants us to leave for the trip right after Christmas, and that's not a whole lot of time for Angie to get on board with this insane plan.

I should've told Bryn the truth. Why did I let her think we were together?

Because you wanted it to be true, asshole.

My thumb shakes before pressing Send on the text I had typed out.

ME

Because I'm outside your house

I step out of my car, and Angie opens her door with her phone in hand. She is dressed in a golden yellow zip-up hoodie and black athletic pants, hair up in a high, messy bun. Her eyes are wide, and her jaw is practically on the floor. That mouth... those lips.

An enormous black lab sprints out of the house and circles my legs, nearly knocking me over. I lean down to settle the hyper dog as I look up at Angie.

"Surprise...?" I say with a shrug. What is she thinking? I can't tell if she's happy or pissed. This was a mistake.

She shakes her head, and that bright, beaming smile appears. "Oh my god, hi! I can't believe— Excuse her, she's a mess. This is Cally."

The dog licks my face as I continue looking up into those deep blue eyes. "Sorry to just show up like this. I got your address from Wes. I hope that's okay."

"Are you kidding? It's great! Just like old times. Come on in." She opens the door wider as I stand and follow her inside her warm, inviting house. Just like all those years when we were younger. A Harris household always feels like this. Like a home.

Bright, bold colors give the room a chaotic, but charming feel. Joy emanates from every surface. The walls are painted a royal blue, behind an indigo couch covered in golden-yellow pillows. A light wood coffee table sits on a large rainbow area rug. It's all so...her.

"Don't mind the mess, obviously I wasn't expecting company," she says, but with no hint of annoyance. The dog trots inside before Angie closes the door as I take off my coat. "Here, let me take that. Would you like something to drink?"

"Oh, no I'm fine." I rub the back of my neck and stand there awkwardly, suddenly forgetting everything I practiced saying on the drive here.

"So, what's going on? Is everything okay?"

"Yeah, everything is fine. Great."

She narrows her eyes playfully as she crosses her arms.

"You...gonna tell me why you drove all the way out here for a surprise visit? You miss me that much?" she teases.

If she only knew.

"Yeah, about that. Can we sit? I promise it's not bad, it's just...a little weird maybe."

"I like weird." She walks over to her soft purple-blue couch and motions for me to sit next to her. "Lay it on me."

Cally joins me at the couch, and I scratch under her chin as I let out a sharp breath. Here goes nothing.

"Okay...so you know how we talked about work and travel agency stuff, right?"

She smiles. "Yeah, I'm actually really interested in hearing more about that."

"Oh, great. That's *really* great, actually. Umm...so I have a proposition for you. It's..."

"Weird," she repeats with a chuckle. "Yeah, you've said that. Just tell me already!" She grabs a throw pillow and holds it in her lap, fidgeting with the fringe on the side. Cally plops down at our feet.

"I'm putting together a vacation package for work, and you actually helped inspire it. It's going to be an all-inclusive pickleball trip...in the Caribbean."

Her hands fall to her sides. "Wait...what? Are you serious?"

"Yeah. But I'm in over my head here, because—"

"Because you don't know the first thing about pickleball?" she supplies.

I click my tongue as I do a finger-gun motion at her. "Correct. I thought maybe you could help me out. Wes too."

"Sure!" Her leg tucks underneath her as she angles to face me. "You needed to come all the way here to ask me to help you plan an itinerary?"

"Umm...yes. And also..." I scratch at my beard.

She laughs as she swats my arm. "What? Just tell me already!"

"My boss wants you to come with me."

Her eyebrows scrunch together in the most adorable way. My fingers itch to smooth over those worried lines. "Come with you? To the Caribbean?"

I open my hands wide as my heart pounds wildly. "Told you it was weird."

"Wait, I don't understand. Why would your boss want *me* on this trip? How does she even know who I am?"

"So, that's the other thing. She...well..." I clear my throat. "She kind of thinks we're...dating."

Her head rears back. "What? Why would she think that?"

I rub at my neck again and realize I'm sweating. "She saw that picture of us together on Instagram and assumed you were my...girlfriend. And then she immediately went on about this trip that I had just made up and how it would be good to have you there with me."

"And you didn't correct her?" Her head tilts curiously.

I wince. "I'm sorry. It all happened so fast and I panicked. I went in there thinking she was going to fire me from the agency, and before I knew it, I was pitching her this luxury pickleball vacation package in Antigua, and she insisted I take the girlfriend I've kept secret from her."

Angie is silent. Contemplating as she twists a silver and blue ring around her index finger. Is she really considering this? Or is she trying to find the right way to politely tell me to fuck all the way off and never show my face here again. I would deserve it.

"Look, you don't have to come," I say to break the silence. "I just wanted to give you the option, and be totally open about what went down and what I got myself into. I don't want you to feel pressured, and honestly I shouldn't have even put you in this position. It's unfair to—"

"I'm in," she says, nodding.

I stare at her. I must have heard her wrong. Surely I'm hallucinating and sleep deprived because I've been torturing myself with this whole situation for days, and I swear I heard her say that she'll do it. Without me even having to convince her.

"I'm...I'm sorry, what?" I ask.

"I'll do it. Why not, it sounds fun! You know I'm always down for an adventure. Plus, I'm unemployed. Why would I pass up a free trip to Antigua to play pickleball?" She shakes her head, eyes wide and glimmering. "Are you kidding? What's there to think about?"

I let out a long, harsh breath. "Wow, okay, I really thought I'd have to talk you into it...or that you'd be pissed at me?"

Her smile is sweet when she says, "Why would I be pissed? Ash, you're one of my oldest friends. You're practically family. Even if we haven't seen each other in forever."

She places a hand on mine, sending a jolt throughout my entire body.

While the word "friend" lands with a bit of disappointment, the idea of family is something I've always longed for. And she and Wes really are my family. I would do anything for them.

"And honestly, it's not that weird. You had me thinking I was going to need to dig up a body or something. Which, for the record"—she pulls her hand away and holds up her index finger—"I would also do for you."

I can't help but laugh. "No exhuming bodies this time."

"So...do we need to pretend to be dating on this trip? Post pictures on Instagram together to convince your boss it's legit?"

"No, I would never ask you to do that. I think that crosses some ethical boundary." Not that I hadn't thought about it. We will have to be deliberate about the pictures we post.

"Oh come on, Ash, lighten up. I'm offering. We don't have to be making out or anything, just pics like the one we took in London together." My breath catches when she flashes me one of those brilliant smiles. God, she could always light up a room.

My Sunshine...

"You're really okay with all this? I mean, it's a lot, asking you to pretend that we're together. Being stuck with me for ten whole days?"

"Stop overthinking it. It'll be fun." She reaches up and tousles my hair.

Fuck, if she keeps finding new ways to touch me, I'm going to combust.

"I'm actually really excited about this! Plus, if it helps you out with your job, what's there to think about?"

Relief floods me as I let out a long breath. "Okay, but only if you're sure. I've already talked with Wes about his new resort out there, but we should probably give him a heads-up about you coming too. Otherwise he might actually kill me."

His words from when we were in high school ring through my mind.

"Stay the fuck away from my sister, do you hear me? Jesus, dude. Don't ever let me hear you say something like that again. She's off-limits."

Angie laughs. "Why would he kill you? He loves you. He'll probably think this is hilarious."

I guess he never told her then. Probably for the best. I would never want them to fight about me. She always deserved better than someone like me.

"So when do we leave?" she asks.

"End of December, between Christmas and New Year's, likely that Sunday. Does that work for you?"

"It's perfect, actually. My mom will be down here for Christmas; I can have her take the dog back up with her again. Oh! That reminds me, I have a bin of your stuff she kept in storage."

"You do? She kept my stuff for me?" My heart clenches. Not even my own parents bothered storing away any old memories or keepsakes.

"I have no idea what's in it. I didn't want to pry. But you're welcome to take it back with you."

I squeeze her hand, hoping it conveys every ounce of gratitude I have for her and her family. "Thank you." Unsure of what else to say, I let go and clear my throat again. "Wow, okay, so we're really doing this?"

"We're really doing this!" she says, bouncing up and down on the couch cushion and clapping her hands, causing Cally to jump to her feet and wag her tail excitedly. "It'll be so much fun!"

She leans in to hug me, and now I know I must be dreaming. I wrap my arms around her back, holding her tight, involuntarily inhaling the coconut scent of her hair again. Coconut mixed with lavender. It immediately takes me back to being a teenager.

How does a smell transport you like that so intensely? Like magic.

When she pulls back, she says, "So I guess I need to teach you how to play pickleball, huh? Not now obviously, since it's..." she looks at her watch. "Oh shit, it's already ten o'clock?"

I cover my face with my hands. "God, I'm sorry. I'm such an asshole. Coming out here so late without any warning." What the hell was I thinking?

"Would you stop it already?" She stands and tosses the throw pillow in my face.

"I'm gonna go."

Her face scrunches up. "Go where? You live three hours away. Plus, you just got here."

I point to myself. "Again. Asshole."

"You're not an asshole. I like that you surprised me. Do you need to work tomorrow?"

"Yeah, but I can work from home."

"Then it's settled. You're sleeping on my couch."

I shouldn't. But I also know I probably shouldn't drive in the middle of the night when I'm already this exhausted. "Okay. Yeah, that would be nice. Thank you."

She smiles and walks down her hallway, returning with another pillow and a large blanket. "We'll get up early so you can head back in time for work. Sound good?"

Warmth expands through my chest. "Sounds perfect."

11

ANGIE

"I'm sorry, you're what?" Willow practically shouts at me. The colorful glow of her Christmas tree lights sparkles in her eyes as we stand around her kitchen. "You're going on a ten-day luxury pickleball vacation to Antigua with your high school crush?"

I raise an eyebrow and shoot her a slow smile that I know will drive her mad.

"Are you actually insane?"

"Maybe." I put my mug of milk in the microwave and lean my hip against her kitchen island, crossing my arms. I thought she might be more interested in the fact that Asher spent the night on my couch last night after showing up on my doorstep unexpectedly. But I guess she can only process so much information at one time. I still can't really believe it all myself. Not that anything happened, but my mind wouldn't stop playing scenarios where he knocked on my bedroom door, or joined me in the shower, or I walked into the living room and climbed on top of him on the couch.

Let's just say it was not a restful sleep.

This morning, I took him to my favorite breakfast spot to talk some more before he headed back to Indianapolis. It was so easy and comfortable, like it's always been with him. And the more I think about it, the more excited I get for this trip. But I can understand how someone who didn't know us back then would see this as a ridiculous idea.

"Just admit it, you're a little jealous," I say with a smirk.

"I mean...yeah. I'm going to be stuck here in the Midwest in the middle of winter while my best friend gets to play pickleball in the Caribbean and suns herself on a hot beach."

I hold up one finger. "First of all, you know I can't tan, I just burn. And secondly"—I put up another finger—"you have your man to keep you warm. Just snuggle up on the couch with him or in front of the fireplace, or whatever weird shit you couples do. You'll be fine."

She shoots me a withering glare. "You know what I'm worried about. Don't bullshit me."

"It's not a big deal." The timer goes off, and I pull the steaming mug from the microwave before stirring in the hot chocolate powder. "He doesn't feel that way about me, he never has."

"Exactly. That's why this *is* a big deal. I don't want to see you get hurt again. I was there when everything went down with John, in case you forgot."

A familiar ache settles in my chest. Of course I didn't forget one of the worst moments of my life. Thinking the man I was deeply in love with felt the same way, only to find out he was... indifferent. Needing to "see what else was out there" as he put it, meaning he wanted to sleep with other people, and probably already was.

"I know. This isn't like that. Asher is an old friend, practically family. There's never been more between us."

"But you *want* there to be?" she guesses.

I hesitate, taking my time to wrap my hands around my hot mug. It's enough to confirm her fears.

Do I still want there to be more? Or am I ready to move on from this fantasy once and for all? Maybe I'll get lucky and being in close quarters with him will show me all his flaws and red flags I've never allowed myself to see before.

My best friend in high school, Christina, once told me a crush is just a lack of information. I could use these ten days to actively look for things I don't like about him. Then I'll finally be free of this curse.

It's time to take off the rose-colored glasses.

She blows on her own drink to cool it down before taking a sip. "Look, I'm not here to tell you what to do. Go, have fun. But...just be careful. Please. I couldn't stand to see your heart broken again. It would kill me."

I blink back tears. God, she's such a good friend.

She adds, "And then I would have to kill him, and I really don't want to go through all that trouble."

I set down my mug and squeeze around her torso, resting my head on her boobs. I wish we had known each other back in high school, and she could've been there during the whole Asher situation the first time around. Christina was wonderful and supportive, but she never saw me the way Willow does.

She is so intense and fierce with her love. I know she would do anything for me, like I would for her. It's why we got matching tattoos our first year of college. A reminder of our unbreakable bond.

I pull back and take a sip of my hot chocolate to distract myself from my overwhelming emotions when the front door opens. Our friends Simon and Faris come inside, not even bothering to knock or ring the doorbell because they know it sends the dogs into a frenzy. Simon is balancing a bottle of wine and a tray of snacks. Faris carefully makes his way to us, hobbling on his walking boot, avoiding said crazy dogs.

"Look at you!" I shout as I walk toward him to wrap him in a hug.

Faris is still in physical therapy after he tore his Achilles four months ago training with Willow for the same pickleball tournament Max and I were in together. That's when she and Luca were paired up and eventually fell in love.

"How do you feel?" Willow asks him.

"Better every day. Glad to be off the crutches finally."

"I bet," I say, gently guiding him to the couch. He eyes me suspiciously.

"What were you two just talking about before we got here? You're being weird." Why does everyone in my life have to be so damn observant? And nosy.

"Nothing," I say at the same time Willow talks over me.

"She's going to the Caribbean with her high school crush. The guy she ran into in London and also let sleep over last night."

I narrow my eyes at her. "Traitor."

Willow crosses her arms with a victorious smile as both Faris and Simon take in a harsh breath, and then immediately start shouting back and forth in a chorus of questions.

"What?"

"Who is he?"

"When were you going to tell us?"

"He spent the night?"

"When do you leave?"

I throw my hands in the air. "You all need to chill! It's not that big of a deal."

"Oh please," Faris says. "Your high school crush? In all the years we've known each other, you've never once told us about him."

"I feel betrayed," Simon adds with a pout.

I roll my eyes as I grab my mug of rapidly cooling chocolate and take another sip. "Fine. His name is Asher. He lived next door growing up and was Wesley's best friend. The three of us hung out a lot. I thought he was cute. Then he moved away to college. The end."

Willow gives a dramatic thumbs-down while blowing a raspberry.

I shoot her a glance that I hope conveys that I really don't want to make a big deal out of this right now. Her face softens a little.

"Look, he was my first crush, but it was a long time ago. We were kids. And nothing ever happened." I shrug. "We reconnected in London. We're going to check out Wesley's resort in Antigua, and I'm going to help Asher put together a pickleball vacation that he can sell to his work clients. Any other questions?"

"Wait." Simon grabs his phone. "Are we talking about that guy who tagged you on Instagram?"

He pulls up the photo of the two of us, and I nod.

"You said he was just a friend!"

"He is!" I shout. "That's what I'm trying to tell you."

Faris looks over at Simon's phone and says, "Jesus. This is your high school crush? He looks like a much hotter Prince Harry."

"I knew I should've done more digging," Simon whispers to himself as he furiously types away.

Faris adds, "And you're going on a vacation with him? Just the two of you?"

"And you expect us to believe you're not fucking?" Simon says without even looking up from his phone.

"We're not! It's not like that between us. Can we drop it

now?" I grab Simon's phone out of his grasp and toss it face down on the couch.

Thankfully, everyone seems to pick up on my urge to swiftly end this conversation.

Simon stands and unwraps the snack tray. "Well, I'm jealous."

"Same," Faris adds. "You all keep going on these trips without me while I'm injured. I feel personally attacked."

Simon nods. "Right? You both owe us big time. I'm thinking...Portugal."

"What about New Zealand?" Willow chimes in as she opens the bottle of wine.

"Yes! Your *friend* can hook us up."

I don't appreciate the way Faris says "friend," but I choose to ignore it. He and Simon start talking about traveling and where they want to go on this make-believe vacation. Willow comes to my side, wrapping her arm around my shoulder as she hands me a glass of wine without saying a word.

"I'll be careful. I promise," I whisper. "I can handle a few days with an old friend."

She nods, but I know she doesn't quite believe me.

Hell, I wouldn't believe me either. But it's too late to back out now.

In three weeks, ready or not, I'm headed to the Caribbean with Asher Hayes.

12

ANGIE

February 14

It's been one year. I've had a crush on my brother's best friend for a WHOLE YEAR. And it hasn't gotten any better. In fact, it's worse than ever! He keeps doing and saying all these nice things, showing off his ridiculous dimples, and it makes it impossible to get over him.

As corny as it is, I love Valentine's Day. But not being able to celebrate with the one person you want is beyond shitty.

Wes went home sick at lunch today, so Asher and I walked home together. We talked about our days, and he said he really doesn't like Valentine's Day. How it's all fake and meaningless. Probably because his parents fight all the time, which I hate.

But I can't help but think about how Dad would always bring home lilies for me and Mom on Valentine's

Day along with giant cupcakes for all of us from the bakery down the street. It was just so nice to feel loved and appreciated. I used to think everyone felt that way on Valentine's Day.

So I said, "I guess every day can't be all sunshine and rainbows, huh."

Then...he tugged at a lock of my hair and said, "Maybe you could be my sunshine."

I swear I stopped breathing and it suddenly felt way too hot with all those layers on. Luckily we were almost home at that point, and we would be going our separate ways since Wes was sick and couldn't hang out.

He called me his sunshine.

I liked the sound of that way too much.

Why does he have to be so dang sweet?

Dammit, I may never get over him.

13

ASHER

I'm not sure if I can go through with this. I should call off the whole thing. Angie seemed so open to the idea of going on this trip with me, but only as friends, because that's all she will ever see me as.

I look around my drab apartment, wondering if putting up some Christmas decorations would cheer me up. But then I think, why bother? Christmas is next week. No one is coming over. I have no one to celebrate any holidays with. No pets, no one waiting for me when I come home. It's pathetic.

Then there's the fact that I'm leaving two days later.

No point in putting up a sad little Charlie Brown tree, which would just make this place look even worse.

Maybe I'll distract myself by starting to pack. Even if there's still plenty of time. Thoughts of traveling with Angie are the only thing giving me a shred of happiness right now. I'm still in shock that she agreed to this whole thing.

I've started watching instructional pickleball videos online to get a handle on this sport I'm supposedly so interested in. Plus, I don't want to look like a complete fool when she's helping me. I think I have the basic concept of it—hit the ball, keep it in the lines, first team to eleven points wins—but I've never been particularly good at racquet sports. Basketball was my thing in high school, and I've been going to the gym regularly for the past few years, but I'm sure I'll look ridiculous out on that court no matter what.

My phone burns a hole in my back pocket as all I can think about is texting her. Would that be weird? I mean, what would I even say? Something about the trip?

I pull it out before I can overthink it.

ME

Hey! Do you need me to grab anything at the store? Or are you all set?

ANGIE

do we have enough sunscreen?

ME

Between the two of us there could never be enough

ANGIE

LOL so true

other than that I think I'm ok???

I'll bring pickleball stuff

ME

Oh right

ANGIE

😜

ME

no second thoughts about this whole thing?

ANGIE

no way

I'm excited 😁

ME

Me too 😎

My heart wants to leap out of my chest.

But then I'm struck by a blinding thought. Sunscreen.

Rubbing sunscreen all over her shoulders...her back.

She'll be in a swimsuit. A bikini, probably.

My cock swells at the images my mind is now conjuring. *Fuck.*

I've been so preoccupied with the logistics of having her on this trip with me in the first place that I didn't even stop to think about the implications of spending ten days together at a beach resort.

Or sleeping in the same room.

What am I doing?

Wes, Angie, and I would spend our summers together at the nearby pool a lot, and those last few years before I left for college were pure torture. She had filled out in all the right places, and it took everything in me to respect Wes's wishes and keep my distance. Especially when the other guys at school were noticing her too, flirting and making her laugh. I wanted to be the one to make her laugh.

But we're not kids anymore.

We're both grown adults who are perfectly capable of making our own decisions.

Although Wes and I didn't end things on the best of terms, he is still like a brother to me, and I wouldn't want to do anything to risk our friendship. Even now.

Wes and Angie are the only family I've got.

I can't even remember the last time I spoke with my parents, nor do I really care to. If they're not going to make the effort to have a relationship with me, why should I? It's like I was an unpleasant phase in their life and now they've moved on. I wish things could've been different, but I've stopped holding on to any hope that it could change.

That's why I can't fuck this up.

I pull my luggage out of the closet with a sigh. I've done a lot of traveling over the years for this job, so packing is like second nature. I know exactly how much of everything to bring for myself and what I'll need while I'm there. But this trip is different. It's the first time in a very long time I won't be going alone.

And it's with one of my favorite people in the whole world.

The thought alone warms me all the way down to my toes.

Even if we can never be together in a romantic way, I just want to be near her.

Being apart from her and Wes all these years really drives home how utterly alone I am. I've been running from all my problems and my fears for far too long.

It's time to grow up.

14

ASHER

It's seven a.m. Sunday morning, and Angie Harris is in the passenger seat of my Honda Civic, our luggage stuffed in the trunk, and we are headed up to Chicago to fly out and spend ten days together in Antigua.

It all feels so surreal.

Like a fantasy I've let play out in my head for years.

I spent the night again so we could leave early from her place, and like last time, I barely slept, thinking about her in the next room. Maybe I can try to get some sleep on the plane.

Five minutes into our forty-two-minute journey to O'Hare Airport for the only direct flight they had, I've barely said a word. Angie is the one to hold the majority of our conversation, thankfully. She's so animated and talkative, I could listen to her ramble on for hours. I'm not even sure I understand what she's talking about right now, but it's the most exciting and important thing I've ever heard.

That's always how it felt with her. I've missed this feeling.

"Okay, so how are we putting this itinerary together?" She turns in her seat to face me, one knee pulled up to her chest as she plays with a lock of hair that has come loose from her braid. "What's the plan?"

I tap on the steering wheel. "I've done some research and have an idea of what other people are doing for these types of trips. We'll be there for ten days, but I think the package we put together should be eight, including travel days. Like Saturday to Saturday."

"That makes sense. I like it. We can try a bunch of things out, and at the end we can figure out what we liked and what works best for the itinerary."

I nod. "I've put together similar packages before, but I'd love to get your input on the pickleball aspect and activities we could add. Find a way to stand out from the competition, you know?"

"Hmm, okay. Right off the bat," she starts, gesturing excitedly with her hands, "I'm imagining like, pickleball clinics in the morning, open play in the afternoon. Do you have any coaches or trainers lined up?"

"I have literally nothing lined up. Except for the fact that Wes's resort is open to a partnership, thank god. He really saved my ass there. Otherwise this whole thing falls apart."

"Okay. Pickleball details we can work out later. I'll keep a running list of things we need to come back to." She pulls out her phone and starts typing in her Notes app with a determined look.

"You're a lifesaver, you know that?" I nudge her with my elbow.

"Once we get there, I can handle your social media too if you like. We really need to get you more followers and engagement on there. You're missing a huge opportunity on trips like these to connect with potential clients."

"You sound just like my boss," I say with a playful roll of my eyes. "I guess I'm lucky to have you here with me then."

We arrive at the airport and get through security fairly quickly by O'Hare standards. After grabbing coffee and a bite to eat inside the terminal, we board our flight and settle into our seats. I lift my hand over the armrest, but quickly realize Angie's arm is already there. Our pinkies touch ever so slightly, and we both pull away at the same time.

I feel my face flame with heat as I turn to look out the window for something interesting to stare at.

Get a grip.

When I let out a long breath and lean back in my seat, the enormity of the situation finally hits me. Ten days together. The same room. Half naked on the beach. Sweating on the courts.

I feel the sides of the airplane close in on me.

The last time I went on one of these trips with Sarah, it was a complete disaster. Spending so much time together in one small space made me realize how incompatible we were. It wasn't long after we got home that it all came crumbling down.

Would the same thing happen with Angie?

My hand finds the left side of my chest, and I squeeze, panic clawing through me. This was such a bad idea.

Is it too late to back out? I think to myself as a flight attendant walks by. I imagine what I could possibly say to her to get me off this plane without looking like a terrorist or like I've lost my damn mind.

Who am I kidding, there would be clips of me all over social media before we even landed.

Angie puts a hand on my arm, jolting me out of my spiraling thoughts. "Hey, you okay?"

"Oh, yeah, fine. Just not a huge fan of flying," I lie.

She quirks an eyebrow. “Isn’t flying, like...a major part of your job? Figured you’d be used to it.”

Of course it is. I’m just a terrible liar.

One lie only leads to more lies.

“I uh...still get a little nervous before takeoff. No big deal.”

“How many flights do you think you’ve been on for your job?” she asks. I know she’s trying to distract me.

“Oh...too many to count,” I reply. “Does that make me sound like a dick? Like I’ve traveled so much I can’t keep track?”

She huffs out a laugh. “Sounds like a good problem to have.”

I drum my fingers on my knees before digging through my bag to distract myself and try to calm my nerves. Not from the flight, but from this entire situation I’ve managed to find myself in.

Her lips twist to the side. “This whole thing is a little weird, though, right? Like it doesn’t seem real?”

I’m flooded with relief to know she feels the same way. “Yeah. Weird, but...nice.”

A bit of awkward silence ensues. If I put on headphones, would that be rude? It’s not that I don’t want to talk to her, but I’m suddenly so nervous I’m afraid I’m going to say something stupid and ruin this whole thing on day one. I need to make it through the next ten days like a normal person.

As if hearing my thoughts, she says, “Anyways...I’m just gonna read. I won’t be offended if you want to put some music on or something.” She nods to the headphones in my hands.

“You sure? I might try and get a quick nap in, but just nudge me if you need anything.”

“Will do.” She smiles sweetly before opening up a paperback novel. I sneak a peek at the front cover. Some deceptively sweet cartoon illustration, but no doubt filthy as hell on the inside.

Now I definitely need a distraction. I can't be thinking about Angie reading smut when she's mere inches from me, close enough to smell. Heat flows toward my dick as I silently curse myself and shift in my seat. Nope, not now.

I place the noise-canceling headphones over my ears and put on some calming music I downloaded to my phone, squeezing my eyes shut.

I can do this.

It's only ten days.

What could possibly happen?

15

ANGIE

Our shuttle from the airport pulls through a set of large white iron gates around five p.m., and my eyes can barely comprehend the sheer beauty surrounding me. Palm trees everywhere, crystal clear blue-green waters, luscious greenery, and flowers spraying the landscape in brilliant, beautiful colors. It doesn't even look real.

We pull up to a sprawling white building with terra cotta roofing, wide open windows, and an enormous stone fountain out front. The grand entrance is surrounded by more palm trees and exotic flowers. Salty air sticks to my skin as two men dressed in fine linen take our bags and proceed to take them inside, beckoning us to follow.

The inside is like nothing I've seen before. It feels both luxurious and cozy at the same time, with large crystal light fixtures hung from enormous rafters with thick twined rope. Natural cottage elements mixed with abstract metal pieces decorate the long, open lobby.

When I look to Asher, he shoots me a wink, sending a wave of butterflies soaring in my belly and heat flushing up my neck.

That one gesture is enough to undo all the work I've done to get over him for Operation: Grow Up Glow Up—other code name considerations included Operation: Crush This Crush and He's Just a Teenage Dirtbag.

In his line of work, he's probably used to staying at all these fancy places where they pamper and spoil you, but this is completely new to me. He must see it written all over my face.

"Holy shit, Wesley completely undersold this place," I whisper. "It's incredible!"

As we walk through the wide-open space, a gorgeous older woman with long, black hair hands each of us a large round glass full of some kind of glittery golden drink. I take a sip and let out a low moan. The sweet, citrusy blend dancing on my tongue is one of the most delicious things I've ever tasted.

Asher is staring at me. I immediately bring my hand up to cover my mouth. "What? Is there something on my face?"

He blinks several times and walks away from me to the reception desk. He's been acting so weird today. Barely saying two words to me on the drive to the airport and on the flight here, and then he *winks*? Now he's back to being all silent and mysterious again. What is going through his head right now?

"Hello hello! And welcome to the Blue Water Resort," a stout man dressed in an aqua blue polo shirt and white linen pants says brightly from behind the front desk. "Mr. Hayes, how are you today?"

I come to Asher's side as he replies low and even, "Very well, thank you."

So professional. *Mr. Hayes, Super Serious Travel Agent Extraordinaire*. Why am I suddenly picturing him in a fitted three-piece suit adjusting his cufflinks?

The energetic man then looks to me. "Mrs. Hayes, welcome! How was your flight?"

I freeze. Asher and I both glance at each other, unmoving.

"Oh, I'm—"

"I see here congratulations are in order," he continues. "We have upgraded your room and hope to provide you with the best experience possible as you start your new life together. Please let us know if there's anything you need. We hope you enjoy your stay."

"Sorry. Upgraded?" Asher asks, his face adorably scrunched up.

"Yes, to our honeymoon villa. At no extra charge, of course. It's our way of saying congratulations, and we hope to be working with you more in the future."

Holy shit. Why would he think we're married? There must be some mix-up with the paperwork. We should correct him.

However...

If we tell this guy the truth now, then we'd be missing out on a once-in-a-lifetime opportunity. *The honeymoon villa?* We can't pass this up. It doesn't hurt anyone, right?

In that moment, I make a wildly reckless decision as I subtly move my grandmother's sapphire ring from my index finger to the ring finger on my left hand under the counter, still balancing my delicious shimmering cocktail.

Asher sucks in a breath, no doubt ready to be grumpy Mr. Truth-Teller and try to talk the receptionist out of letting us have this new room, but I stop him with a gentle hand to his forearm over one of his tattoos.

"Babe, did you hear that?" I say, beaming up at him. "The honeymoon villa! Gosh, this is so exciting!"

I feel him tense beneath me, and I squeeze his arm in warning. When he doesn't move, I look back to the receptionist with a wide grin.

"What a lovely surprise, thank you so much. This just made our whole honeymoon unforgettable."

"Of course." He turns to Asher. "Sir, if you will just sign these forms, we'll have you all set."

Asher slips out of my grasp and takes the pen from the counter to sign the papers. All the while it's like he's in a trance. Still acting so weird. He must really need this vacation if he's this tense.

This version of him is so different from the carefree one I remember. What's happened to him these past ten years to make him so anxious and worrisome? He had mentioned an ex before, but didn't seem to want to talk about it. Maybe it ended badly and he's not completely over her.

Does he feel guilty taking me on this trip when he still has feelings for someone else?

"Perfect! Your bags have already been taken to your room. Here are your keys," he says, handing us two keycards. Asher takes them both and puts them in his pocket, still showing no hint of emotion. "Your villa is number twelve. Down that path, second building on the right."

I wrap an arm around Asher's waist, leaning into him as I say to the kind man, "Thank you so much." Looking up at Asher, I add, "Come on, Shmoopy. Let's go."

Asher tries to suppress a smile, finally getting the hint to play along as he takes my hand, leading me out of the main building toward the outdoor villas. Sparks ignite in my palm and up my arm at the physical contact.

What have I gotten myself into? I'm supposed to be trying to get over him, not convince people we're married. If we keep this up, we're going to have to be affectionate in public all week.

Once we're out of earshot of the resort employees, Asher drops my hand and says, "What was that?"

I instantly miss the warmth of his touch, even though it's insanely hot and humid out.

"Oh come on, were you really gonna say no to an upgraded room?" I gesture around us. "I mean, look at this place!"

"But...now they all think we're married."

"So what? We were already going to be pretending to be dating, what's the big deal?" Even though I know exactly why it's a big deal.

He turns away from me without saying another word, and I roll my eyes as we continue to walk the distance to our villa in silence, taking another sip of my drink.

"Look, if we're going to survive this vacation together, you're going to have to lighten up a little, Ash. Come on! Where's the guy I remember from high school? He was always up for adventures and having fun. Forget about acting married or what the people here think of us. Let's just have a good time, okay?"

Without thinking, I reach up and pinch his left nipple. He flinches and turns to me with wide eyes.

"Ow! Did you just purple nurple me? You know that's not fair." He tries to sound annoyed but a tiny smile creeps across that gorgeous face of his, making my stomach flip as he rubs his chest. "Okay, fine. I'm sorry. Let's have a good time."

We continue walking as a cluster of villas appear along the pathway, each angled so the back faces the water. I wonder what the honeymoon villa will look like. If the rest of this place is any indicator, it's going to be way more than just "nice."

We approach villa number twelve, and Asher waves the keycard over the black box on the door. He opens it to let me in first. The sight in front of me takes my breath away.

Wide bamboo screen doors open to the view of a sky alight with brilliant shades of orange and pink, reflecting off the waves of the vast open waters. Sounds of the ocean drift through the large open villa as a soft breeze gently lifts the sheer white curtains. It's an honest-to-god paradise.

I step up to the open doors to get a better look, and a gasp slips from me.

"We have our own private pool? Are you kidding me?"

Asher comes to my side, taking in the view. Two lounging chairs point toward a pristine infinity pool overlooking the small, private beach. "Damn, this is nice."

"Nice? It's spectacular!" I turn and walk into the connected bedroom space and notice the king-size bed, my mouth falling open. "Umm...Ash?" I say as he steps closer.

He nearly drops his drink.

Flower petals spread out to read "Mr. & Mrs." inside a heart over the white bedspread. A large bouquet of red roses on the nightstand sits behind a bottle of champagne on ice and two glass flutes, with a small envelope propped against them.

I pick up the envelope to read what's inside.

Congratulations on your wedding! Wishing you a lifetime of love and happiness. - The Blue Water Resort

Holy shit. I guess we're really doing this.

"Well..." I look to Asher with a growing smile. "Let's get this honeymoon started!"

16

ASHER

Of course there's only one bed. What could I have possibly expected the moment the man at the front desk said we would be in the goddamn *honeymoon villa*? Making the assumption that Angie and I were newlyweds, and her gleefully going along with it for some reason. Why did he think we were married?

I should have corrected him immediately. Just like with Bryn, this is getting out of hand.

Why is it so hard for me to convince people we are not actually together?

You know why, my brain claps back.

Lies, lies, and more lies.

"This is crazy," I finally say.

"I wonder why he thought we were newlyweds?" She crosses her arms.

"You mean aside from the fact that you went along with it and called me 'Shmoopy?'"

She lets out a deep laugh that warms me up. "Yeah, I mean,

I can only assume *you* didn't tell them we were married when you booked the room, based on your reaction back there."

"No, I would never do that. You know I was already against having you pretend to be my girlfriend."

Girlfriend.

If she only knew how long I've wanted that to be true. But not like this. Not through coercion or lying.

"Is the idea of being married to me that horrifying for you?" she asks with a pout, and my stomach drops like an anchor.

I try to think of something to say, but no words come out.

"Angie, I—"

"Ash. I'm fucking with you." Her face splits into a wide grin. "Will you lighten up already? Stop worrying so much and start enjoying this vacation."

I instinctively cover my nipples in case she tries to pinch them again. She used to do that all the time, because she's a menace.

Angie finishes the rest of her drink in one long gulp and sets it down on a nearby table before taking her phone out and snapping photos of the room and the incredible view. No doubt for my Instagram page.

Thank god she offered to help me with all that. Social media is not my strong suit. I'd much rather live in the moment instead of worrying about "making content." Who the hell is interested in what I'm doing anyway? But she insists I need to start trying if I want to get new clients and move up in the business.

"Maybe don't post the 'Mr. & Mrs.' part?" I say half-jokingly. But part of me is deadly serious, because if Wes found out we were now pretending to be married, he might actually put a hit out on me, and I can say goodbye to our companies forging a partnership for more of these vacations.

It was hard enough convincing him that we were playing the dating card to appease my boss and that it didn't actually mean anything.

I hate lying to him.

"Good call." She pushes and scatters the rose petals all over the bed, making it look like a simple romantic setup. That could be believable as something they would do for regular non-married couples, right?

I need to stop overthinking it. Angie's right, I really do need this vacation. When was the last time I actually relaxed?

"So...what do you want to do tonight?" I ask her. "I figured we'd just want to keep things low-key after a long day of travel. Maybe hang out in the pool for a bit and then go grab some dinner?"

She looks over at me. "Oh yeah, I meant to ask, what's the food situation here?"

"The resort has eight restaurants on-site, plus eleven or twelve bars. Everything, including drinks, is all included, of course."

"Oh wow. We should try to hit up as many of them as we can while we're here. I am getting hungry, but a dip in the pool sounds perfect right now. I'll go get my swimsuit on."

She digs around in her suitcase while I decide to busy myself with...something else. Anything besides imagining what kind of swimsuit she is going to torture me with once she comes back out of that bathroom. The bathroom with a frosted glass door, a wide-open shower, and barely any privacy.

That whole situation is going to be a problem. Not only taking showers, but what about when I need to take a shit? I'll have to go find another restroom on the property, far away from her.

I drain the last of my welcome cocktail. I have a feeling I'm going to need a lot more of these to get through this trip in one piece.

Speaking of one-piece, the opposite of that is what enters my view when Angie steps out of the bathroom. A bright yellow string bikini barely covers her perfect body. Hard nipples poke through the tiny triangles clinging to her chest, and I think I might pass out.

Is she trying to kill me?

I turn away, my forehead suddenly damp, my neck prickling with heat. It's fine. Only nine and a half more days of this.

"Yeah, I'll...me too, yeah," I mumble to no one in particular, taking my entire suitcase with me into the bathroom like a maniac. Barely any space for me to hide away and change in peace.

After stripping down and changing into my swim trunks, I stop to look at myself in the mirror, silently cursing to myself. The tattoo on the left side of my chest is clear as day. Shit. I need to cover it up with something.

I notice her makeup bag on the sink and get an idea. Foundation maybe? Only one way to find out. I smear a dollop on my skin, hoping it's enough to blend in. My chest hair provides a little cover, but the dark ink against my pale skin is striking. This will have to do for now, and if not, then I guess we're going to be having a whole other conversation real soon.

Can I really keep it covered this entire trip?

I chicken out and decide to put my shirt back on. We'll be going to dinner soon anyway.

"So do you want to hang out at our private pool, or go down to the resort pool?" she asks when I walk back into the bedroom. "I'm good either way."

"Let's just hang here," I reply. "I think I need another drink though."

"Same." I hear some rattling behind me as I put my suitcase back on the luggage rack. "Hey Ash?"

"Yeah?"

"Did you know we have a fully stocked bar?" she says in a sing-song voice.

"Oh yeah?" I turn in her direction, forcing my eyes to focus anywhere but that teeny bikini. For the first time, I notice she has a tattoo of her own on the inside of her wrist. A small watercolor heart that I definitely need to know more about.

"And it says if we push this button here, we can place an order for anything we want, and they'll just bring it to us."

"Oh, I've never sprung for butler service before. It felt too weird when it was just me."

She presses the sleek black button on the wall, and a deep male voice comes through. "Yes, Mr. and Mrs. Hayes. What can I get you?"

I'm still not used to hearing "Mr. and Mrs. Hayes." I ignore the buzz rushing through my blood.

Her jaw drops dramatically as I whisper, "Okay, that's pretty cool."

Without missing a beat, Angie replies, "Two strawberry margaritas, please."

"Right away," the man says.

"Okay, but that's excessive, right?" she asks. "Who needs a butler?"

"Nobody, but it's part of the package. And you were the one who wanted to have the *honeymoon experience.*" I feel my face flush when I realize how that could be taken, but she is unfazed.

"It's too bougie for a pickleball vacation, though."

"What if I went and fetched you whatever you wanted this week?" *Please let me wait on you hand and foot. Spoil you. Treat you like the queen you are.*

"That I can get behind," she says with a laugh.

Angie grabs two towels from the side table as she lowers her sunglasses from the top of her head, sauntering through the open doors toward the lounge chairs. A knock on the front door stops me from staring at her ass for too long. When I answer it, a man in the same blue and white uniform as every other staff member stands there with two pink drinks on a serving tray.

"Your drinks, Mr. Hayes," he says.

"Thank you so much," I say, taking the glasses.

"Can I get you anything else?"

Checking out his name tag, I respond, "No, Alvin. I appreciate it. Thank you so much."

I head toward our private pool and set the drinks down on the table between the two lounge chairs. One occupied by the most beautiful woman I've ever laid eyes on.

Angie adjusts her chair to lie flat as she looks up at me. "Thanks, Ash. Or should I say 'hubby?'"

I wince. "Yeah, I don't think I'm the 'hubby' type."

The nickname, but also as a husband in general. I've never wanted to get married. Most of my life, I've felt content either being on my own or having passive relationships with other people. Never believing I was marriage material or that I would be good enough for anyone in that way. And it's worked out for me so far.

I wonder though, what it would be like to be loved unconditionally by someone you felt the same way about. If that could even be possible for me.

She smiles softly as she takes a sip of the margarita, and then flips herself face down onto her lounge chair, so her perfect, round ass—barely covered by a tiny strip of yellow fabric—is pointed right up at me.

Goddammit.

17

ANGIE

March 4

I'm sixteen!!! Mom surprised me with the keys to the Buick this morning! It's not the nicest or fanciest, but it's mine. It used to be Grandpa's so it holds a special place in my heart. After getting my official driver's license, I drove around and hung out at Christina's for a while. Then I came home for dinner and Asher was there...he sat next to me at the table while we ate, and then asked me to drive him and Wesley around.

First he handed me a present wrapped in sparkly colored paper. I opened it up and it was a keychain. Dangling from the metal ring was a wooden sun painted golden yellow. He said he made it in wood shop class for me for my first set of car keys.

A sun.

Sunshine.

We stood there for what felt like an hour just staring at each other before Wesley rudely interrupted the moment and brought us outside to go drive.

Wesley sat in the passenger seat and Asher was in the back. I was so nervous having him there while I drove that I bumped the curb turning on Waterson Street. SO EMBARRASSING! My face was probably bright red the entire time as I tried to ignore him staring at me from the back seat. I avoided looking in the rearview mirror the entire time.

When we got back home I started bolting for my room, unable to face my colossal embarrassment, when Asher put his arm around my shoulders and said, "You did great. Happy Birthday, Sunshine."

18

ASHER

Angie and I get seated at a large hibachi table with a group of six other people. This Japanese steakhouse looked amazing on the website, and I have been dying to try it since this ridiculous plan got set in motion. Sizzling grills and lively conversation fill the room, and Angie and I are sitting so close our knees are almost touching. Just like in London at the tiny Italian restaurant.

After putting in our drink orders, Angie says, "So tell me more about college. I always wondered what you did after you left us."

The words stick like a barb. I know she doesn't mean for it to hurt, but it does, and she picks up on my hesitation.

"Or...we can talk about something else? The economy? People who put pineapple on pizza?"

"You mean monsters?" I shake my head. "Nah, it's fine. A lot went down that summer; I think about it all the time. College was okay, but I don't want you to think it was easy for me to leave."

She puts her hand over mine. It's soft and warm and everything all at once. I fight the urge to interlace our fingers.

"Hey," she says. "I didn't mean to upset you. I'm sorry."

"Please don't apologize. I don't know, it's just—" Cheers erupt around us when the table next to ours goes up in flames. I find myself leaning in closer. Too close. My mouth barely an inch from her ear. "I knew you'd all be fine without me. But I wanted to reach out so many times to see you guys again."

"So why didn't you?" She says it so softly I almost didn't hear it. Not accusatory, but almost hurt. Then she pulls her hand away. That simple movement is enough to break something deep within me.

I shift in my chair, ready to spill everything I've been holding in, when the waiter sets down two tiny ceramic cups and a large carafe of sake in front of us and proceeds to take everyone's food orders. Angie and I both order the steak and chicken combo.

"Do you know that it's customary in Japan to pour your companion's drink?" I ask as I pour the hot sake into her cup, the clear liquid steaming.

"I think I did hear that somewhere. Have you been?" She takes the carafe and pours my drink.

"Not yet, but I'd love to someday. My clients have told me incredible stories." I lift my cup and hold it out to hers. "*Kanpai.*"

She taps hers to mine and repeats, "Kanpai."

We both take a sip and savor the rich, crisp flavor.

"So...back to what you were saying before," she says, filling my cup again. "I wouldn't have expected you to reach out to *me* necessarily, but Wesley said you guys didn't speak again until last month in London. What happened there?"

I sigh, wishing there was a way to avoid telling this story. But I want to be honest with her, and I certainly don't want her to think it was her fault. "Something happened between us right before school ended that summer. We had a fight, and it ended badly. I went off to college before we could really put it behind us. It all just fell apart, and neither of us reached out to make up. Which, looking back now was so dumb and immature."

Her eyebrows are scrunched, those ocean blue eyes searching. "What happened?"

I rub the bridge of my nose. "I'm really not sure you want to hear about this."

"Are you kidding? You guys were like brothers; I've always wanted to know what could ever keep you two apart. Spill it."

I pour more sake into her cup and take a breath. "Okay...do you remember Prom night?"

She shifts awkwardly in her seat and looks down at the table. Taking a sip of her drink as she nods her head. I still remember that night well, wishing it was her I was taking to Prom as she stood off to the side, her mom taking photos of me and Wes with our dates. She looked sad, and I thought maybe it was because her dad wasn't there for it.

"Well, my date ended up ditching me halfway through the dance for some college guy, so I ended up hanging out with Wes and his girlfriend all night."

"Ah, yes. I remember Stacy very well."

"Right? I always felt like the third wheel with them. But... that night, she was...flirting with me. I brushed it off, pretended not to notice, but she started getting more insistent and touchy. In front of Wes."

"He didn't care?" she asks before taking a sip of her sake.

I bite my lip. "He seemed...into it? Or at least he wasn't putting a stop to it."

Her eyes go wide.

"So, that night...she invited me back to the hotel room they had gotten. To be with...her and Wes." I wince, unable to gauge her reaction.

"Huh." She sets down her cup and crosses her arms, resting them on the table.

I quickly add, "I said no. I mean, it would've been weird, right? I didn't feel comfortable crossing that line. Multiple lines, really."

She leans her head on her palm, a smile tugging at her lips. "Without too many details of my brother's sexcapades...did *he*? Want you to, I mean?"

"I don't think so. I think it was more like...a thrill to see her flirting with another guy. Not so much that he actually wanted us all to..." I wave my hand around, letting her fill in the blanks.

She nods, cutting me off with a raised hand. "Got it. Okay, so then what?"

I take another deep breath. "After that night, things just soured between us. He started shutting me out. I think he was pissed knowing that his girlfriend was attracted to me, or was worried I wanted to be with her. They broke up that summer too, if you remember."

"I remember, but I thought they just didn't want to do the long-distance thing."

"That was part of it, but I think Prom night sealed the deal. He didn't trust her...or me after that. Eventually, we had a huge fight about it." I shake my head, trying not to let all those emotions rise back up. I've spent the better part of a decade keeping them in check, and I'm not about to lose it in front of her or all these strangers. I drain my cup. She fills it back up.

"But...I don't understand. You didn't do anything wrong. You didn't go through with it."

"Trust me, I know. I've overanalyzed the whole thing for years. What I did wrong, what I could've done differently. I remember driving away feeling so lost and empty inside. Like I had no one left in my life who cared about me."

Tears well in her eyes as she puts a warm hand on my leg. "Oh, Ash. I had no idea."

"Hey, no crying." I reach out and swipe one away just as it falls down her cheek. "This is our honeymoon, remember?"

She huffs a wet laugh and sniffles. "I hate that you thought no one cared about you. That couldn't be further from the truth. I'm so sorry about everything that happened, and...I can't speak for Wesley, but...I really missed you."

My head rears back. "You did?"

She scoffs, pulling her hand away again. "Are you fucking serious right now? You were one of my best friends. You, me, and Wesley were always together. The infamous trio. I can't believe you would ever think that didn't mean anything to me."

A lightness grows in my chest.

She missed me.

Before I can pick that notion apart too much, the animated hibachi chef arrives at our table, ready to put on a show.

When we get back to our villa, warm and buzzed from too much sake, a moment of silence washes over us. We probably should have figured out the logistics of how we're going to sleep tonight before this moment.

I clear my throat. "I'll, uh...take the couch tonight."

"What?" she says, like I offended her.

"There's only one bed, so of course you should take it. It's fine. How many times did I sleep on your couch growing up? I slept on your couch last night for crying out loud!"

She smiles. "True, but this bed is huge. There's plenty of space for both of us. It doesn't have to be weird."

But it is weird. And sleeping next to her would be torture. My dick is already trying to get hard at the thought. Nothing good can come of that.

"Don't worry about me." I quickly turn away from her to set up a blanket and a pillow on the couch in the main living space. "I've slept on worse."

"How about another drink first?" she says, toeing off her sandals. "I'm not tired yet."

That is also a bad idea, but I find myself saying, "Okay, but you have to order it and answer the door when Alvin gets here."

"Deal."

She calls up our butler and orders our drinks in between fits of giggles. Then she excuses herself to the bathroom to change as a text buzzes on my phone.

WES

Everything good with the room? All settled in?

I think I'm going to throw up. What does he know? Is he messing with me, or just checking in? My fingers hover over the keyboard while I figure out how to reply.

ME

All good, thanks again for hooking us up

I mean, setting this up!

Super chill. Nothing weird about that.

Then suddenly I don't care, because Angie comes out of the bathroom in a pair of tiny pink sleep shorts and a tight gray tank top that nearly stops my heart. Her hair is down in long, loose waves that my fingers itch to get tangled in. Mercifully, she plops down next to me on the couch and immediately covers her bare legs with the blanket.

This is fine.

She smiles softly. “Thank you for telling me. About you and Wesley? I know that must have been hard to talk about.”

I shrug. “I’m trying not to worry too much about the past anymore. I’m more excited about what’s to come.”

Pink tints her cheeks as she tries to suppress a smile, just as Alvin arrives with our drinks.

We stay up talking for another two hours.

19

ANGIE

Asher and I head down to the main restaurant for breakfast and coffee. Here, they make custom gourmet omelets and offer a variety of savory meats, fruits, and pastries. The space is covered, but open to nature, so a few birds swoop in from time to time, grabbing crumbs off the ground and occasionally an unattended plate. The ocean waves are a peaceful backdrop to the scenic wonderland.

I'm still waiting for this to feel real.

I take out my phone as we set our plates on the table, snapping a few aesthetic photos of our meals for his Instagram.

"I'm so glad you're in charge of that because I would never think to take a picture of my food. Do people really want to see that?"

"Food pics aren't nearly as big as they used to be, but some people may want to know what kind of food is offered at the resort you're trying to sell them on."

He nods, taking a sip of his coffee. "So, did you sleep okay last night?"

Honestly, I was a little disappointed that he slept on the

couch instead of the bed. Not that we would do anything scandalous, but there was plenty of room, and it really was comfortable. I could tell he was stressing about the sleeping arrangements when we got back from dinner, so I tried to loosen him up with more drinks.

"I slept great," I answer. "Probably better than you, at least."

"Yeah, that couch was a bit small."

"Then why did you insist on sleeping there? I told you there was plenty of space in the bed. I promise I won't take advantage of you," I tease, placing a hand on his arm. He tenses beneath me, and my heart sinks.

Is the idea of being near me so awful for him? I thought we were having fun, but it's like he can't even stand the idea of being too close to me. Maybe he really is hung up on his ex and wants to prove to her that he is faithful by not putting himself in a situation where something could happen with me. I should respect that.

I pull my hand away. "You still okay with this arrangement? Am I making you uncomfortable?"

"No, of course not." He wipes his mouth with his napkin, looking away. "I'm sorry, it's not—"

Asher is interrupted when the stout man from the front desk who checked us in yesterday approaches us. I suddenly remember we're supposed to be newlyweds, and right now we look like two awkward coworkers at a business conference. I scoot my chair closer to Asher and lean my body into him as I wave at the receptionist. When he's at our table, I see his nametag says "Greggory."

"Good morning, Mr. and Mrs. Hayes. How was your first night with us?" he asks with a hint of mischief. No need to make this weird, dude, we're already there.

Asher puts his arm around me, rubbing my shoulder, and

I'm relieved that he's playing along. A little too relieved. I like the feel of him wrapped around me more than I'd like to admit. His strong hands massaging me.

As hard as I'm trying to get over him, I can't help but wish this thing between us was real.

Asher says, "Excellent."

"This is so wonderful, thank you for everything," I say. Asher and I look at each other, and I want to kiss him. Right here in front of Greggory the front desk guy. Asher's smile is warm and genuine, and I can't pull my gaze from his lips. My stomach flutters wildly. All I would have to do is lean forward and I could know what those lips taste like.

"Well," Greggory says, breaking the spell. "Please let us know if you need anything at all."

"We will," Asher says.

We.

If only there was a real "we" to speak of.

Asher pulls away the moment the man is out of sight. Like he couldn't wait to stop pretending.

What is going on with him? Why is this so hard for him? I was disappointed when he said he didn't believe in marriage, but I assumed it was because of his parents. Did something else happen that he's not telling me about?

For now, I won't push, but I hope he knows he can be honest with me. I'm not going to be able to relax if he is like this the whole trip.

I take a sip of my coffee, swallowing with it the disappointment that this fake marriage will never be real.

About an hour later, I'm guiding Asher to the middle of the

court up by the net, just behind the kitchen line. "Let's just start with hitting the ball back and forth. No pressure."

"Okay, sounds good."

I walk to the other side of the net and drop the bright yellow ball on the ground before hitting it softly to him with my paddle. He follows suit and hits it back. We go back and forth several times, and he misses almost half the shots.

"Damn, I suck at this."

I laugh. "We'll just blame the delayed hand-eye coordination on those mimosas at breakfast, yeah?"

We hadn't planned on drinking this morning, but it's hard to resist when everything is already included. It seemed like we both needed it to break the tension after Greggory left.

"No, this is all me. I'm terrible. Although I am still pretty full." He rubs his belly, pulling my gaze down where it shouldn't be. Luckily he can't see where I'm looking with my sunglasses on. "We should consider adding another hour between breakfast and play time when we write up the itinerary."

"Probably a good idea," I say. "We don't want everyone puking all over the courts every morning."

He holds the ball in his hand, looking down at it with a frown. "What was I thinking telling my boss I played this game and then building an entire vacation around it?"

I walk up to the net. "Hey, it doesn't matter now. It's not like she's going to demand proof of your skill level. I'll teach you everything I know, and we'll come up with a kick-ass trip. Easy peasy. I promise, people are going to love it."

His shoulders slump as he walks up to his side of the net. "How do you know that?"

"Because I'm already having the time of my life." I tap him on the arm with my paddle.

"Are you?" he asks with a raised eyebrow.

"What's not to like?" I put my arms out wide. "We're in the Caribbean, we've got a kickass view from our villa, and I get to play pickleball with you every day. Plus, it's the middle of winter and we're here instead of the Midwest." I shiver at the thought of how cold it must be back home. Makes me think of Willow, and now I want to call her.

"That's true."

"And I'm here with my husband," I add with a wink.

Husband. That word definitely does something to me. I probably shouldn't keep egging him on with how he's been acting, but I'm also hoping to get some kind of reaction out of him. Maybe if I can push him hard enough, he'll finally tell me what's really bothering him.

I walk backward to the middle of my side of the court as Asher hits the ball to me. After a while, he's finally relaxed enough that he's hitting it consistently without getting frustrated.

"See? You're doing great!"

"Yeah, but these are just dinks," he says. "Just wait until we get into bangers and topspins and all that."

I let the ball bounce past me. "Where did you learn those words?"

His eyes dart down to his feet as he rubs the back of his neck. "I may have watched some YouTube videos. I had to get a sense of what I was getting into before I came out here."

"Look at you! What a great student."

I notice his face is getting red and wonder if he forgot to put on sunscreen. The ball ricochets off his arm when I serve it to him. He flinches and blinks several times.

"Where did you go just now?"

"Sorry. Didn't you ask about having a professional on these trips to run the morning clinics?"

"Yeah, like a semi-pro player or a coach. Someone known in the pickleball community."

He crosses his arms, tucking the paddle under his armpit. "How do we book someone like that?"

"Let me talk with Darrell back home. He runs that indoor facility we go to all the time. I'm sure he has some connections."

We move on to playing a one-on-one match, showing him how to serve and keep score. After about an hour of this, he's already getting better. He really is a good student. My mind flashes with images of me standing over him, telling him how he can earn extra credit and a gold star.

Well that's not appropriate.

Neither are the thoughts I have when he raises the hem of his shirt to wipe the sweat off his forehead. Ridges outline his toned abs, and a trail of coarse reddish-brown hair disappears below the waistband of his basketball shorts.

Jesus H. Christ.

I haven't seen him without a shirt since those summers we went to the pool together, and even then, he looked nothing like this. When he rakes a hand through his damp hair like he's in a Calvin Klein underwear ad, I have to make sure I'm still breathing.

I decide if I can't have the real thing, then at least I'm going to enjoy pretending.

Because my fake husband is hot as fuck.

20

ANGIE

March 21

I was trying to find something to watch on TV after school when Spaceballs came on (Dad's favorite movie) and I lost it. I ran to my room sobbing uncontrollably.

It's just so unfair. It doesn't matter that it's been six years, because I miss him every day. I'll never understand why bad people are allowed to live their lives and get everything they want, when one of the kindest and funniest people in the entire world is taken away. I hate it.

But later when I came downstairs for a snack, Asher was in the kitchen. He stopped talking to Wesley the moment he saw me, and I realized I must have looked terrible after crying so much. He asked me what was wrong, and I said it was just a really bad day, but I'll be fine.

When Wesley started texting Stacy, Asher sat me down on the counter stool and said, "I'm really sorry you had a bad day. Can you tell me one GOOD thing that happened today though?"

I thought it was so weird that he was asking me that, but I indulged him. Because I can never say no to him. And after thinking about it for a moment, I remembered that I got a lead part in the school play.

When I told him, he smiled so wide I couldn't help but do the same.

He said he was proud of me and that whenever I'm having a bad day, I should try to think of just one good thing that happened. Because you can almost always find at least ONE thing, and then you'll see that the whole day wasn't bad.

Now I can't stop thinking about the play!!!

...and those dimples. :)

21

ANGIE

Later that afternoon, we decide to take a walk along the beach so I can get some good photos for Asher's Instagram. We had a productive morning of pickleball, an incredible lunch at the Latin fusion restaurant, and then some lounging down at the resort pool. I was quite disappointed when Asher kept his shirt on the entire time. That sneak peek of his abs on the courts earlier put me in a tailspin, and I was secretly hoping for another show.

He's probably worried about getting sunburned, which is a serious concern for both of us.

Also, we had to figure out the bathroom situation. There isn't enough privacy to do what we each need to do in there every day, so we've agreed that the other person either needs to go outside or hang out on the opposite side of the villa. It seems to be working out okay so far, even if it is a little awkward.

The sand is hot beneath my feet as I snap some pictures of the beach. A section of large rocks getting battered by the waves. A round white wicker swing surrounded by palms and red hibiscus.

"So, what did you think of your first experience with pickleball?" I ask as I sink to my knees in the sand, redoing the messy bun atop my head.

He takes a seat next to me. "To be honest, I enjoyed it more than I thought I would."

"You didn't think you'd like it?"

"I guess my impression was that it was a slow sport for aging grandparents. But I can admit when I'm wrong. It was fun."

I smile. "You picked it up quickly, I'm impressed."

"Well I had a good teacher," he says, elbowing my side.

I fight the excess heat creeping up my spine at the inappropriate thoughts drifting back into my mind.

"How often do you play?" he asks.

"A few times a week," I reply, picking up a handful of sand and letting it fall through my fingers.

"Oh wow, that's a pretty big time commitment."

I shrug. "Not really. I mean, you make time for the things that matter to you. Willow and I love playing and spending time together, so that's what we choose to do."

"Sounds like you have it all. Great friends, hobbies. I'm kinda jealous."

I don't have it all. Not everything.

My brows furrow. "You've got a whole life out in Indy, though. You like it out there, right?"

He twists his lips to the side, tossing a small shell toward the ocean. "I'm starting to think I don't know what the hell I'm doing anymore."

I'm not sure what that means, so I wait for him to elaborate. But when he doesn't say anything else, I wrap my arm under his and lean my head on his bicep, watching as the sun begins to set.

Asher points toward the water. “Hey, look at that.”

I follow his line of sight, shielding my eyes from the light. “Oh my god, dolphins!” I squeal. “I love dolphins!”

“They’re pretty close too.”

I jump to my feet and take about two dozen photos, practically bouncing on my toes. There have to be at least twelve of them surfacing over and over. Smooth, gray fins cut through the waves, making my heart soar. The quality isn’t great, so I won’t be posting the pictures. These are just for me.

“The pics don’t do it justice, but I’m so glad we got to see them.” Dolphins are the most beautiful and magical creatures out there. After a minute or so of clutching my phone to my chest, and long after they have disappeared from sight, Asher comes to my side and takes my hand, urging me to keep walking.

I note that there’s no one around we need to pretend for, but I’m enjoying the unexpected contact. I take a chance interlacing our fingers together, and fight back a smile when he doesn’t pull away.

Up ahead is a man standing behind a booth filled with shiny trinkets. Asher elbows my side, angling his head toward the booth. “Come on.”

“Do you want to get something?” I ask. He has a mischievous look on his face that I can’t quite figure out.

He ignores my question and approaches the man selling various bracelets, necklaces, shells, and rings. “Hi, what kind of rings do you have?”

I shoot him a glare. “What are you doing?”

“If we’re going to be married, you should have a ring. Don’t you think?” Then he winks at me. The second wink this trip, which is unusual for this version of Asher, and more in line with the one I knew growing up. Maybe he's finally getting on board with making the most of this trip and relaxing together, but I can't quite figure out these sudden mood changes.

We both look at the display of rings. I glance up at him, still thoroughly confused by this side quest and what he's hoping to accomplish.

"Come on, lighten up a little," he says, echoing my words from earlier. His smile is wide and carefree, and it's doing crazy things to my insides.

I nod, mirroring his easy smile. "There's the Ash I remember."

Most of the rings are made from gorgeous rocks and shells, colorful and smooth. He lets go of my hand as my eye catches a golden yellow stone with a spiral carved into the middle.

A sun.

Immediately I reach for it and notice Asher rubbing at the left side of his chest.

"You okay?" I ask.

He clears his throat. "Huh? Oh, yeah I'm good."

I hold up the ring. Our eyes meet, and I can't help but laugh. "This looks just like that keychain you made me for my birthday, doesn't it?"

"Sure does, Sunshine."

I will never get tired of hearing him call me that. I know in that moment it was meant to be, and I must have this ring.

"I'm gonna get it."

He puts a hand out. "Nope, my treat." He gives the man some cash as I move my grandmother's ring back to my index finger and place the new sun ring on my left ring finger.

I hold my hand up for him to see, but he doesn't say anything, just nods. His throat bobs, and it's like a switch has been flipped. I guess we're back to quiet, moody Asher.

But I'm not dwelling on him and his weird behavior anymore.

This ring is everything.

I pull my hand into my chest and can't help but squeeze like I'm hugging myself. My heart is so full I think it might burst.

Taking out my phone from my back pocket, I hold it over my left hand, snapping a photo like we just got engaged, and I feel him stiffen next to me.

"Calm down, I won't post it."

But I do send it to Willow to rile her up. When I told her about the room upgrade and how we have to pretend to be married now, she was predictably concerned. I love her for it, but I assured her I had everything under control and that we're just having fun. It's our mantra for this trip, after all.

WILLOW

very pretty!

I just hope you know what you're doing

I look down at the ring again. It's perfect, and everything I've ever dreamed of.

Except...it's not real.

It will never be real.

If I keep up this fantasy, I'm going to wind up getting hurt. Maybe Willow is right and I shouldn't have let it get this far. Was I a fool for thinking I could just enjoy this trip and it not mean anything?

I plaster on a smile, still determined to make the most of this vacation. Because regardless of what I do, it's already too late to avoid getting my heart broken.

22

ANGIE

The next morning after a light, early breakfast and two hours of pickleball, we arrive at the meetup spot for our snorkeling excursion. Asher and I take our time slathering on the SPF 50 sunscreen. This Caribbean sun is brutal. I've already gotten fairly pink on my shoulders and face from being outside all day yesterday. Asher was smart to bring a shirt to stay covered while we are on the boat. In fact, I still haven't seen him without a shirt on this entire trip and he hasn't gotten burned, so he may be on to something.

The boat arrives, and we meet our tour guides, Mateo and Sean. After putting on our life vests, we sit back and let the two enthusiastic men take us out on the water. It's about a ten-minute ride over the choppy waves, and the entire time I'm bouncing up and down on the vinyl seats, getting sprayed by a cool mist. I grab Asher's arm instinctively when we hit a particularly rough wave to try and steady myself back on the seat.

The view from out here is incredible, the water transforming into a deep, rich blue the farther from shore we get.

Salty air tickles my nostrils, and wind whips my hair around in a frenzy. I tip my head back, letting the sun warm my face as I readjust my sunglasses.

"Oh my god, it's so beautiful out here," I say. "I suddenly want a boat. Is that weird?"

"Not at all, I could totally see myself out on a lake every weekend. Getting away and reconnecting with nature? Sounds amazing."

An image forms in my mind of Asher and me taking a boat out on the water together, just the two of us. Maybe us and a few kids.

Stop. Being a couple is just an act, I remind myself.

But when will I have the chance to be this close to him again?

I scoot closer to him and lay my head on his shoulder. His arm pulls me in to his side without me having to remind him to play along, and my heart thrums in my chest. After years and years of pining over him and being apart for so long, I would have thought I'd be over him by now. Clearly, that's not the case. I'm failing at my mission.

I need to take my own advice and stop overthinking it. Asher is one of my oldest friends, and I am lucky to be able to call him that. Just because we can't be romantically involved doesn't lessen how much he means to me as a friend.

Even if I am frustrated that he chooses to sleep on the couch every night.

"Almost there!" the guide steering the boat announces. I think it's Sean.

My stomach flutters with excitement. I angle my head up and shoot Asher a wide smile, and he returns it eagerly. He's excited too. It's nice to see him happy again.

So many times he would come over to our house looking defeated, like his home life was slowly sucking the life out of him, and Wesley and I were the ones who could always bring that sparkle back. It made me feel important to him, like I was lucky to be in a position to make him happy.

The boat slows to a crawl and eventually stops by a landing of jagged rocks. They set down the anchor, and we proceed to take off our life vests to put on a set of snorkeling goggles and mouthpieces. The guides climb out of the boat and both extend a hand to me. I take their hands and jump off the first step, excited to finally get in the water and explore.

My feet sink into the sandbar below, the water cool against my skin, and I hear a splash behind me as Asher follows. When he approaches my left side, I realize too late that he finally took off his shirt, and I'm a little disappointed I missed the show. But I need to pay attention to the guides and stop ogling Asher's wide, muscular shoulders. Stop thinking about what they felt like under my palms as I rubbed sunscreen all over them twenty minutes ago, before he put that damn shirt on again.

Shit, pay attention.

The four of us wade through the waist-deep water for a bit until the guides motion down with their hands, and they sink into the water to swim just below the surface. Asher looks back at me, and we laugh at our ridiculous snorkeling gear, but I can tell his smile is wide. We both follow the instructors and dip under the water. The sight has me gasping in my rubber mouthpiece.

Exotic fish in every color imaginable. Ripples in the crystal-clear water send sunlight in every direction, bouncing off the bumpy coral covering the sea floor. Bright blue and yellow fish dance around us, and critters skitter across the sand below, just out of reach. The sheer beauty of it has me awe-struck.

I'm kicking myself for not getting an underwater camera

for this. Do those even still exist? Rookie mistake. This would be perfect for his social media.

I tap Asher's arm, and when he looks over at me, I mime taking a picture with my hands to let him know I wish we had a camera. He reaches into his board shorts, where he magically procures his phone encased in a waterproof sleeve and hands it to me.

My eyes go wide. He really did think of everything.

After about an hour and a half of snorkeling, we reluctantly head back to the boat. We take off all our gear, and I hand Asher his encased phone right as he is putting his shirt back on.

Ugh, my timing is the worst.

"Good call on that case!" I say. "I never even thought to bring something like that."

He shrugs. "Figured you'd want it for social media. Anything worth posting?"

"Oh my god, so much. It's gorgeous down there. Thank you for letting me tag along for all this." I lean in, wrapping my arms around his torso and pressing my face to his chest. His arms circle my back, and I breathe him in. Salty and fresh like the ocean itself. I could stay here forever.

When I pull back, a slight blush has crossed his cheeks, or maybe it's just tinted from the sun. We probably should get back in the shade soon.

A few minutes into our boat ride back to the resort, Mateo and Sean look at each other and nod suspiciously, then look to us.

Sean says, "Do you guys mind if we stop for a few minutes and dive for some conch?"

"Oh, fine with me," I say, looking to Asher, who nods as well.

They drop anchor again and dive down into the water,

coming up after less than a minute, each with one or two large conch shells in their hands. They motion to us, and we both get up and help load the shells into the boat before they dive back down for more.

Absolutely stunning. The outer shell is rough, sand colored, and spiky, giving way to glossy bright pink and white on the inside.

I laugh. "So this is happening." Moments like these make the best memories. I live for this kind of thing. "Are we even supposed to be doing this? They gave each other a weird look right before they asked us."

"It's a little strange, but I'm into it," he says as the men breach the water and hand us four new conchs.

"These shells are so beautiful."

"Look inside," he smirks. "It's not just a shell."

I tip back the one in my hand, getting my face closer when I spot a slimy black creature living inside. "Oh shit!" I yell, nearly dropping it.

Asher bursts out laughing—a real laugh, deep and rich—and I realize it's the first time I'm hearing that sound in years, and it warms my heart. "Did you think these were just empty shells at the bottom of the ocean?"

Splaying my arms out, I say, "I mean, that's the only way I've ever seen them! Never really thought about them being part of an actual sea creature, but it makes sense."

Mateo and Sean keep resurfacing with more and more conchs, and Asher and I dutifully place them on the floor of the boat shiny side down, but we are quickly running out of space.

After loading what has to be at least fifty conchs, the guides bring up the anchor, and we continue our trek back to shore. Once we arrive, Mateo points to the pile of conch and says to us, "Pick one."

I look back at him, confused. "What?"

"Which one?" he continues pointing.

"Oh." Still unsure exactly what he means, I pick up one of the shells near my feet.

The man takes it, washes off the sand and says, "You want him?" pointing to the creature inside and then jabbing a thumb toward the resort. "You can give him to the cook."

My eyes go wide, finally understanding his meaning. "Yes, please!" I bounce on my toes, clapping my hands. I love trying new things.

I watch curiously as the man uses a gigantic knife to cut out the dark slug-like creature and then drops it in my awaiting palms. He dips the empty shell into the water before handing it to Asher. I don't miss him peeking inside as if making sure there are no more surprises living in there.

This thing is kind of gross and slimy, but I can't stop laughing. Asher fishes out his phone and snaps a few pictures of me holding out the sea creature like I just won a prize.

This is what it's all about. Adventure, new experiences. I want it all.

Later that evening as we eat another amazing dinner at the resort—where we both tried our delicious conch friend battered and fried—the backs of my legs feel raw and itchy. I probably still have sand on me from the beach earlier. But it only gets worse as the night goes on. By the end of dinner, I'm nearly howling in pain.

Asher looks over at me with concern in those deep green eyes. "You okay?"

"I don't know, my legs are really hurting." I keep shifting in my chair, trying to ease the discomfort, but nothing helps.

"Let's finish up and we can take a look. Hopefully you didn't get a rash or a bug bite or something."

"Yeah, I don't know what this is."

When Asher and I walk back to our villa, he pulls me off to

the side away from the other guests and says, "Okay, let me see." We stop on the dirt trail, and I lift my skirt past my thighs, and his eyes go wide.

"What is it?" I ask. "Is it bad?"

"Uhh, did you forget to put on sunscreen today?" he asks. The horror lacing his voice makes my stomach drop.

"What? No, you saw me. I put on extra cause of the snorkeling. Why, am I burned?"

He pauses.

"Asher!"

"Yeah...you could say that. Come on, let's hit up the gift shop for some aloe."

"How bad?" I ask again.

He takes my hand, but doesn't say a word.

A sunburn would account for this searing sensation, but I was so careful today. I retrace my steps after we applied our sunscreen. We spent nearly ten minutes bouncing up and down on those wet seats on the boat getting to our snorkeling spot. It must have washed all the sunscreen off the backs of my legs.

Oh god.

And then I was face down in the water for ninety minutes. All the while, that part of me was unprotected from the brutal Caribbean sun.

A wave of dread rolls through me. Oh no, this is going to be so bad.

When we finally get back to the room, I immediately go to the full-length mirror to see the damage. Lifting my skirt, I gasp at the sight.

My ass and my thighs...are purple.

23

ASHER

I was not prepared.

First, for her to lift her goddamn skirt like that. But then, to see how burned she was. As a redhead, of course I've been sunburned before, but nothing like this.

My heart squeezes at the thought of how much pain she is in. It has to be sun poisoning.

I feel like I've let her down. I should've been paying attention. On the other hand, when I do pay attention, I freak out about my feelings for her. It's like I'm losing my mind.

I want her, but can't have her.

We pretend to be married, holding hands or hugging, and I find myself enjoying it way too much, so I try to put some distance between us. But she feels me pulling away, and I can see she's disappointed, so all I want to do is get close to her and make her happy again.

It's torture.

Then this happens, and all I can think about is taking care of her.

After her initial shock wears off of seeing it for herself in the mirror, I have her lie face down on the bed so I can rub cool aloe gel over the burn. The whimper she lets out when I slowly spread the green goo around makes my heart crack.

This is not how I imagined touching her ass for the first time.

I need to get it together. This is not the time to be thinking about that. Nothing good can come of it.

"That feels nice, thank you," she says softly into her pillow.

"I'm so sorry you got burned. I didn't even think about the sunscreen rubbing off on the boat." I give her ankle a reassuring squeeze when I'm finished, and lie down next to her on my side. "What do you want to do? Watch something on my iPad? Read your book?"

She pulls her face out of the pillow to turn in my direction, her eyes puffy and lined with tears. Strands of blonde hair cling to her forehead before I tuck them behind her ear.

"I don't want to do anything." She sniffles. "It really hurts. I'm sorry I ruined this trip."

"Hey," I say, wiping away a tear streaking down her face as she squeezes her eyes shut. "You didn't ruin anything. You could never. It's just one bad thing that happened."

I sit up on the bed, propping myself against the pillows on the headboard, and poke her arm. "Tell me one good thing that happened today."

She opens her eyes slowly, blinking several times before smiling softly. Wistfully. I know she remembers. "There were a lot of good things today."

"Okay, then tell me your favorite."

She sighs, propping herself up on her elbows. "The snorkeling. Pre-butt-burn, obviously. When we were swimming with those bright blue and yellow fish, they led us to that enormous sea turtle. It was...magical. Like nothing I'd ever seen before." She closes her eyes as if trying to imagine it all again.

"I bet you got some good pictures too," I say.

She nods. "I did. You came in clutch with that waterproof case. Now we'll have those memories forever."

I can't help but smile. "See? Wasn't such a bad day, right?"

"You're right. But...maybe we should keep snorkeling off the official trip itinerary?"

"Yeah, you're probably not gonna be able to play pickleball much in this condition."

She flops back down on the bed with a groan. "Ugh, that was the whole point of coming here."

When she starts sobbing, my hand reaches for her windswept blonde hair. I want more than anything to tell her everything will be okay. That I would do anything to make her feel better again.

"Sorry. I'm being weird," she says in between hiccups.

"Would you stop apologizing?" I didn't realize she would be this upset about not getting to play pickleball. "It's fine, we can play as soon as you're healed when we're back home."

She turns her head to me. "No, it's not that. I mean, yes I love pickleball, but that's not why I'm crying."

"Then what is it?" I lie back down facing her, closer this time, and my hand finds its way to the small of her back. A soft, reassuring touch.

"Just thinking about...the first time you did that. The 'one good thing' trick. Did I ever tell you why I was so sad that day?"

My mind races to recall that moment with her, but all I remember is that she looked devastated, and I would've done anything to cheer her up, so I said the first thing that came to my mind. And it worked.

I shake my head.

She sniffs. "I was thinking a lot about my dad that day. Something reminded me of him, and all these memories with him came flooding back. It's crazy how something so small can do that. Even after...what, sixteen years?"

Another tear rolls down her cheek, and I wipe it away.

"I miss him," she says. "I still think about him every day."

"Do you want to talk about him?"

She shrugs. "Not really. I'm sorry for bringing the vibes down."

"Are you kidding? You couldn't bring the vibes down if you tried."

"Can I ask you something?" She twists her lips to the side. "And you don't have to answer if you don't want to."

"You can ask me anything," I reply honestly. And I wish she would. I want her to ask me everything because I need her to know me.

"Do you still talk with your parents?"

I shake my head. "Nah. They barely acknowledge I exist. Only when they think they can get something out of it."

"God, I'm so sorry, I shouldn't have even brought it up. That was insensitive of me."

"No, no, it's really okay. It doesn't upset me, it's more like... I feel nothing for them. My dad is a complete dick, and my mom doesn't have a nurturing bone in her body. Of course, I wish things could've been different, but I've learned to accept how it is. I'm not angry or sad anymore, I'm not...anything, really."

That feels true of so many things in my life lately. My parents, Sarah, my job.

But in that moment, I realize, I don't want to feel *nothing*. What kind of life is it to just get through each day feeling numb and merely surviving? When I'm with Angie, I feel everything. All the highs and lows, everything in between, and I've never felt so alive. I want to feel like this every day.

She reaches her hand out and rubs her thumb over my

wrist. "You're nothing like them, you know. If that's something you're worried about. Quite the opposite, actually."

I blink away the stinging behind my eyes. I was not expecting her to say that, but it's nice to hear all the same. "Thank you."

"I'm so glad you moved in next door," she says.

That makes me smile. "Me too, Sunshine."

She pulls her hand back and groans. "Ugh, this burn really sucks. I need a distraction."

"Okay, what can I do?"

"Would you..." She shakes her head and closes her eyes. "Never mind."

"No, what is it? Anything you want."

She doesn't know I would do anything for her. Anything to make her smile again. The smile that can light up a room. Every day I get to see that smile is a good day.

"It's silly, but would you read me some of my book? It's about to get really good, and I'm dying to know what happens."

"You want me to read your book to you?" I ask.

"See? It's dumb, you don't have to." She buries her head back into the pillow, and I rub her back gently.

"No, no, I will. I'll go get it." I roll off the bed and head to the beach bag by the back door, where I know her book is. When I return, I ease myself down next to her, careful not to jostle the bed too much and risk moving her legs. Taking out the bookmark, I clear my throat. "Chapter twenty-three."

She looks up at me from beneath her long, wet lashes, a content smile playing on her lips.

It's a romance, but it doesn't look to be a particularly spicy chapter, thank goodness. I'm not sure I could handle that right now.

"*The absence of her was overwhelming. She's everywhere in this house we built together, but she's gone. Because I pushed her away. Right into the arms of my twin brother, Fabio, who faked his own death last Christmas in an attempt to start a new life as a street performer in Portugal."*

What the hell is this book? I flip over the front cover before looking at her, but her eyes are closed and her breathing has already slowed down. A soft snore stirs with every inhale.

Grabbing a soft blanket from the chair, I cover her top half and turn off the bedside lamp. I lie next to her, watching the adorable micro expressions cross her face as she sleeps.

Our conversation about my parents replays in my mind. I can't help but think about the last time I saw my dad. Telling me how disappointed he was that I wouldn't come visit them and deciding then and there I could go the rest of my life never seeing or talking to him again.

That was four years ago.

At Sarah's funeral.

24

ANGIE

October 2

OMG last night was so much fun. Christina and I smoked weed for the first time!

Wesley bought some from a friend and asked if we wanted to try it. Asher protested at first, which I thought was kind of sweet, but then he said he wouldn't have any to make sure our first time was safe. (awww) I ended up coughing so much my throat STILL hurts, but once it kicked in, I felt amazing.

Asher started telling us all this ghost story about the farm just outside the county line, and how the family there was murdered over a hundred years ago. And if you go to the exact right spot at night, you can still see a mysterious light off in the distance, which is supposed to be the caretaker searching the property with a lantern. We were just high enough to decide to drive down there and see for ourselves.

Asher parked Wesley's car at the far end of the field, pointed toward the farmhouse and the woods beyond. We piled on the hood of the car, laughing our asses off. We kept saying how creepy and stupid this all was, until after about a half hour of waiting, we saw it. A tiny flash of light swinging back and forth around the forest. It was actually terrifying, and we all screamed. Asher took my hand and pulled me off the car, and the four of us bolted out of there as fast as we could. On the car ride home, we could not stop laughing.

I swear I kept catching Asher staring at me, but I was so high I probably just imagined it.

We came back to the house and raided the pantry and spent the next several hours scarfing down Doritos and Zebra Cakes.

It was the most fun I've ever had.

25

ASHER

A strange noise awakens me. I jolt up, noticing the bright light filtering in through the room, and twist to the side to make sure Angie is okay. She's grunting a little as she stretches, her eyes slowly fluttering open.

"Morning, Sunshine," I whisper, swiping her hair out of her face, because I keep finding excuses to touch her. "How you feeling?"

"Ugh, like someone took a cheese grater to the back of my legs. How's it look?"

I glance down, trying to avoid any lingering stares. "Still pretty bad. Let me get the aloe." I slowly rub the gel along the burn as she inhales sharply. "This okay?"

"As good as it can be, I guess," she mumbles into the pillow.

I finish covering her legs and walk to the bathroom to wash my hands.

"What do we have planned today?" she asks with a hint of trepidation once I return to the bed.

"Mountain biking in the hills for six hours," I say, deadpan. "What do you think?"

She laughs, and I mirror her smile. "Oh cool, sounds perfect. Wait..." She rolls on her side toward me. "Isn't today New Year's Eve?"

"It is, and there's a big party down at the beach tonight, but we can do anything you want. Whatever you're feeling up for. If you just want to stay in the room today, we can. Or lie by the pool with a fat margarita? You tell me what sounds good."

"First of all, I need food," she says before running her tongue along her teeth. "And to brush my teeth. I totally forgot last night."

"Same," I reply.

She rubs her eyes and yawns. "I was not expecting to crash like that."

"Yeah, I slept like a rock." I couldn't bring myself to leave her alone on the bed last night, not in her condition. I guess I have been making it a bigger deal than it is, and damn if this bed isn't the comfiest I've ever slept in. It only felt natural to stay by her side and take care of her.

"Okay." I jab the ticklish spot on her hip. "Figure out what you want to eat, and then you can take care of that morning breath."

She smacks my chest. "You're one to talk, you haven't brushed either."

Standing up, I grab my pillow and playfully whack her in the head before jogging to the other side of the room.

"Hey! No fair, I can't chase you! You're such a cheater."

"That was for the purple nurple earlier," I say victoriously. "Hurry up, I'm ordering breakfast. Lox right? Extra onions?"

She carefully peels herself out of bed and stands on shaky legs. "I will murder you. I don't suppose they have Starbucks anywhere nearby?"

I shake my head. "Sorry."

"Ugh. Coffee and French toast then. God, I would kill for a Caramel Macchiato right now." Slowly making her way to the bathroom, she adds, "Don't forget the bacon."

With the push of our magic button, our breakfast arrives at our door in under fifteen minutes. Angie eats standing up to avoid anything touching the back of her thighs. They're still beet red and look insanely uncomfortable.

The protective asshole in me vows not to let anything else happen to her out here.

On our way down to the resort pool, we stop at one of the bars to grab some mango guava margaritas. I set us up under the shade of a large palm tree, laying out our towels on side-by-side lounge chairs. I'm taking a risk having my shirt off today, but I applied her foundation over the tattoo and I don't think she'll notice. It's too hot to keep wearing it, and at this rate, I'll be going home with a farmer's tan.

I help Angie with her back and shoulders like yesterday, taking my time to make sure I cover every inch with plenty of sunscreen. No need to rush the process when her skin feels this soft.

We sit by the pool for a while, Angie careful to keep her burned skin from touching anything. We've fallen back into our old dynamic where the conversation flows so easily, and any silence between us is completely comfortable. There are no expectations for how we act or talk to each other. It's so...easy. Natural. And I finally stop overthinking it.

"Okay, so I have to know more about this twin brother who faked his death and fled to Portugal," I say, turning toward her and resting my arm above my head. Something flashes across her face so quickly I can't tell what it was.

She smiles, pulling her sunglasses to rest on top of her head. "You mean Fabio?"

"What the hell is happening in that book?"

"I guess you'll have to read it to find out," she says with a smirk, lowering her sunglasses. "Hey, have you been to Portugal?"

"*Sim*," I reply.

Twisting toward me, she whips off her sunglasses completely. "Do you speak Portuguese? Wait, how many languages do you know?"

"Fluent in Spanish, but I know enough to get around in... let's see..." I start counting in my head. "Eight other languages."

Her mouth is wide open like I just blew her mind. If I knew it was this easy to impress her, I would've been speaking Portuguese from the start. Or maybe French.

Before she can say anything, we get a whiff of a very strong, pungent scent. We both look at each other with wide eyes.

"Is it legal here?" she whispers.

"I think so, in small amounts. Are you thinking what I'm thinking?"

She bites her bottom lip, and my eyes drop to her mouth. "I haven't since college. But it would probably help with the pain, don't you think?"

"I mean, it sounds medically necessary to me," I argue. "Let me see what I can find out."

I climb out of the lounge chair and casually walk toward a guy who looks to be in his early twenties with dirty blond shaggy hair and a few intense-looking tattoos along his thigh and biceps.

Approaching the guy, I clear my throat and ask, "Hey, man,

what's up?" I suddenly feel old and completely uncool. I might as well have just waved and said "*How do you do, fellow kids?*"

"Aw hey, chief," he replies in his drawn-out surfer boy accent. I'm all too familiar with guys like him from my days in California.

I point to the joint in his hand. "Mind if I ask where you got that?"

Fear flashes in his eyes as he looks around. God, I must look like some old man ready to complain and narc on him. I lift my hands and quickly add, "Just...wondering where I can get some too."

Relief washes over his face as his mouth splits into a wide, goofy grin. "Oh right on. I got you covered, my man."

I never could have imagined I'd be spending New Year's Eve buying weed on my fake honeymoon.

26

ASHER

We decide to wait until after dinner to light it up, not wanting to make fools of ourselves in front of the other guests. Neither of us has done this in years, so this could get interesting.

Now we're back in our villa, giddy and excited to get high, much like we did those handful of times together back in high school. For whatever reason, we're both whispering and acting all secretive, even though it's totally legal out here.

"You ready?" I ask, practically buzzing from excitement. How sad is it that I haven't done anything this fun in so long? What have I been doing?

She nods excitedly before opening the wide doors to the back porch, walking to the far end overlooking the water. "Why does it feel like we're about to be caught?"

"Because it's all we've ever known with this," I reply, holding up the joint in cheers as I hand it to her. "Ladies first."

I light the end for her as she inhales deeply, almost immediately coughing, and I can't help but laugh. "Oh my god, just like your first time. Do you remember?"

The same night the four of us—me, Wes, Angie, and her friend Christina—went out to the McAfee farm after I made up that ghost story. We freaked ourselves out so badly, but it was one of the most fun nights I've ever had with her. I felt just as protective of her then as I do now.

Once she's able to catch her breath, she nods and hands me the joint. "You're right, I could not stop coughing!"

I take my first inhale in ten years, my lungs filling with fire. I fight the urge to cough as I hold it in for as long as I can. When I let it out, the thick gray smoke wafts toward the ocean.

The New Year's Eve party on the main beach will be starting soon, but I don't want to risk Angie getting sand on her sunburn, especially if we're high. If she ended up falling, it would hurt like hell. No, I'd much rather spend the evening alone with her, laughing until my face hurts.

We pass the joint back and forth until there's nothing left. I lean over the railing, already feeling my entire body relax as I let out a deep sigh. Every muscle releasing in waves.

"How you feeling now?" I ask. I can already feel my eyelids getting heavy.

She nods. "I'm feeling it. This stuff is strong."

"How's your butt?"

"Honestly, not too bad right now. Thanks for scoring us the doobie."

I snort. "I don't think anyone calls them doobies anymore. The kids these days would laugh at us."

"We are getting pretty old, aren't we?" she says with a raised eyebrow.

I shrug. "It's not so bad. Most of the time."

"Another year ends tonight." She rests her chin on her palm, leaning on the railing. My hands ache to touch her again. To swipe her long hair over her shoulders. To rub my thumb over the pulse point on her neck.

"They say how you bring in the new year is how you can expect the rest of the year to go." I can't remember where I heard that, though. It's probably bullshit.

"So, sunburned ass and high as *fuck*?" She says "fuck" in a comedically low voice, causing me to burst out laughing.

I was thinking more along the lines of us being together, but it would be foolish to get my hopes up. I suddenly can't remember why I've been fighting this so hard.

Only three more hours until midnight, and lord, how I want to kiss her. I could always laugh it off as "just a New Year's kiss."

I'm overthinking again.

Shit.

I'm so high, I forgot how much my thoughts go crazy when I'm like this.

Some people smoke to calm their minds down, but it seems to have the opposite effect on me, making me more paranoid and anxious. My body is relaxed, but my brain is overanalyzing everything. What I'm doing with my hands. Do I really need to pee or is everything just a little tingly? What if I pee my pants? What if I say something inappropriate or somehow confess all my long-buried secrets about how much I'm still hopelessly in love with her?

Chill.

Breathe.

We stand there, the crashing waves filling the silence between us.

After a while, Angie says, "So what do you want to do?"

I feel like I need a distraction so my thoughts don't go haywire. "Watch a movie? We could see what's streaming."

"Yes! And room service too." She gasps. "Oh, I love Alvin so much. He really is the best. I'm gonna call him up."

I shake my head as she giddily orders room service. For

someone hesitant about having a butler, she sure is enjoying that magic button. Of course she's already made friends with Alvin and has learned all about him and his family. I don't know how she does that, connecting with people so easily and letting them into her heart.

Scrolling through the app on my iPad, I try to find a lighthearted comedy for us to watch. I land on a section of classic comedies and find one of my favorites. "Oh my god, I love this movie. You've seen it, right?"

When I flip the iPad around, she goes still, then blinks several times before a small smile slowly forms on those beautiful lips. "Yeah. Me too. Start it up."

We settle on the bed next to each other, propped against the headboard with pillows all around us as I press play. Angie keeps her legs bent and pulled into her chest, leaning slightly on me.

Spaceballs begins playing, and I'm already chuckling at the scrolling text on screen. We watch the entire movie snuggled up together, quoting nearly every line, the two of us going back and forth as Lone Star and Princess Vespa. We pause for only a few minutes to eat the junk food she ordered once it gets delivered to the room. My arm finds its way around her shoulder as I pull her closer, the two of us laughing until our sides hurt.

I realize this is what it's all about. These moments right here. If this is all I'm ever allowed to have with Angie, then I'll protect it with everything I have.

When the movie ends, we get ready for bed and fall asleep spooning before midnight.

She's the big spoon.

27

ANGIE

What the fuck…?

Where am I?

What day is it?

I'm struggling to comprehend what's happening to me in this moment and why my brain feels so fuzzy. I can't even open my eyes.

Why does my ass hurt so bad?

Then it all comes trickling back.

Right. We got high as shit last night to dull the pain of my sunburn and fell asleep before midnight. I don't think I've ever missed the ball drop. A part of me is a little disappointed because I was hoping to kiss Asher at midnight. The perfect cover in case he went on another one of his internal freakouts.

I couldn't believe out of all the movies he could've chosen for us to watch, he picked *Spaceballs*. I never even told him it was my dad's favorite movie. It had to be another one of Dad's signs, letting me know he wanted me to be happy, and maybe that he likes Asher too.

I wish they could've met.

Then a thought strikes me. I never once wished Dad could've met John. Never had that ache of knowing they never would. Did I know deep down John wasn't the one for me, but needed a rebound, and he was there saying all the right things?

Did I really love John, or was he a poor replacement for Asher?

Am I still high? Why am I dredging up all these old memories?

Prying open one eye, I find bright sunlight flooding in through the sheer curtains, with no concept of what time it is.

Grabbing my phone off the nightstand, I see that it's ten a.m. and I have a ton of missed calls and texts from my friends back home.

GROUP CHAT

WILLOW

Happy New Year!!!!

FARIS

YES! Happy New Year!!

SIMON

Love you all, happy new year! 😽

WILLOW

...Angie??

Hello??

Unbelievable

FARIS

She's already forgotten about us

SIMON

Too busy with her husband

Honestly I get it

It was only a matter of time

FARIS

Sad. Now both of you are too busy getting laid to hang out or talk with us anymore

WILLOW

Oh cry me a river

I just saw you this morning!!!

I can't help but laugh. I miss them. The four of us have been close from the moment we met, Willow and I eight years ago when we were assigned as roommates in college. Then we met Faris and Simon three years ago when we moved into the West Brook neighborhood. They came to a house party down the street from someone Simon worked with, and when Willow and I walked by, they invited us to join them. That ended up being Max and Kayla's house.

ME

You're all so dramatic

Happy New Year!!

FARIS

She's alive!

ME

I was asleep before the ball dropped

got high to help with the pain

SIMON

Look at you!

Well stop talking to us and get back to your man already

ME

he's not my man

and Willow was NOT supposed to tell you about the fake marriage thing

WILLOW

like I could possibly keep that to myself

FARIS

where are you registered?

ME

you're all insufferable

LOVE YOU MISS YOU

WILLOW

Love you more

FARIS

LOVE YOU MORE

SIMON

LOVE YOU MORE!!!!

I click off my phone and gently roll to my side. The sunburn is not as raw as yesterday, but still tender.

A smile breaks out over my face when I see Asher sprawled out on his stomach, a glistening dollop of drool clinging to his perfect lips, his shirt hiked up nearly to his armpit. I'm glad he finally came to his senses and has joined me on the bed the past two nights instead of that tiny sofa.

We fell asleep cuddling, and it was the soundest sleep I've had in a long time.

I think about the exceedingly gentle way he rubs aloe over my skin, like I am something precious. It feels nice to be taken care of like that.

Is that enough for me? Will I ever stop wanting more from him?

My hand moves of its own accord, swiping away some loose auburn hair that has fallen over his forehead. He stirs a little, prying open one eye, looking about as disoriented as I felt a few minutes ago.

"Morning, Sunshine," he says on a yawn. "Happy New Year."

"Happy New Year, Ash."

If it's true that how you start the new year is how the rest of it will go, then I'll be ecstatic. Waking up next to each other, with sleepy eyes and messy hair. A dream come true.

God, he really is beautiful. I want to kiss him.

"How's the sunburn?" he asks.

"A little better. Not sure how much I'll be able to do today though."

"That's okay, we can just chill by the pool again if you want, or grab a cabana at the beach."

True, we still have half the trip left and plenty of adventures to go on. Memories to be made. I'll just slap some more aloe on my legs, down some Tylenol, and suck it up.

I can't stay cooped up in here any longer. I hate missing out.

"Don't you have a bunch of activities planned? I don't want to derail anything."

He rolls onto his back, his arm draped over his eyes when he realizes how bright it is. "I think the snorkeling covers us for a while."

"Are you sure? You can go do stuff without me, you know."

He lifts his arm, his brows furrowing. "You trying to get rid of me, Sunshine?"

I huff a laugh, sinking back down into the bed and pulling the soft white sheet up to my neck. "Just trying to think about your business and all the stuff we should be doing and posting. Like research for the trip."

He tsks. "Don't worry about all that. There is no 'should.'

We have plenty of time. Let's just relax and recover. Maybe some light pickleball this afternoon if you're up for it."

My chest warms. He's always so considerate and accommodating. I don't want to feel like a burden. I hate that he's had to completely rearrange his itinerary for me, all because I managed to get myself burned. But he's always been selfless; it's who he is.

He looks over at me with those deep emerald eyes, his smile soft and content. My fingers beg to reach out and touch his face. To feel that scruff along his cheek, to swipe my thumb over those soft lips. He's so close I can feel the heat emanating from his body. If I scoot a few inches closer, what would he do? Would he press his body to mine? Would he get upset?

I'm about to do it, determined to get an answer out of him, when he says, "I do have a quick meeting with the resort rep after lunch, though. Getting some more info on the accommodations and hopefully work out a deal for selling these vacations."

"I'm really proud of you for all you've done here." I put my hand on his arm over his intricate swirling black tattoo and give him a gentle squeeze.

He smiles, moving to get out of bed, and I stop him without thinking, pulling back on his arm. I don't want him to leave yet. I need him close.

So I say the first thing that pops into my head. "Tell me one good thing that happened this year."

A small tilt of his lips. "Easy. Marrying my best friend."

He shoots me a wink before sliding out of my grasp and walking to the bathroom.

Those words have no business making my stomach flip like that.

28

ASHER

"This all sounds great, Asher," Tony, the resort sales rep, says as he collects the papers and takes back the iPad I just signed. The man is easily in his thirties, but has the energy and enthusiasm of a teenager, and insisted we start off on a first-name basis. He and Angie would get along great. "We look forward to working with you. I'll have these contracts sent over to your office in Indianapolis right away."

"Perfect, thank you." I stand and extend my hand, Tony shaking it firmly as he rises from his black leather chair.

"And congratulations again. Mr. Harris had nothing but nice things to say about you."

I freeze when he mentions Wes. "Mr. Harris" to him, being so high up on the corporate ladder.

"Oh. Yeah, Wes and I go way back. Since we were in middle school, actually."

"Wow, and now you'll be brothers-in-law. Sounds like you're living the dream, man."

I can only nod, my stomach twisted in knots. God, I feel like such a fraud. I wish I was living the dream, but none of this is real. Angie and I are just pretending. Pretending to be a couple, pretending to be married.

"Please enjoy the rest of your stay, and let us know if you need anything at all."

"Will do," I say, turning on my heel and hurrying to get the hell out of there.

What am I doing? Playing honeymoon with my best friend's sister, who I am definitely still pathetically in love with? This is all going to blow up in my face if I keep it up. Is Wes going to hear about our fake marriage and our upgraded honeymoon villa from the staff here? I don't see how he doesn't find out about all this.

Unless he already knows.

Tony could've already let it slip when they talked.

One lie only leads to more lies.

We need to come clean before this charade puts everything at risk.

Later that afternoon, I'm finally able to get Angie back onto the pickleball courts. She said her legs felt good enough to play, but it's probably because she is wearing the shortest tennis skirt I have ever seen in my life. Every time she takes a step, the light, airy fabric dances around her perfect, round ass, her breasts barely contained in the tiny tank top she has chosen to torture me with.

My god. How am I supposed to focus on playing when she looks like that? Just one more reason why we need to stop this. I thought I could play along. Enjoy the perks of "being together" without the fear of commitment, but every second I'm with her just hurts that much more, knowing it's all a lie.

I can't do this anymore.

I'll tell her tonight.

After a few minutes of warming up, two older women—likely in their fifties if I had to guess—arrive at the court in matching pink and green outfits and gym bags. One is petite with brown curly hair, and the other is tall and lean, her short hair graying.

"Y'all want to play doubles?" one of them asks as they wave to get our attention.

Angie's face lights up. "Sure! We were just warming up."

The women approach us with their hands outstretched. One says, "I'm Jessica, and this is my wife, Amalya."

They shake hands. "Hi, nice to meet you! I'm Angie. This is my husband, Asher." So much for not pretending anymore. I ignore how the word "husband" pulses through me, and how I actually enjoy the way it sounds coming from her.

And because it's too late to back out, I lean into the lie one last time. Shaking their hands, I add, "We're on our honeymoon."

Angie beams at me.

"Oh, congratulations!" Amalya says. "Where did you get married?"

My whole body tenses up. We never discussed any backstory, but I'm sure Angie has this covered. I look to her, but her eyes are wide, as if coming to the same realization about our lack of preparation.

"It was a small backyard wedding," she blurts. "Back home in the States. Just close friends and family."

"How wonderful," Jessica says. "Have you two been together a long time?"

I jump in, trying to play the role of the love-struck husband. "We were next-door neighbors growing up, so we've pretty much known each other forever. One day it just turned into more." None of which is technically a lie. I pull Angie to my side and gaze down at her, the story of us flowing so easily from my lips. "And we've been deliriously happy ever since."

Angie's expression is hard to read. Her smile is wide but not quite meeting her eyes. I kiss the top of her head, unable to look at her any longer without bursting.

Our new friends both say "Aw" at the same time.

"So how long have you been married?" Angie asks them after she pulls away from me.

"Twenty years today," Jessica says. They look at each other with such fondness, I almost can't wrap my head around it. Married for twenty years and they still love each other so easily? Still so obviously happy and in love? How?

Angie clasps her free hand over her heart. "Wow, twenty years is incredible. Congratulations!"

After a few more minutes of chatting, we warm up with them by hitting the ball back and forth, not worrying about scoring or where it lands on the court. I try to work on improving my hand-eye coordination and hitting the ball more intentionally, but I still can't quite focus.

I was ready to end this arrangement with Angie, but what if I told her how I really felt instead? How I don't want to fake this anymore. Am I willing to risk our friendship for her to know my truth? Because if she doesn't feel the same way, how could we keep going on as friends?

A sharp pain on my arm pulls me from my dizzying thoughts. Angie waves the paddle she just smacked me with in front of my face. "You good?"

"Yeah, totally," I lie.

"Ready to play a match?" Amalya asks from the other side of the net. Angie gives an enthusiastic thumbs up, and I have to force my eyes away from the drop of sweat disappearing in the crease between her breasts.

We all get in position, Angie readying to serve first. "Zeros on start," she calls out.

We weren't prepared.

These kind and lovely, happily married lesbians absolutely destroy us.

I shouldn't have been surprised, considering I've only played for about six hours total in my life, and Angie is still hesitant with her sunburn. But I think even if we were both decent and played together every day for a year, we would still get obliterated.

We managed to get one whole point out of the entire first match, zero on the second, and two on the third and final. And only because I think they were taking pity on us. Like I said: destroyed.

"I think we need to call it while we still have some dignity left," I say.

Angie laughs. "I think mine has been gone for a while now."

We say "Good game" to Jessica and Amalya, and they offer us another round of congratulations on our fake nuptials before we pack up our stuff by the fence.

"Quick thinking back there with our wedding details," I say once we're out of earshot.

She laughs. "Yeah, we probably should have coordinated stories a while ago in case someone asked. You really should come up with an epic proposal story. People love those."

Proposal story. How *would* I propose to her?

No, I shouldn't even be thinking about that. We'll never actually get married, and Angie deserves someone who can give her that. Someone who can give her everything she's always wanted.

But I still long to reach out and touch her. To brush away her wild, blonde hair from her face and kiss those plump pink lips. To hold her close and inhale that sweet smell of lavender and coconut.

We can pretend all we want, but in the end, it only serves to remind me that I'll never have the real thing. And it's starting to hurt a little too much.

29

ANGIE

May 12

Being in love with someone who doesn't feel the same way is a special form of torture. Everything revolves around him. He's all I think about. When I close my eyes, I can't help but picture these elaborate scenarios where we are actually together and happy. But then I come crashing back down to reality and the ache in my chest grows even stronger.

Why can't I get over him?? It's been more than two years.

TWO YEARS OF THIS.

Tonight Asher and Wesley are going to Prom. Wesley of course is going with Stacy, and Asher is taking Priscilla Parker, who always gets whatever she wants. What's it like to be God's favorite, PRISCILLA?

The four of them came here to take pictures and everything before going out. Like it wasn't bad enough imagining them together in my head, but to have it shoved in my face and have to pretend to be happy? It took everything I had not to cry in front of all of them. I'm sure Priscilla would have loved to see that.

Watching the one person you wish would love you back, laughing and touching someone else? It hurts more than anything I've ever experienced. They're right in front of you, but you can't have them. It's like dying of starvation and staring into the window of some fancy restaurant where everyone is full and content. Why does everyone else get to experience love? Why does everyone else get to have what they want?

Priscilla could never love him like I do.

It's not fair.

I just hope he is happy. He deserves that. Even if it's not with me.

Even if it makes me want to disappear.

30

ASHER

"That was incredible," Angie says as we board the taxi back to the resort.

"We're definitely putting that restaurant on the itinerary."

I was so glad when we woke up this morning and Angie said her burn was feeling better, and that she wanted to get out of the resort and explore a little. We opted for an easy hike at Greencastle Hill.

The views were amazing, and Angie made sure to take plenty of photos. Afterward, we found a small local restaurant in town called Islands to eat lunch.

Of course, I chickened out talking to Angie last night about what we're doing. I'm terrified to have that conversation, and honestly, I don't even know what I'd say. Do I tell her how I really feel? Or say I'm not comfortable pretending anymore? Is there any scenario where I don't hurt her feelings?

When we arrive back at the resort, a tall woman at the front desk waves at us. "Welcome back, Mr. Hayes. Mrs. Hayes. Are you enjoying your stay with us?"

My heart thuds in my chest. Maybe this is my chance to

finally put an end to this charade. Tell the resort, tell Angie all at once. I'm about to respond when Angie slides under my arm and wraps hers around my torso. A shiver runs down my spine as her palm rubs my chest, her breasts pressing into my side as I fight for air. My cock twitches of its own accord.

She looks up at me while saying, "Yes, we are. Thank you so much for everything. This place really is amazing!"

Angie's eyes are mischievous and daring. It's the closest our bodies have been before, even counting when we spooned on New Year's Eve. I lean down, my lips barely brushing the shell of her ear as I whisper, "What do you think you're doing?"

I feel her smile against my cheek. "Just play along. We're supposed to be on our honeymoon. I'm your wife, remember?"

Can she feel my heart hammering against my ribs?

My wife.

Goddamn, it's the first time I'm hearing her say that word, and I shouldn't like the way that sounds. Like yesterday when she called me her husband on the pickleball court. I've been firmly against the idea of marriage my entire life, but when it comes from Angie, those words don't sound scary. They sound...right somehow. I'm suddenly lightheaded as I pull away from her enough to search her face. Could she really want me like that?

My gaze lands on her lips, plump and curved into that Cheshire cat smile of hers, as the air around us turns thick and heavy.

What is happening?

I can't think straight. It's like she's cracked some code within me I didn't even know existed.

My wife.

She is my wife.

Those deep blue eyes pin me in place. I'm not in control of

myself as my free hand slowly finds her cheek, and for a split second she leans into my palm, never breaking eye contact.

I've forgotten all the reasons why this was a bad idea. There's nothing in the world that can stop us from being together if we want it badly enough. And I know I do. God, I've never wanted anything more.

What happens next alters my brain chemistry.

Our lips press together lightly, and the rest of the world falls away. I'm not entirely sure if I'm the one who kissed her or if she kissed me, or if we came together at the exact same time.

For years, I've imagined what kissing Angie would be like. It doesn't even come close to the real thing.

Our first kiss.

Soft at first, the contact between us is new and surprising. Slow, lingering movements as our mouths feel each other out. Then our kiss deepens, and I know it was me this time. My other hand slides to the back of her neck, pulling her in closer as every moment we've shared collides into this one kiss, for the first time, and suddenly everything makes sense.

Dreams manifesting into reality.

A throat clearing off in the distance wakes me from my trance as we quickly pull apart. The woman at the front desk clears her throat again, and my head whips in her direction, reminding me of where we are and what just happened. Jesus.

"Sorry," I say breathlessly to the receptionist as I rub the back of my neck. "We just—"

She places her hand over her heart. "You two are truly in love; it's so beautiful. Enjoy it." She goes back to typing something on her computer, effectively dismissing us. Probably wishing we would take our display of inappropriate affection somewhere more private.

Angie and I stand there in stunned silence, trying to recover from the monumental shift that just took place. What is she thinking right now? Did she feel what I felt, or was it all for show?

Angie grabs my elbow and pulls me away giggling. I take her hand and squeeze, unwilling to let her get away. Not after that. Not now, not ever.

She leads me around the far edge of the lobby, and we nearly run into an older gentleman with a huge rolling suitcase.

"Ope!" Angie squeals, stopping suddenly in her tracks as I barrel into her, pulling her down with me and crashing to the floor, narrowly avoiding the man as he continues walking around us with a confused look on his face.

We both erupt in laughter, but I'm hyper aware of her body pressed on top of mine. I tuck a strand of golden blonde hair behind her ear, no longer sure of what we are to each other. But I know I could stay here forever with her.

"You were very convincing back there," she says once the laughter has died down.

My stomach sinks. Something about the way she says it makes me think it *was* just part of the act. That she isn't nearly as affected by that kiss as I was. For one single moment, I let myself believe that something really had changed between us, but just as quickly it's gone, and reality settles back in. Why do I keep doing this to myself?

She pulls herself off me and offers her hand to help me up. We stand and head toward our villa, but it's hard to focus on anything except her. The memory of that kiss lingers on my lips.

Fuck, it was the most electrifying experience of my life.

And yet she doesn't seem affected by it at all.

We make our way across the promenade, avoiding each other's stare, my hands buried in my pockets to keep from touching her. The silence between us is unbearable.

"So..." she says, picking at her nail. "Can we just pretend that didn't happen? It doesn't have to be a big deal, you know?"

My heart squeezes to the point of physical pain, but I shrug, trying to appear casual. "Right. Not a big deal."

Except it is. I can't keep doing this.

I need to work out or go for a run or something. I'm too wound up right now and can't make sense of anything. It's too much. Because we can never go back to how things were before, and I'm terrified our friendship won't survive what happens next.

31

ASHER

When we arrive back at our room, we've still barely said a word to each other. What is she thinking right now? Did she feel what I felt back there? How is it possible for a kiss to completely tear someone apart, while the other person feels nothing?

I need to clear my head, far away from her. "I think I'm gonna hit the gym, if that's cool with you."

"Go for it!" she says cheerfully. Again, completely unbothered. "I'll probably lie down for a quick nap now that I can sleep on my back again."

"Okay," I say, plastering on a smile. "Reconvene in a few hours?"

"You got it."

After quickly changing into my workout clothes, I grab my stuff, barely sparing her a second glance as I slip out the door. This has gotten way out of hand. I feel like I'm going crazy thinking about her. And those lips. Her breasts pressed against my side.

It doesn't help that I start to get hard every time she pops into my head. I'm not sure when I'll even be able to take care of my aching cock because of our non-private bathroom situation. After six days with her, I think I might actually be dying. Maybe there are some locker room showers down at the resort gym where I can find some release.

Maybe that's my problem. I'm wound too tight and haven't jerked off in almost a week. Meanwhile, she's walking around in a bikini that leaves little to the imagination, touching my arm and my chest, smiling and laughing. Then that kiss sent me careening over the edge.

Right on cue, there's my dick, who hasn't gotten the memo about waiting until I'm in the shower. I quickly adjust myself in my shorts behind a large flowering bush on the walking path, so I don't get kicked out of the resort for being a creepy pervert.

The door to the gym beeps as I swipe my keycard over the sensor. I set my water bottle down at one of the treadmills by the windows, but immediately realize I forgot my phone when I go to turn on my music. "Goddammit," I whisper to myself, letting my head fall back. I can't work out in silence like some psychopath.

I reluctantly grab all my stuff again and jog back to the villa, huffing my annoyance at no one in particular. Hopefully Angie hasn't fallen asleep yet and I won't wake her when I get there.

I enter the villa as quietly as I can, peeking into the bedroom area to find the bed empty. The faint sound of running water tells me she must be taking a shower. With little more than a thin pane of frosted glass separating me from her naked body, I avert my eyes and head to the side table to grab my phone.

I'll just sneak back out, and she won't even know I was here.

Walking to my side of the bed, I unplug my phone from the wall charger. I'm tiptoeing back out when I hear a faint noise coming from the bathroom.

I stop moving so I can listen better. There it is again, and I recognize Angie's voice. My mind can't help conjuring up inappropriate images of her in there, and my phone clatters loudly to the floor.

Oh fuck. I need to get out of here.

I bend to pick up my phone when I hear her say, "Asher...?"

Shit, she must have heard me. Maybe I can still sneak out and pretend I was never here.

"Oh god..." Her voice sounds strangled, and I can't tell if she's pissed or embarrassed or both that I didn't stay far enough away from the bathroom like we agreed. I should apologize and leave. No need to make this awkward.

She then cries out clear as day, "Asher!" and it sounds like she might be in pain.

Shit!

"Angie?" I yell as I burst through the door, expecting to see her injured on the tile floor, my heart climbing out of my chest.

She lets out a blood-curdling scream as my eyes find her wet, naked body inside the open shower. Standing there, perfectly fine. Perfectly...breathtaking.

"Oh my god! What are you doing in here?" she yells as she turns off the water and grabs a towel from the rack to cover herself up.

I shield my eyes. "Fuck, sorry! I thought you were hurt."

"Why would you think that? Jesus Christ, you scared the shit out of me!" Her breaths are heavy, and now I feel like a complete asshole.

"I'm sorry! It sounded like you were crying in here. You called out my name like you needed help."

The tiny bathroom goes deathly silent as my words settle

between us, and I realize I've read the situation all wrong. She clearly didn't know I was in our room.

But...she was in the shower...alone...crying out my name.

No. There's no way.

There has to be some other explanation.

"Angie?" I say slowly, still averting my eyes, trying to keep my self-control in check. "Why were you saying my name in here?"

I know I should leave. Pretend this never happened. It's what a gentleman would do. But my patience has run out. That kiss from downstairs has scrambled all the neurons in my brain, and now I'm running on pure animal instinct.

When she doesn't answer, I dare to drop my hand from my face. My eyes take in the sight of her clutching a white towel at her chest, barely covering her thighs. Her soft, fair skin covered in droplets, blonde hair sopping wet. Her cheeks and her chest tinted pink, either from the heat of the shower, or...from me.

I take several deep, steadying breaths before forcing my gaze higher and higher until I finally meet her wide eyes. Her expression is soft but searching as I take a step closer.

Now I know I'm not in control anymore.

Because there's still time to walk away from this.

I should stop.

But I can't.

"Angie?" I say again, my voice low and gravelly.

She looks down at her feet. Her freckles barely visible on her deep red cheeks.

I need to know for sure she was doing what I think she was doing in here. That I didn't imagine it.

Another step closer, now almost within arm's distance. Her chest rises and falls over and over. My hands itch to pull on that towel until it falls to the floor.

"I...um..." she says on a shaky breath, but goes silent again.

The final step closes the distance between us, my nose barely brushing hers when I angle my head down and whisper, "What could you possibly be doing in here...screaming my name...if I wasn't even here?" Drops of water fall from her hair onto my shoes.

"Ash," she says breathlessly, pressing her forehead to mine, still not looking at me.

"Use your words." I barely even recognize my own voice, but I don't miss how she squeezes her thighs together at my command, how her breath catches. It's enough to confirm it. I was right.

Holy fucking shit.

Things will never be the same again.

"I was...touching myself," she says just above a whisper.

Pulling back, I pinch her chin between my thumb and index finger, angling her head up, forcing her to meet my gaze. "And what were you thinking about while you were touching yourself?"

Her throat bobs as she swallows audibly. I almost get lost in those sparkling blue eyes, like pools of water I could drown in.

"Say it." I need to hear the words.

"I was thinking about you." A tear falls beneath those damp lashes. "It's always you."

32

ANGIE

Asher squeezes his eyes shut. For a moment, I think he might be embarrassed for me and is trying to figure out how to let me down gently. Like I'm still Wesley's annoying little sister and that's all I'll ever be.

But I know it's not true. I saw the look in his eyes. Those hungry, green eyes roving over my body inch by inch as I stood under the weight of his assessing gaze. Then there's the obvious bulge in his athletic shorts.

He wants me too.

And now I've confessed to him that I was masturbating to the thought of him.

He presses his forehead to mine again as he slides his large, calloused hand from my chin across my cheek and into my wet hair. His chest brushes mine as it heaves up and down. I need him to make the next move, because I don't have the courage to ask if that kiss earlier was real. It certainly felt real.

"Angie," he says, his voice strained. "I can't do this anymore. No more games. Tell me what you want from me."

I can't do this either. It's too much to keep to myself

anymore. Being near him this week has been torture. And now he's right here within reach, and I finally know he wants this too. So I stop pretending.

"I want you, Asher," I cry. "Please just kiss me again."

"*Fuck*," he groans.

Time slows to a stop, the universe compressing around us.

His lips finally find mine, and I think he might devour me. It's urgent and hungry and feverish, his beard rough against my chin. Nothing like the soft, methodical kiss from an hour ago. No, this is something else entirely.

Insatiable, untamed. Wild.

Raw.

Holy fucking shit, this is really happening.

I feel like I might die from how much I need him right now.

Can't think. Can't breathe.

With my free hand, I fist his shirt to pull him closer. A moan escapes me when he pries the towel from my grasp, and it falls softly at my feet. Goose bumps erupt all over my body as the cool air hits my damp skin.

His fingers glide up my stomach to my aching breast, where he squeezes a palm full before brushing his thumb over my hard nipple. When he pinches it, I gasp. Never have I felt like this before, and he's barely touched me.

Fuck, I may not survive this. I had already gotten myself close to the edge before he caught me, and now I think I might explode.

He pulls back and looks down at me. His eyes dark and hooded with lust. The hand that was on my breast slides down my arm, to the same fingers that had been rubbing my clit to filthy thoughts of him. He grabs my wrist, slowly bringing it up between us.

"Was this the hand you pictured was mine?"

I bite my lip at the memory, at his commanding tone. I've

never heard him talk like this before in all the years I've known him. All I can do is nod.

He looks at my fingers, his pupils blown wide. Slowly, he brings my hand up to his face, and he inhales deeply, his eyes rolling in the back of his head.

Oh my god...

Then he surprises me again by opening his mouth and licking my fingers clean, his dark eyes locked on mine. This is absolutely, without a doubt, the hottest thing I've experienced in my life.

Asher Hayes is standing in front of my wet, naked body, licking off the fingers I just had in my pussy. This can't be real life.

My fingers release from his mouth with a pop before he says, "Would you like the real thing?"

What is happening? I'm not even sure I know what he means, but I know I want whatever he is offering. So I nod again.

This man continues to leave me speechless.

He comes to my side as he holds his hand underneath mine, and I shiver. "Take *my* hand. Show me what you like."

My heart is in my throat. I can barely think straight. So I do what he says. I wrap my fingers around his hand, bringing it to the inside of my thigh, slowly guiding him up and up until he reaches my soaking wet center. We both suck in a harsh breath at the same time.

I press his fingers into my clit, and move them around in circles. He takes over the movement as my head drops back to his shoulder.

"Like this?" he whispers in my ear before claiming my mouth again. His tongue finds mine as we share breath. My hand reaches back to tangle in his hair, pulling him closer. But it's not enough.

His fingers press harder, but he slows his movements. When he breaks the kiss again, he wraps his other arm around me, pinning my back to his front. His erection digs into the base of my spine as he says, "What about this hand?"

I feel like my legs might give out. It's too much. "I want that hand inside me, Asher. Please, take me to the bed."

In an instant, I'm spun around and off my feet, his hands under my knees as I wrap my arms around his neck and kiss him deeply again. God, I always knew it would be like this with him if we ever got the chance.

"Is this okay?" he asks between heaving breaths. "Your burn."

"It's fine. Don't you dare stop."

He tosses me backward on the bed, and I don't have time to tell him how unfair it is that he's still fully clothed before he presses my legs open wide and takes my throbbing clit in his mouth, his facial hair tickling the sensitive skin of my inner thighs. He alternates between sucking lightly and lapping feverishly with his tongue. One finger teases my entrance before plunging deep inside me. I arch off the bed, the sensation so intense I might be ready to come already.

My hands fist the sheets as I try to anchor myself, slowing down my thoughts and just feeling him on me. In me.

He adds a second finger, curling them both up along my sensitive inner walls. His moans are almost as loud as mine as he keeps up the steady movements. My lower belly floods with heat as I feel my insides tightening and coiling. Holy fuck.

I can barely think straight, can only feel what he's doing to me. What I've fantasized about for years. I've never felt like this before, like I might explode from so much pleasure.

I won't be able to hold it together much longer as he continues thrusting his fingers inside me, licking and sucking my clit. Adding a third finger and stretching me wide, he takes his free hand and presses his palm down just below my belly button.

That's when I completely lose it.

I just...explode.

Blinding pleasure rips through my body as I scream, pulsing around his fingers, digging my nails into his shoulders as everything I am and ever was and ever could be breaks me apart.

It doesn't stop. It never ends.

I don't even know how long it takes, but Asher is moaning as he continues his movements until I finally come down slowly, matching my pace and rhythm. My chest still rising and falling rapidly with my ragged breaths, sweat slick over my skin.

The sheets beneath me feel wet, like really wet.

I peer down at him, his beard and his lips glistening with my release, turned up into a wicked grin.

"Goddamn, baby. I didn't know you could squirt like that," he says against my thighs with a groan. He pulls away from me as I let out a long exhale, my body melting into the bed, my arms and legs heavy as lead.

Fucking hell. I've never squirted before. Part of me wants to be embarrassed, except the look on his face tells me he liked it. Really, really liked it.

I bring myself up to kiss him, my hands coming around his neck to pull him closer, tasting myself on him. I want more. My hand reaches for his hard length, but he quickly grabs my wrist to stop me and breaks the kiss.

"I want to feel you," I whine. "Let me take care of you."

"There's..." he starts, letting out a harsh breath. "There's nothing to do...at the moment."

"What do you mean?" I look down to see a large wet mark on the front of his shorts. When my eyes find his again, he turns away, cheeks stained a deep red as he rubs the back of his neck. "Oh."

"Yeah...sorry, I...that's never happened to me before, but there was no way I was going to keep my composure after that. You were...goddamn, there are no words. That was the most beautiful thing I've ever seen in my entire fucking life."

I feel my own cheeks flush as I press my forehead to his. He was so turned on by me that he couldn't stop himself from coming in his pants? "I don't know what to say."

"You don't have to say anything." He chuckles as he pulls me to the edge of the bed and drops to his knees between my spread legs. He leans in to kiss my lips. "That was incredible."

"No, it's just..." I shake my head.

"What is it?" His hand comes up to rub my cheek. "Tell me." The gentleness in his voice strikes something deep within me, and I melt into his palm.

"I can't believe that just happened. I never thought...with you?" I stammer. "I always assumed you didn't think of me that way."

His eyes go wide, and he laughs. *Laughs.*

My heart sinks. "It's not funny. I'm being serious." I smack his chest. "Stop!"

He leans in, still smiling, and nuzzles his nose with mine. His voice is an octave lower when he says, "Oh, Sunshine. If you only knew."

I feel my heart pounding in my ears. "Knew what?"

His lips brush softly over mine. "That I'm fucking obsessed with you, and I've dreamed about calling you mine for almost fifteen years."

33

ANGIE

What?

My head rears back, and I search his eyes for understanding, because I've obviously heard him wrong.

My hearing must have been severely damaged during my mind-blowing orgasm. An Asher Hayes orgasm is apparently so life-altering that hearing loss should be mentioned as a possible side effect.

"What did you just say?" I ask.

"Angie—"

"That's not funny." I stand up, wrapping the bed sheet around myself, and step past him. Leaving him kneeling on the floor.

Why would he say something like that? He clearly doesn't know how cruel it is to lie about having those feelings for me. To whisper sweet nothings in my ear that I so desperately want to hear.

In my experience, guys will say anything to get you to sleep with them. But Asher wouldn't do that, would he?

"Please don't freak out," he says from behind me, his tone

suddenly serious. "I'm not asking you to do anything or say anything."

I whirl around to find him on his feet, his palms open. That cool, sultry demeanor from moments ago has given way to sheer panic.

"What are you even talking about?" I ask. My heart is in my throat and my brain is still mush. Another side effect.

He rakes a hand through his auburn hair. "I'm not trying to be funny. It's the truth." He takes a hesitant step forward.

I shake my head, unable to process what he's saying right now. "Excuse me if I have a hard time believing that. I have spent half my life hopelessly in love with you, and have had to live with the pain of knowing you've never felt the same way."

To hide the tears welling up in my eyes, I quickly turn and walk to the other room. I hear footsteps following me, so I add, "This was a mistake. I thought I could finally get over you on this trip, but it's just too hard. Even after all these years, you still have the power to completely wreck me. Congratulations."

It hurts too much.

Willow was right. I was a fool for coming here and thinking I could move past these feelings. And now he knows, and we can't go back to the way things were.

Especially not after what we just did...

His hands come to my shoulders to spin me around, but I can't bring myself to look at him.

He comes within an inch of my face. I clutch the bedsheet tighter to my chest, needing something to distract me as the weight of his attention becomes almost too much to bear.

"Angie. I need you to listen to me." He gently angles my face up to his. "I'm telling you the truth. I don't know exactly when it happened, but we were young. It started as a crush, but I never thought I could have you, so I never said anything. You were my best friend's sister. It killed me to leave for college, to leave you. Not a day went by that I didn't think about dropping out of school so I could be with you. To tell you how I really felt about you."

"Then why did you disappear?" My voice cracks, and I hold back the tears threatening to spill over.

It's the question I've held on to for so long. It never made sense to me that he would leave and cut off all communication like that so abruptly.

His hands drop from my face. "It's complicated."

My lips twist to the side. "Is it your ex? Are you still in love with her?" I can't help but ask the other question I've been obsessing over this week.

"What? No, she has nothing to do with this. I hadn't even met her yet. I was in love with you when I left, and I still am to this day."

I shake my head. "I don't believe you."

He steps back and pulls his shirt over his head, letting it fall to the floor. Taking my hand, he brings it up to his chest, where there are dark markings on the left side just above his nipple. A tattoo.

How have I never seen this before?

My fingertip traces the shape—a spiral with wavy lines sprouting outward. A sun. *Sunshine.*

I feel like the earth has opened up and swallowed me whole, my life completely upended. I no longer know what's true anymore.

"When did you..." I swallow, my throat suddenly dry.

"My first night away at college. The first night away from you."

No. None of this makes sense. I search his deep green eyes again, but only find truth. "Why?"

"That night...being so far away from you was torture. I needed a reminder of you. My feelings for you were real, and I just wanted to hold on to that. Even if it was all I could have of you."

My heart cracks. "I wish you had told me how you felt."

"I didn't think it would matter," he says. "That you would even miss me."

"How could you believe that?" I lean in and press my forehead to his chest. "You broke my heart when you left."

"I'm sorry. I didn't know." He wraps me in his arms, pinning mine between us as I sink into his warmth. His breath is hot on my neck when he murmurs, "So all this time? You felt the same way?"

I try and fail to hold in a sob.

"Angie?" He pulls back with his hands on my shoulders. His face is pained, pleading.

I squeeze my eyes shut as tears slide down my cheeks, nodding because I can barely string two words together.

"This is real?" he asks with so much hope I think I might burst. His thumb swipes the tears away, but more follow in their wake.

I suck in a deep breath and open my eyes. "It's always been real to me. I am so fucking in love with you."

34

ASHER

She loves me?

She has been in love with me for as long as I have?

Years and years of memories flood my brain as I re-evaluate everything I've ever felt or thought about her. The feeling is so overwhelming I think my heart might leap out of my chest. All I can do is grab her by the face and kiss her fiercely.

There will be time for talking soon enough, but right now I just need to feel this. To settle into this new reality.

She's in love with me, too.

After all this time.

I pour every ounce of myself into her. Every feeling I've had for this woman, as I spear my hand into her damp, tangly hair, deepening this kiss I never want to end. She drops the bedsheet and wraps her arms over my shoulders, pulling me closer.

My other hand runs down her back and over her round, perfect ass. I'm about to squeeze when I remember her sunburn, and instead bring my hand up to dig my fingers into her hip.

She moans as she pulls away, breaking the kiss. Both of us trying to catch our breath as the enormity of our situation finally sets in.

"What do we do now?" she asks, and it's the most adorable thing I think I've ever heard. I can't help but smile wide as my hands rub up and down her sides.

"Whatever we want." I lean in to kiss her forehead.

For the first time, our future is wide open.

"Will you lie down with me?" I ask. "I'm feeling a little... overwhelmed at the moment. This is a lot to take in."

She nods as her fingers trace the sun tattoo over my heart again. I hoped it wouldn't scare her away, but I had to show her I was serious. That I was being honest about my feelings for her.

And she's still here.

She's in my arms and I never want to let her go.

"Actually, let me change out of these real quick," I motion to my cum-stained shorts as I reluctantly pull away from her.

After changing into a fresh pair of briefs in the bathroom, I find her brushing her wet hair in front of the full-length mirror. She looks ethereal, like a goddess.

I grab her and pull her down on the bed, causing her to squeal before we both erupt into laughter. I snuggle her into me; her back to my front as I squeeze around her tightly, breathing in the sweet scent of her hair. Her skin warm against my chest. I want to stay like this forever.

I can't believe any of this is real.

The taste of her still lingers on my tongue.

Her skin is like velvet under my touch. I want to trace every freckle, every line. Kiss every inch until I've memorized it all. When my thumb skims over the heart inked on the inside of her wrist, I say, "Speaking of tattoos...tell me about this. It's your only one, right?"

She lets out a contented sigh. "Yeah. Willow has the same one. We were roommates in college, and one night I convinced her to get matching tattoos to commemorate our friendship. She designed it herself."

"You two are really close, huh."

"Like sisters. When we met that year, it was like we already knew each other somehow. It just clicked. And we've been inseparable ever since."

I'm glad she has someone like that in her life. It reminds me of how Wes and I used to be. I press slow kisses to Angie's shoulder, still trying to make sense of what just happened between us.

"This is weird, right?" she says, as if reading my thoughts. "Like, we're naked and you're kissing me."

I can't help but laugh. "Weird...but in a good way, I hope?"

She laughs too. "Well, obviously. I mean, first you give me the best orgasm of my life, and then I find out you've had feelings for me this whole time?"

My hand stills on her forearm. "Wait...did you say *best* orgasm of your life?"

"Easily."

I lean my head closer to hers. "The one where I jizzed in my pants?"

She laughs again, and the sound warms me up from the inside. "I don't think you realize just how fucking hot that really is."

"I think the word you're looking for is 'pathetic.'" My cheeks warm.

Turning in my arms to face me, she says, "Are you kidding me? The fact that you were so turned on by me that you lost control? If that's pathetic, then please keep being pathetic for me."

"Always have been when it comes to you," I say as I brush her hair over her shoulder.

Her hand comes to rest on the side of my face, but her smile is fading, and she's gone quiet. Her brows furrow as the wheels turn in her head. She must have so many questions, like I do. We have a lot to talk about, but now that I have her here, I'm willing to do whatever it takes to keep her.

It should scare me, the endless possibilities of *us*. A future together. But it's actually the opposite. I finally feel a strange sense of calm, like everything has led us to this moment, and this is how it was always supposed to be.

I've never felt that before.

So I claim her soft lips again, because I will never get enough. We will never make up for all the lost time, but at least I can try.

"What are you thinking?" I ask when we finally pull apart. "You can tell me anything."

"I know I can, it's just...it's you. It's *us*. There's a lot to process."

I pull her closer, her head fitting into the crook of my neck as my arms circle her. "I know. But I'm here, we're here. We have all the time in the world to figure this out."

"Do we though?" she asks quietly, pulling away to look up at me with those big blue eyes. "What happens after this trip and we both have to go back to the real world?"

In just a few words, she manages to vocalize the one thing that really does scare me. How do we protect what we have now? It took so long to get here, and it's not going to be easy once we're out of our little vacation bubble.

I force a smile as I take her hand and interlace our fingers, pulling them to rest between us. "The real world is whatever we want it to be. We'll figure it out."

She wants to say more, and I already know what's holding her back. It's the biggest question that's kept us apart.

"I know you said it was complicated...but if you felt this way for so long, then why didn't you ever say anything? Why did you move away and change your number? I feel like...before we move forward, I have to understand. Please."

I nod as I let out a breath, feeling my heart rate pick up. "Okay. After Wes and I had that falling out, I guess I just thought it would be better for everyone if I gave you all some space. Then a few months later, in a moment of weakness...I looked at your social media...to see what you were up to."

She closes her eyes, no doubt understanding what I'm getting at. All those images of her and some guy. I looked at all of them, even though it killed me. Even though it sent me into a dangerous spiral.

"You looked so happy. Whoever that guy was...I could tell you were in love. I knew then I had missed my chance with you. I wanted you to be happy, so I told myself you were better off without me. I would never want to get in the way of your happiness, so I had to move on."

It would be another four years before I met Sarah. But even then, I still thought of Angie. I never really moved on from loving her.

"I'm sorry you had to see those pictures. Knowing now that you had feelings for me...that must have been hard."

"You don't have to be sorry," I say, shaking my head.

"I guess it's kind of like when you went to Prom with Priscilla Parker."

My stomach drops. Angie was there that night, watching us take pictures before the dance. She looked so sad, but I never considered it was because of me.

"I was never really into her. But I am sorry. I had no idea." My hand finds her waist, my lips pulling up at the sides. "And...

not that it's an excuse, but you also never said anything to me about *your* feelings."

She smiles at that. "Okay, fair. But I feel like...god, there were so many chances for us to cross that line, but we never did. Why? I still don't get it. I mean, Wesley might've been weird about it at first, but who cares? He would have gotten over it."

I avert my gaze, pulling my tingling arm from underneath her and unlinking our hands. Sitting up, I try to figure out what to say, but I come up empty.

"What?" She pushes up to her knees in front of me and grabs my face with one hand, turning me back toward her as she narrows her eyes, searching. "Did he say something to you?"

I chew my lip. I don't want to throw Wes under the bus. They're so close, and I wouldn't want to do anything to jeopardize their relationship. But...I'm also done using him as an excuse. We're not kids anymore.

"Oh my god. He told you I was off-limits or some other bro code bullshit, didn't he?"

I reach for her, rubbing her arms. "Please don't blame him. He had every right to say what he did."

She buries her face in her hands. "Ugh. This is so fucking typical."

"Angie." I pull her wrists away gently, but she won't meet my gaze. "It was for the best. I would've been a shitty boyfriend. Don't you remember how fucked up I was about everything? I wasn't good enough for you back then...and if I'm being honest, I'm not sure I'm good enough for you now, but—"

"Don't ever say that," she snaps. "Of course you are. You are a kind and decent man."

Shaking my head, I say, "I think about it all the time. I

thought I was doing the right thing, but what did it even matter? In the end I lost you both. You were my family, and I was too scared to stay and fight for you."

She's quiet for a moment before placing her hand on my cheek again. "You didn't lose me. It just wasn't our time yet."

I swallow around the lump in my throat, tamping down the hope blossoming in my chest. "Do you really believe that?"

"I have to," she says softly, placing a gentle kiss on my lips. "Otherwise we've spent all these years pining over each other for nothing."

I can't help but laugh. "Yes, that would be a tragic waste of time, wouldn't it?"

"You know...we met you at such a difficult time. We had just lost our dad, and things were really hard for us. I like to think you came into our lives for a reason. You were exactly who we needed at the time."

My heart swells as I tuck a strand of hair behind her ear. "You all were who I needed back then, too."

I lie back down, pulling her into my side. I just need to feel her. Give myself time to believe this isn't some beautiful dream. No more words are needed as our breaths slow down, and I drift off to sleep to the faint smell of lavender and coconut.

35

ANGIE

I blink my heavy eyes open to find the room dark, except for a soft glow from the bedside lamp. I don't even remember falling asleep, and...yep, I'm definitely naked. Asher's arm is laid over my waist, our legs a tangled mess. Everything comes flooding back as I lean into his warm chest and squeeze his arm closer.

He stirs a little, our legs untangling as I turn in his arms and take in his messy auburn hair and slightly slack jaw.

God, he's gorgeous. And adorable. And irresistible.

And...mine.

He was worth the wait.

The memory of what he did earlier with his mouth and his fingers has heat rushing to my core, and I giggle softly to myself.

Wait, how long ago was that?

I look around the dim room. Outside our window is pitch black.

How long were we asleep? What time is it?

Grabbing my phone off the nightstand, I gasp.

ELEVEN P.M.

Holy shit. We slept the entire day. No wonder I'm so hungry all of a sudden.

I turn back to Asher, ready to wake him, but I stop myself when I see the tattoo on his chest. My finger gently caresses the spiral shape, following its pattern. I can't believe he got this the first night after he left. It's like I was there with him the whole time.

His skin is warm under my touch as I spread my palm over his chest, my fingers moving through the coarse hair. "Hey, wake up."

He groans something indecipherable as I lean down, nibbling softly on his earlobe. His eyes fly open at the same moment he grabs me by the waist and rolls me on top of him in one fluid motion. My legs land on either side of his hips, straddling him and hovering a few inches.

"Good morning," I croon. "Or should I say...good night?"

His hands slide over my hips as he looks up at me sleepily. "Hmm...what time is it?"

I tilt my phone toward him. "It's eleven. Can you believe it?"

He scrunches his face together as he squints at the screen. "Eleven? At night?"

"Yeah. I'm gonna need some food soon." I look back at my phone screen and realize I have several missed calls and texts from Willow.

WILLOW

Hello??

I'm bored

You haven't been texting me

You said you would keep me updated

Call me pleeeeease

I told you not to go on this trip

If he murdered you I'm going to be so pissed

I let out a snort. God I love her.

ME

I'm fine, just woke up

Asher's hands tighten on my thighs as he pulls me over him back and forth. My core lights up at the sudden intense friction. A thin pair of clean boxer briefs is all that separates my naked body from his already-hard dick. Which I still haven't seen with my own eyes yet, but from what I can feel right now, it might be the biggest one I've ever come across. I'm already getting wet, but I want to tease him a little more first.

WILLOW

Thank god you're okay

Wait, just woke up??

Isn't it like 11 pm over there? Or do I have my time zones mixed up

One of Asher's hands moves up my torso, sliding over my breast as he softly brushes the sensitive skin around my nipple.

"Who are you talking to?" he says with a fake pout.

"Just texting Willow back. I hadn't talked to her all day, and then we got...distracted."

"Would you like more distractions?" He continues his maddening movements, thrusting his hips up as he pinches my nipple hard between his fingers.

"One second," I say on a gasp as I type out my response to Willow, needing to assuage her worries so I can get back to more important things. But also seeing Asher lose his composure a little is super satisfying.

ME

Yeah we're all good here

No need to worry

WILLOW

wtf

You guys were fucking weren't you

I laugh out loud. Shit, she knows me so well. I'm so lucky to have landed her as my best friend.

ME

not exactly

...not yet

👀

WILLOW

OMG

you dirty slut

Asher pinches my other nipple even harder, eliciting a sharp gasp from me as a jolt shoots down my spine. "I can do this all night, Sunshine." He sits up, one hand sliding up my back to hold me in place where my neck meets my shoulders, licking the sensitive spot below my ear. His breath is hot on my skin as he says, "But I'd rather not be inside you for the first time while you're on your phone."

I set it down beside me as he takes my breast in his mouth, his tongue making quick circles over my nipple before sucking hard. When he moves to the other breast, I frame his face with my hands, shifting my hips to straddle him better.

Grinding on his rock-hard cock, a nagging thought suddenly enters my brain. "Wait. Do you have condoms?"

His eyes go wide as he pulls back. "No. Shit. Do you think maybe there's some in the gift shop downstairs?"

"I think it closed at ten."

He lies back down, covering his face with his hands. "Goddammit. Can we...ask the concierge for that, you think?" His voice goes into a higher octave, making me giggle.

"You want my best friend Alvin to deliver us..." I lower my voice to a whisper as I press a hand to my bare chest. "...condoms?"

I'm pulled down abruptly within an inch of his face. "Hey, they did want us to enjoy our honeymoon, and said to let them know if we needed *anything*." He punctuates the last word with a thrust of his hips as he starts kissing me deeply.

For a moment, I consider going without one, because right now I need this man to fuck me so hard I forget my own name. To fill me up until I'm screaming. But I'm not on any birth control, and the idea of getting pregnant scares me more than my fear of clowns. Plus, it hasn't been that long since Chad and his infamous PPP. It would be massively irresponsible.

When I pull away, my phone buzzes with another text.

WILLOW

I hope you found that surprise I left for you

I pick it back up to reply, wincing at the bright screen, and rest the phone on Asher's forehead.

"Hey, what the fuck," he says as I ignore him and start typing.

ME

What surprise?

WILLOW

front big zipper on the wheely bag

you're welcome

I whip my leg over his hips, grabbing my phone off his face, and crawl to the end of the bed—still completely naked—where my bag is lying on the floor below.

"What in god's name are you doing?"

I smile at the exasperation in his voice, but I'm too curious to see what surprise Willow left me. She never does stuff like this. Opening the zipper on the front, it takes me a second to see what it is in this dim light, but it's not long before I'm letting out a screeching laugh.

WILLOW

Two different sizes just in case

I saw the size of his hands

ME

OH MY GOD I love you bitch

WILLOW

Have fun

ME

I toss my phone on the floor as I grab what's inside my suitcase and sit back up in bed, turning to Asher and hiding Willow's timely presents behind my back.

His gaze lingers on my bare breasts, which I may be sticking out a little. "What's that?"

I hold up the two boxes of condoms like I'm a model on *The Price is Right*. "Looks like Willow saved the day."

His mouth forms into the most wicked grin. "Oh,

Sunshine," he says with a raised eyebrow, propping himself up on his hands. His bare chest and toned abs on display, making me bite my lip. "We should really order room service first. You're gonna need your strength for this."

36

ASHER

I make Angie put on one of the fluffy Blue Water Resort robes while we eat our room service dinner side by side at the small table in the main living space. Her exquisite naked body is way too much for me to handle right now. It's a miracle I've kept my hands to myself this long, and I can hardly wait to have more of her. But I've waited this long, and I'd wait another fifteen years if I had to.

We graze on flank steak, roasted rosemary chicken, garlic mashed potatoes, flaky pastries, and an enormous cheese platter while reminiscing about the past.

"Sleepovers at your house were always my favorite," I say between bites of Manchego.

She eyes me curiously, and I put my hands up.

"Not in a creepy way or anything, but...honestly, I loved when you would come down the next morning. Hair all rumpled, sleepy eyes. No makeup. The purest form of you I ever got to see."

Her cheeks take on a shade of red, and I take her hand in mine.

This feels so much like it did when we first met. Innocent, fun. Back when there was just some invisible pull toward each other, but none of the stress or trauma we've both accumulated over the years. When life felt so much simpler.

Just two good friends enjoying each other's company with no expectations.

But as our bellies fill up, and the memory of what we did together earlier today creeps in, I become hungry for something else. I need to be closer, to feel every inch of her skin. I need to taste her again.

Need to be inside her.

"You're staring," she says as she wipes her mouth with the cloth napkin and sets it aside.

"I can't help it." I kiss the back of her hand and make my way up her arm, her skin soft as silk. "I still can't believe you're really here. I keep expecting to wake up from this dream."

A sharp pain on my arm makes me jump. "Ouch!"

Did she just pinch me?

"See? Not a dream." Her face is lit up, a wide grin taking over her face. How is it possible for someone to be this beautiful? It's unreal.

"Is that how we're going to play this? You like a little pain with your pleasure?" My free hand slips into the front of her robe and finds her nipples hard and pointed. I pinch one just as hard as she pinched me, and she gasps. I lean in and claim her lips, pulling her up to standing.

God, I cannot get enough of her. I will never tire of kissing her.

And she wants *me*.

"Take off your robe," I say as I pull her toward the bedroom. She bumps into the table, knocking a plate of something onto the floor.

"Shit!" she cries.

I pull her hand to keep walking. "Leave it. Undress and get the fuck over here, Angie. *Now.*" My hand slips out of hers, and I climb onto the bed, positioning myself with my back up against the headboard.

A slow, feline grin spreads across her face as she unties the robe, letting it fall in a puddle at her feet. Just like that, she's completely naked again, and I'm hard as a fucking rock. I rub myself over my briefs, and her wide, hungry eyes follow the movement.

She climbs onto the bed, crawling toward me. Her hand replaces mine as she continues the slow, torturous movements.

Fuck.

When her fingers hook into the top of my briefs and pull down, I suck in a breath as my cock springs free. Her jaw drops, my underwear stalled at my thighs as she's frozen in place.

"You okay?" I ask with a teasing smile.

"It's..." Her eyes finally meet mine again as my eyebrows raise innocently.

"It's what?" I'm such an asshole. That primal instinct deep down begs to hear her say it. I prop one hand behind my head, the picture of arrogant nonchalance.

"It's huge," she finally says. "I mean...I figured it was big, but...holy shit. Do you think it will fit?"

There it is. I shouldn't get so much pleasure from hearing her say it. Some leftover genetic code from millions of years of biology and evolution, making me feel like a goddamn king right now while she drools over the size of my dick. I can't help it.

"It'll fit. You were made for me."

"Extra-large box it is, then," she says with a smirk.

Before I can say anything more, she continues pulling my briefs all the way down my legs and tosses them aside. Then her hand is eagerly gripping me at the base, and I hiss at the sudden overwhelming sensation.

"Easy, Sunshine. I want to make this last."

She smiles again before opening her mouth, her tongue teasing my tip slowly. I swipe at the strands of hair in front of her face and gather the golden locks behind her head, holding it all there while she licks me to perfection and I hold on for dear life.

Her tongue glides up the side, leaving a wet trail. She spits more onto the tip as she slides her hand down and back up, never letting up on her tight grip, and nothing has felt so good before.

Fuck me, I need to hold out longer. I can't prematurely ejaculate in front of Angie twice in one day. I might as well walk into the ocean right now and end it all.

She doesn't even get a chance to see if she can take me all the way into her mouth before I drop her hair and pry her off me.

"Stop, stop." I'm panting, taking her face in my hands and bringing her close for a kiss. I feel like I'm going to explode already. Her body hovers over mine as I run my hand over her entrance, finding her soaking wet.

"Is this for me?" I murmur against her lips.

"It's always for you," she replies breathlessly. It reminds me of what she said in the shower when I asked her what she was fantasizing about.

"It's always you."

My heart swells. I think I was too shocked and distracted to let the words sink in the first time, but now it feels like they're imprinted on my soul. What else did she say?

"It's always been real to me. I am so fucking in love with you."

Something warms within me. She's here and she wants me. She's in love with me.

This is not the time to overthink things though. I want to remember every second of this.

Plunging two fingers into her soaking pussy, I marvel as she arches her back and moans. I use those same fingers to draw slow circles over her clit, then sink them back in, adding a third finger, and repeat the movements until she is a panting, sweaty mess. Stretched and ready to take me.

"You want to grab that present?" I brush her hair over her shoulder with my free hand before cupping her cheek.

She looks dazed as she lets out a long breath, our foreheads pressing together as we take a moment to ready ourselves. Knowing what is about to take place between us.

Once the condom is rolled on, I look up at her as she straddles me. "We'll go nice and slow, okay? You control how fast and how deep. Any point you want to stop, we stop."

She nods.

"Angie? Look at me." I wait until our eyes meet. "You tell me if you want to stop, okay?"

"I'll tell you," she whispers.

I take my cock and slide it back and forth, gliding through her wetness, before notching it at her entrance. "Ready?"

She leans down and kisses me deeply. Passionately. It takes my breath away.

I could hold her here like this forever.

How is this real?

She slowly lowers herself down an inch, and we both gasp.

"Oh fuck," she says, eyes squeezed tight.

I grit out, "Nice and slow, Sunshine."

She takes her time, thank god. Pausing to adjust to the stretch every time she takes more of me. Her tight heat envelops me as I fight for control of my body. Everything just feels so...right.

How is she so perfect?

"You're doing so well," I say between heavy breaths, cupping her face with both hands. "Do you see how well you're taking me?"

She looks down between us where we're joined. "I'm only like halfway?"

I smile against her lips. "We'll get you there. You're just so fucking tight."

"I won't be after this," she says, and I can't help but laugh. Then she does too. My chest warms at the sound.

"Ready?" I say again once our laughter has died down, and I realize she's already slid down another inch. "You're almost there."

She whimpers. "I'm so full. I've never felt like this before." The tenderness behind her words nearly takes me out.

Our eyes meet, and it's like a jolt to my system. I say on a shaky breath, "Me neither. God, Angie you're so perfect."

She comes down the rest of the way, fully seated, and we stay there for a moment. Still, embracing. Kissing. I slide my hands down her hips to her ass, caressing her soft skin, her breasts pressed into my chest. After a minute or so, I push her hips slightly, urging her to move when she's ready. And when she does, I'm pretty sure I might die.

Yep, I'm dead.

RIP me.

What a way to go, though.

Slow, gentle rolls of her hips eventually give way to faster, more intense movements. Our moans grow louder and deeper, almost feral. It's all I can do to hang on as long as I can, but fuck does she feel so good. She feels like...

She feels like home.

Something in me shifts, and my heart feels like it's going to give out. Tears form in my eyes as I try to blink them away. Am I seriously crying right now?

But then I notice...so is she.

I swipe at a tear falling over the dusting of freckles on her cheek with my thumb. When another comes right behind it, I kiss it. I kiss them all. All the while, our movements turn more frantic, unrestrained. The pressure building and building at the base of my spine as I start to lose control. My balls tighten, and I know I can't hold on much longer.

"I'm close, baby," I say on a moan. I don't even care how pathetic I sound. I want her to know how much she affects me. She can see me cry and beg for her all she wants. I am hers, and she is mine.

"Me too," she says on a whimper.

Grabbing her hips, I take control and pull her off me, rolling her onto her back. With one hand pushing her knee up to her chest, I thrust into her and begin pressing circles over her swollen clit with my thumb.

She grabs my shoulders and shouts, "Oh god. Oh fuck, Asher. *Fuck*!"

The walls of her pussy contract around me as her nails dig into my skin, and I can't hold back any longer. I explode from within to the sound of my name on her sweet lips. I yell out with her, wondering how anything could possibly feel this good. How nothing will ever compare to this moment, right here.

I unload everything I have as I hold on to her for dear life.

Unable to think of anything but her.

It'll only ever be her.

Once we finally come down, I lower to my elbows, kissing her softly as my hand comes to the back of her neck, slick with sweat, and I feel her shiver.

I am never letting her go.

37

ANGIE

Asher and I are still in bed fourteen hours later. We fell into a pattern of making love and napping pretty much nonstop since last night. I'm completely exhausted and sore in the best possible way, but I think I'm ready to throw in the towel. I'm all sexed out.

"I don't want to leave this bed," Asher groans, squeezing me tighter.

"Me neither." I lean into his warmth, savoring this feeling.

His heart beats slow and steady against my back, our hands interlacing together as I pull them into my chest.

"But..." I continue. "We do leave in three days, shouldn't we do more for the trip?"

"There's still plenty of time." He buries his face in my hair and inhales. "Besides, I've stayed at tons of resorts like this. The only missing piece of this vacation package was pickleball, and I think we've already got a good plan for that. Thanks to you."

I spin in his arms to face him, my palm coming to rest over the scruff on his cheek while his hand slides down to my ass and squeezes. "You do need some more practice, though," I tease.

He gasps dramatically. "How dare you."

"You've made some improvements; I'll give you that. But you may still need to convince your boss you've played for more than six hours in your life."

"Mmm...that's fair. How's this...we have more food delivered..." He kisses me. "I make you scream my name two more times..." Another kiss, except this time he tugs my lip with his teeth. "And then we'll play some pickleball and go relax on the beach."

My thighs clench involuntarily when he kisses me deeply, his tongue hot against mine. He pulls my leg up over his and presses our hips together.

"What about off-site?" I say between heavy breaths. "Shouldn't we visit a few more places outside the resort? Things that are unique to Antigua?"

He pulls away sighing, but still has a wide grin painted on his face. "Okay, you run a tight ship, Sunshine. Tomorrow we'll do a whole adventure day. We'll get someone to take us out and explore, or maybe we just go and get lost together," he says, repeating his words from our day in London.

Getting lost together.

"Sounds perfect."

After a late lunch delivered by my bestie, Alvin—and not two, not three, but four more orgasms—we finally leave the comfort of our warm bed and get dressed and ready for pickleball.

On the court, I give Asher a run-down of ways to improve

his game. Though he seems more interested in touching me every chance he gets.

"Focus!" I say, swatting him on the arm. "You want your shots to stay low. A high ball is a disaster waiting to happen."

He's nodding, but his eyes haven't left my ass. Perhaps wearing my shortest tennis skirt was not the best decision for today. Or was it?

"Asher!"

His eyes fly up to meet mine. "What? I can't help it if you have the most phenomenal ass. And now that I know how it feels in my hand, I'm completely obsessed. I'm not the same man I was two days ago."

He runs his pickleball paddle up my thighs and pulls it away slightly, but before he can smack me with it, I yell, "Don't you dare! My burn is still recovering! It's bad enough your fingerprints are practically branded there now."

"Ugh, fine," he says, playfully rolling his eyes. "What were you saying about balls?"

I nudge him away and walk to the other side of the net, unable to keep the smile off my face.

"Keep it low, just above the net." I lob it to him, and he returns it, but the ball smacks into the net. "Okay a little higher now."

He grabs the ball and lets out a huff of a laugh. "Yes, I worked that out for myself, believe it or not." The ball flies a few inches over the net, and I hit it back to him.

"There you go! Just like that."

"Are you saying you like my dinks?" he says with a smirk as he returns it.

"The way you handle your balls is quite impressive," I say in a sultry voice, causing him to miss the next shot.

We practice for another ten minutes or so before moving

on to serving. I have him copy my movements side by side, and he picks it up fairly quickly.

"You're a natural at this," I say.

"This is the easy part. It's once I'm playing an actual match that I can't quite keep up. It goes too fast and I never know where to be."

"Honestly it just takes practice and repetition. Let's play a match. It's the best way to learn."

"I can think of some other things I'd like to repeat with you," he says, his hand coming to the underside of my skirt and slipping underneath before I pull away.

"You are the worst!" I go to swat at his hand, but he grabs mine and pulls me close.

With his arms around my shoulders, pinning me to his chest, he says, "Hmm, that's not what you were saying this morning." Warmth floods my core as he kisses up the column of my throat like we're not out in public with several people around.

I force myself not to show any reaction. "Yeah, but now you're interrupting my pickleball time, so I'm rethinking my priorities."

"Ouch." He kisses me again, and I fail to suppress a moan. "Okay, big shot. Let's play."

"I'll make it up to you after." I shoot him a wink as I walk to the other side of the court. When I turn back, his cheeks are tinted red and he's trying to adjust his shorts discreetly.

We play a few matches, ending with me whooping his ass by at least eight points every time. He's actually pretty good for a beginner, and he seems to be enjoying himself, but I refuse to go easy on him. It's the only way he'll learn.

After pickleball, we decide to take a quick shower together. Except a quick shower turns into me getting on my knees for him, determined to finally take him all the way into my mouth

—which I do, finally. He returns the favor before washing my hair, bringing me to the bed, and folding me like a pretzel until I see stars.

Now I really am all sexed out.

We finally head down to the beach for the rest of the day. No activities, no agenda, just the two of us splashing in the waves and relaxing. Together.

As I lie under a cabana, I snap some photos of the gorgeous ocean scenery for his Instagram. I've already managed to get him up to two thousand followers since we got here, with no signs of stopping. I think I've probably taken about three hundred pictures this week, but I've only scratched the surface. Everything here is a visual masterpiece.

The past twenty-four hours with Asher have been a chaotic, amazing whirlwind. I can't believe I told him I was in love with him. I couldn't just play it cool.

Although he all but expressed the same thing, even if he didn't say the word "love." He has a sunshine tattoo for me, for crying out loud.

It all feels so perfect right now, safe in our perfect little Caribbean bubble, both of us trying to avoid having "the talk." I know I'm not ready to think about what might happen when we get home and the bubble bursts. But we still have three more days before we have to deal with all that and face reality.

But I do love him. I always have.

And I want to tell the whole world he's mine.

By the time we finally pack up our beach stuff and head back to our villa, we are both famished. We walk hand in hand through the hot sand until we reach a secluded cobblestone path we haven't seen yet. Surrounded by palm trees and hibiscus bushes, we pass by a tall black lamplight that looks eerily similar to the one we had back home growing up. I immediately stop in my tracks.

The memory of that lamp magically fixing itself all those years ago, and all the signs Dad sent after he died, hits me like a ton of bricks. I rub at the ache in my chest, tears burning the back of my eyes.

What is going on with me? This is the second time this trip that something so small has triggered all these old memories of my dad, and I can't control the overwhelming emotions flooding to the surface.

Asher's hand is already at my elbow, steadying me. "Sunshine, what's wrong? Are you okay?"

Grief threatens to pull me under as a tear falls down my cheek, and I look away from him.

"Hey, hey. What just happened?" He puts the beach bag down, placing both hands gently on my face.

"I just...started thinking of my dad again all of a sudden. I'm really missing him right now for some reason." I sniffle, wiping my nose on my arm. "Sorry, I'm being weird."

He pulls me into his chest, stroking my hair. My hands wrap around his torso as I seek that familiar comfort he always provides.

"You're not being weird. I remember how hard it was for you guys."

"Yeah, but it happened so long ago. I feel like I should have my shit together by now, right?"

He chuckles softly. "I don't think it works like that. Grief is complicated. You could be out there living your life, and something just triggers it out of the blue."

He says it like he knows from experience, but I don't remember him telling me about any family members dying or anything.

"I wish I could've met your dad," he adds wistfully. "You think he would've liked me?"

I smile as I pull away, looking up at him, reaching for his face and tracing his prickly jaw with my thumb. "He would've loved you."

He would love you because I love you.

He kisses the top of my head, and a nagging thought reminds me I need to be careful. He said he never wants to get married. Will he always feel that way? Am I okay with being with someone knowing we'll never be married?

Did his ex want to get married and that's why they broke up?

He doesn't seem to want to talk about her, which feels like a bit of a red flag. Shouldn't we be open and honest about our past, so we can build a real future together? That would also mean opening up about John.

We need to talk about this. Soon.

I need to know if this is as real for him as it is for me. If we even have a shot at a future together once we leave this place.

We walk back to the honeymoon villa, hands intertwined, no longer needing to pretend for anyone that we're crazy about each other.

I just wish I didn't have to pretend that whatever this is might have to end before it even begins.

38

ANGIE

June 13

I haven't slept in over thirty-six hours. Asher came over yesterday (or the day before??) and the three of us decided to have a movie marathon and watch the original Star Wars trilogy. I told him and Wesley that, despite watching Spaceballs a bunch with Dad, I had never actually seen Star Wars, which seemed to set them off. Hahaha. Asher insisted we watch all three movies back-to-back. Since it's summer break and we didn't have any plans the next few days, Mom said it was fine.

We set up pillows and blankets in the basement and watched them all in one go, only stopping for meals and bathroom breaks. I think my eyeballs might fall out of their sockets, but it was so worth it.

Wesley and Asher were acting strange the entire time though. Not talking much, avoiding eye contact, sitting on opposite sides of the couch. Something is off between the two of them, and I'm going to get to the bottom of it.

There were a few times when we were all lying down on the floor and Asher was next to me, and his intoxicating smell was all I could think about. I know I missed some important parts of the story, but I couldn't help it. I would look over at him and he would turn his head quickly back to the screen, almost like I caught him looking at me too. Or maybe I imagined it? I am a bit delirious.

ANYWAYS...I wasn't sure if I'd actually like the movies, but I loved them. I finally understand more of the jokes from Spaceballs and wish I could've watched them with Dad too.

Despite the boys being weird all night, Wesley did say something that stuck with me. There was a part where Luke, Leia, and Han were together laughing, and he pointed at the screen and said excitedly, "Hey, just like us!"

Sigh.

Except the trio is breaking up soon.

This is my last summer with Asher.

What am I going to do when he leaves in a few months?

I wish he would stay.

I need sleep.

39

ASHER

After an early breakfast, Angie and I head inland on the shuttle bus for a day full of sightseeing and activities. Since we've already had our fill of water excursions on this trip, we decide to stay on dry land.

She's practically bouncing in her seat next to me. Her openness to explore and to try new things reminds me of myself when I first started out in this business. Wanting to experience everything and never saying no to something new. A life with Angie would be exciting and rich and full of adventure.

My beautiful, wild ray of sunshine.

We start with a walking tour through St. John, a charming, vibrant city, full of colorful buildings and rich history. The guide takes us to St. John's Cathedral and Fort Barrington, and in between we explore lively streets and bustling markets hand in hand.

"Beautiful, isn't it?" I say to Angie as we pass by another historical building.

She smiles, looking around in awe. "It's incredible."

"I always try to include some kind of educational tour or

location on my trips. Not everyone takes advantage, but I think it's important to offer it and encourage people to learn more about the culture and the history of where they're staying."

Her arm wraps around mine as she leans closer. "I love that. What made you start doing that?"

I shrug. "I've seen people act totally disrespectful to a place they're visiting, and it's really upsetting. Like, you're a guest in someone else's home, show some respect, you know?"

She tugs on my arm to stop me before pushing up on her tiptoes to kiss me. I take a moment to get lost in those sparkling blue eyes.

We finish our tour with lunch at a fantastic seafood restaurant with a signature lobster dish that has us both moaning. The atmosphere is lively and warm, with friendly people talking and laughing. It's like having dinner with your neighbors.

Our next stop is ziplining. This is only my second time doing it, and Angie's first. The rainforest tour includes twelve ziplines that crisscross through the canyon, along with various aerial-view walking bridges. The lush green surroundings, exotic flowers, and the melody of birds chirping are so calming and therapeutic, a contrast to Angie's blood-curdling screams as she flies down the zipline.

She takes several pictures of us together in our gear, along with a few videos as she careens through the forest. I can't keep my hands off her every time we meet at the next drop point.

We finish our adventure with horseback riding along the bay. Our brown and white horses take us through a village with trails and a ravine with spectacular views. It's almost too beautiful to put into words. And to have Angie by my side to experience it with has my heart overflowing.

"Good day?" she asks with an easy smile.

"The best."

"Out of all the places you've been, where does this trip rank?"

Number one. No question.

I pretend to ponder it over, rubbing the scruff of my beard as I look off in the distance. "Hmm...easily top ten."

She snorts. "You're such a bad liar. What are your other favorite places?"

This time, I do have to think it over a bit. There have been so many amazing trips that I can barely remember them all.

"Let's see. If we're talking within the US, my favorite cities are Austin, Nashville, New Orleans, and...Portland. Favorite countries? Well, Argentina was incredible; the beauty of it took my breath away. Italy, especially Venice and Florence. Tanzania."

She hums. "Sounds perfect. You've experienced more than most people do in a lifetime. Do you realize how incredible that is?"

Our horses walk side by side as we continue down the trail, and I can't stop looking at Angie. This is everything I could ever want. Could it really be that simple? Could marriage with her actually be like this? Just adventure and love and companionship and laughing? This trip has me questioning everything I thought I knew about relationships, and I'm not sure how to process it.

All I know is I need to protect this. Whatever happens, I believe we could work it out together.

We arrive back at the resort late afternoon, completely wiped out. Both of us too tired to even make love, we just flop on the bed and snuggle up together.

I lie on my back as she hugs me at my side, one leg draped over mine. My hands find her hair as I brush through the strands and lightly scratch her scalp.

She lets out a contented sigh. "That was awesome. I can barely move."

I kiss the top of her head as I pull her in closer, melting into the bed and enjoying her warmth. If we stay like this for too long though, I know we'll fall asleep. To keep us awake, I ask, "What's your dream vacation? You know my top places: What do you want to see?"

"I mean, I want to experience everything, you know? All the popular touristy stuff, but also just wandering around and seeing where the day takes you. Discovering those unique little places you can't find anywhere else and could never plan for."

"It's the best," I say, rubbing her arm up and down. "We should make a list."

"For your travel business?"

No, so I can take you wherever you want to go. Experience everything life has to offer with you by my side so I can see your face light up in wonder. My heart overflowing with love and happiness knowing I did something, anything to make you smile, I yearn to say.

"Yeah, of course. Travel agent stuff. Could be good to have a diverse set of packages for clients and whatnot. Then we could do some research and you could practice putting something together. If that's still what you want."

"Sounds fun," she says. "Can't wait to get started."

"Okay, so what are your top three places?"

"We're making the list right now?" Her eyebrows shoot up as she rests her chin above my armpit.

"Yeah, why not?" With my free hand, I pull my phone from my pocket and open the Notes app.

"Hmm, let's see." She rolls out of my grasp so I can type with both hands as she sits up, crossing her legs. "Okay, definitely Paris... You know, Eiffel Tower and bistros and all that.

I'm kinda sad Willow and I didn't get a chance to go on our last trip."

"*Oui*. You will love it. I mean...*would* love it," I catch myself. I've got to stop acting so needy, but I can't help it with her. Now that I have her, I want to do everything together.

"Say something to me in French." She beams at me.

I'm certainly not fluent, but I've studied up enough to get around the city and have simple conversations. Nothing incredibly romantic though.

"*Où se trouve le café? Puis-je commander un espresso?*"

"Mmm, that's hot. I'm imagining you in a beret right now, and it's really doing it for me."

I look up at her with wide eyes. "Really?"

"Oh yeah, you could definitely pull it off."

"Noted," I say, chuckling. I add a few notes from my last Paris trip, and also a reminder to buy a beret. "Okay, where else?"

She taps her finger to her chin. "Anywhere in Japan. I've always loved the culture out there, and it just looks so fun."

I keep typing in my notes. "Agreed. I know I already said this at the hibachi restaurant, but I've had clients tell me amazing stories and I've always wanted to go."

She snuggles back down next to me. "I'm surprised you haven't made it out there yet."

"I know, just haven't had the right opportunity. But soon hopefully." I can already picture it: walking through Kyoto holding hands as cherry blossom petals float around us. Visiting shrines and castles, as well as the busy cities.

"Did you know that Burger King is the official sponsor of pickleball out there?"

My head whips toward her, waiting for the punchline. When she raises her eyebrows, I ask, "Are you just making things up now?"

She huffs a laugh. "No, I'm serious, it's a whole thing. I just read about it. They even have a special burger for it."

"Well shit, looks like we have another pickleball vacation to plan." I type in my Notes app *Burger King Pickleball???*. "Anything else?"

Her eyes take on a dreamy look as her hand comes to rest under her head. "I really want to see the Northern Lights. Where's the best place for that?"

"I usually recommend Norway," I say as I add *Northern Lights* to the list. "It's cold as hell, but there's so much to do there. Whale watching, fjord excursions, skiing, dog sledding. Plus, the food is incredible."

"So you've been?"

"Once, yes. And I've booked a few packages up there."

"That is so cool," she says, turning to lie flat on her back, closing her eyes. "Are you coming with me on all these hypothetical vacations?"

I put down my phone to look at her. "Only if you want me." I mean to say "to" at the end of that, but don't for some reason, making me sound wimpy and pathetic. I clear my throat.

Her eyes fly open. She sits up, eyebrows scrunched together as she hugs her knees to her chest. "What are you talking about, of course I want you. I want you with me on all my fake vacations. We can be fake dating or fake married there too," she adds with a smile that doesn't quite meet her eyes.

I try to keep my expression neutral. Is she being serious about all this, or are we just joking around here? We're still clearly avoiding having the conversation we need to have before moving forward, but I don't think we can dance around it anymore.

My eyes meet hers. "Sunshine..."

"We need to talk," she finishes for me, nodding. "I know."

I sit up, propping myself back against the pillows at the headboard. My heart pounds in my chest.

She starts picking at her nail, avoiding my stare. "I'm scared of what happens next. When we leave this place and go home."

Taking her hand in mine, I say, "I meant every word I said before. I want to make this work with you. We'll figure it out."

She lets out a long breath, her shoulder sagging. "I know we already kind of confessed our love for each other in a weird roundabout way, but then—"

"Then we never talked about it again. I know, I'm sorry." I shoot her a weak smile, hoping she's not already growing tired of my flakiness. "I'm a mess when it comes to you, and I've been kind of in my head about all this the past two days."

"Me too," she admits.

"I mean...it's you. It's *us*. I've wanted this for so long and never thought it would ever happen. I guess I'm still wrapping my head around everything."

She takes my hands and kisses my knuckles. "I feel the same way."

Warmth floods my chest, and I feel like I could fly. She loves me. I love her.

"Also...I'm only now realizing I never actually said the words back to you. I guess I assumed you knew, but..." My hand comes to rest on the side of her neck, my thumb caressing her jaw as I lean in to kiss her gently. "I love you, Angie."

She presses her forehead to mine, relief written all over her face. "God, I love you so much."

"Let's make a deal. From now on, we talk about it. About everything. I want you to tell me what you're thinking and never hold back. And I'll do the same."

"I like that." She smiles, and my whole body warms.

"You can ask me whatever you want. I haven't always been an open book, but for you, I want to be. I will always be honest with you." The words settle between us like a vow as I twist her sunshine ring between my fingers. Our ring.

Part of me hopes we don't have to talk about everything right this very moment, but I will say and do anything to prove to her I'm ready to make this work. That we can do this.

Because I love her.

And she loves me.

This is real.

"It's okay," she says dreamily. "We have time."

I kiss her and pull her on top of me, wanting to feel her pressed against my body. We stay there embracing each other, a silent promise of our love.

Our past, our present, our future. In every place, and in every time, it's always been us. Together.

40

ANGIE

With our last full day here, we decide to get up early and enjoy our breakfast and coffee overlooking the clear blue-green ocean waters from our private deck. I almost suggest going down to the courts to get some game time in, but I'm pretty sure Asher is pickleballed out.

So instead, we stretch out on our lounge chairs, enjoying each other's company. Content to be together without needing to fill the silence with anything but our presence. I'm almost done with my book, but I haven't been able to concentrate much on it the past few days for obvious reasons.

Barriers on either side of the pool provide cover from any prying eyes, which immediately has my mind going to all the nasty things I could do with him out here without anyone seeing. All in full view of God and the ocean.

Looking over at him, I bite my lip, appreciating the sight of him. No shirt, so his sunshine tattoo is on display. Wide, muscular chest with a spray of coarse red hair that I just have to run my fingers through.

I'm only now putting it together that he wore his shirt so

much at the start of the trip to hide the tattoo. He thought he could go this whole trip without me finding out.

Wearing only a pair of green boxer briefs, the outline of what he's got underneath is clear as day. He's half-hard as if he's also thinking about what we could be doing out here.

His head turns to me as he lifts his sunglasses, flashing that gorgeous smile of his. "Hey, you."

I set my book down, rising to my feet to walk over to him as he puts his phone on the table. My leg raises over his lap and then the other, until I'm fully straddling him. His arms wrap around my waist as I pull him close and claim his lips. The warmth and softness of his mouth has me moaning immediately, his cock now fully hard and rubbing against my sensitive center.

Our kiss quickly turns frenzied until I pull away breathlessly. "I want you to fuck me out here. In the pool."

"Hmm, who am I to deny my wife such a request?" he says as he rubs his hands up my bare thighs under my shorts.

My heart flutters wildly. He keeps saying "my wife" like it's real. There's no one else here to pretend for. It's things like that I'm sure will continue to give me false hope and eventually break my heart, but I can't help it. Maybe one day it could be real. Maybe he would want it with me.

I instinctively look at my left hand, to the finger that holds the sunshine wedding ring he bought me at the start of this trip, and smile, thinking about how far we've come since then.

"Wait. Are you...aren't you supposed to avoid using condoms in water?" he asks. "Did I make that up?"

"Oh, maybe. I think you're right. Ugh, I really need to go back on the pill as soon as we get home. It's wrecking all my plans for you." I just *had to* stop taking it right after Chad broke up with me in such a humiliating fashion. Like going celibate in protest would do anyone any good.

"I have an idea...if you're willing." A hint of mischief glimmers in his eyes.

I arch an eyebrow at him and lower my voice. "I'm always willing."

"That's one of the things I love about you, Sunshine." He swipes my hair over my shoulder, peppering it with kisses. "Now take off your clothes and get in the water."

A wave of heat rolls over me, and I do as he says because I'm at his mercy. I would literally do anything for him.

Once I'm completely naked, I lower myself backward down the steps into the cool water, never taking my eyes off him as he stands.

His briefs come off, and I take in the sight of his perfect, naked body. Standing there, looking like a fucking god. Tall, muscular, devastatingly gorgeous. Monster-sized cock. Knowing exactly how he feels inside me, my core lights up. What does he have planned?

He follows me slowly into the pool like a hunter stalking his prey. When he's close enough, he grabs the back of my neck, pulling my body flush against his hot skin, and kisses me with everything he has. His hands slide down to my ass, squeezing so hard it makes me gasp.

Asher Hayes is an ass man.

I know he was holding back in the beginning because of my burn, but now he can't keep his hands off it.

His hard dick presses against my belly as I curse myself again for not being able to have him bare inside me right now. Filling me up with nothing between us.

For a moment, I almost say fuck it and fuck the consequences, but the logical part of my brain still works enough to tell me to shut up and wait a few more days until we're home.

Home.

I still can't think too much about what happens when we leave this place.

I moan into his mouth as his hand slips down between us and rubs my clit in slow, agonizing circles. God, I love these skilled fingers.

"We may be out of view of any people here," he says, kissing along my collarbone. "But our neighbors might still be able to hear us. You think you can keep quiet, Sunshine?" He nips my earlobe as his other hand slides up my waist and pinches my nipple.

Shit, I don't want to be quiet. I want to cry out his name and let the whole world know he's mine and to know exactly what he's doing to me in here. To claim him as my husband.

He stops his movements and pulls away to look at me as I shiver. "Ooh, it's going to be so...*hard* for you to stay quiet, huh?" He pushes his erection into my torso for emphasis. "You are a screamer. Fuck, how I love hearing my name on those lips." He tugs at my bottom lip with the pad of his thumb. "But you have to try for me. I'd hate for us to get kicked out of here, wouldn't you?"

I whimper, but nod my head.

"There's my good girl. I know you can do it. Now turn around."

"Wha—"

He plants his hands on my hips and spins me so I'm facing away from him. He walks us forward a few steps until the water is at my breasts as he kisses the back of my neck, goose bumps erupting all over my skin, and already I want to cry out. It's torture. But I hold it in.

His grip tightens as he lifts me out of the water, my hips bending at the edge of the pool, and he presses my top half forward, laying my chest flat on the tiles. I can barely see him from this angle, but suddenly I feel a hard slap on my ass cheek.

"I thought we were trying to be quiet," I tease.

He spreads my knees wider, hoisting a leg over each shoulder, gripping the backs of my thighs before leaning in to lick me from my clit all the way up to my tight hole. I suppress another moan as he continues licking me all over. Suddenly my right knee comes up to my side, resting on the tiles, before he plunges two fingers inside my entrance. He strokes back and forth, pressing down on my inner walls.

Oh my god.

He already knows every place that drives me wild.

He keeps going until I'm sure I've died, because this must be heaven. The hand holding on to my thigh tightens as I feel his hot breath against my pussy, his beard tickling the sensitive skin on my inner thigh.

"I know you're missing my cock right now, filling you up." He adds a third finger, and I bite down on my fist to keep from screaming out, only letting out a soft, strangled hum. Fuck, I'm not going to last like this.

As if he can hear my thoughts, I'm suddenly flipped on my back. I look down at him as he thrusts four thick fingers inside me and then sucks on my clit so hard I completely unravel. I scream out, my orgasm surprising me like a slap to the face, before I pull my arm over my mouth to muffle the sound. I come so hard, so violently, I think I might actually pass out. My soul leaves my body as I jolt and writhe against the cool tiles.

As I start to come down, I feel something warm drip onto my chest. My eyes fly open to find Asher putting water between my breasts. No, not water. Is that...?

"Look how much you squirted on me, baby. Fuck, you're soaking wet."

I stare down at myself in awe. I still can't believe he can do that to me. Never have I squirted with anyone before.

"I was just going to use the pool water for this, but what a pleasant surprise." He continues spreading my release between my breasts, massaging my nipples, his eyes hooded with lust. He climbs out in one fluid motion and straddles my torso. "Press them together," he commands, nodding at my chest.

My breaths are still coming in quick as I obey, pressing my soaking wet breasts together. I finally understand his plan, and I feel that pressure swoop low in my belly again.

He plants one hand next to my head, leaning over me as he takes his rock-hard cock in the other. He lines it up right where my breasts meet, and then thrusts between them.

This has to be the hottest thing I've ever seen or done. Slick with the release he gave me, his dick slides in between my aching breasts as I continue pushing them together, squeezing him tight as he rocks in and out.

Angling down, his lips brush the shell of my ear. "I got you a ring. I think it's only right that I give you a necklace too."

Oh fuck, I think I might come again from his words alone. So goddamn filthy. I didn't even know he was capable of talking like this. It completely scrambles my brain like a 1990s anti-drug commercial.

He whispers, "Touch yourself and come with me, Sunshine."

I take one hand off my breast and rub circles over my clit, just as he grabs his cock and starts stroking himself. I'm so fucking turned on it only takes seconds before I'm tipping over the edge again. I start to scream when he kisses me, reminding me to keep quiet through another astral-projecting orgasm.

When he pulls back, I feel something warm land below my chin. I look down at myself as Asher pumps thick ropes of his cum onto my neck and my chest. His head falls back with his eyes squeezed shut and his mouth wide open, like he's letting out a silent roar, continuing to coat me in his release.

We come down together, our chests rising and falling in sync. He climbs off me, rolling me over with him until I'm on top, straddling him. When he pulls me down to kiss him, he doesn't seem to mind that everything he just spilled onto me is now getting smeared all over his own chest.

"I fucking love you," he whispers softly.

"I love you too," I reply, breathless.

I've never felt anything like this before. Everything with him is so perfect. How is it even possible to feel this good? For everything to feel so right.

But then a nagging ache in the back of my brain has me wondering how long it will last.

Cold sluices through me.

I have everything I've ever wanted, so why does it feel like it's going to get ripped away from me?

The first time I was in love with Asher Hayes and thought there was a chance we could actually be together, he left.

How long until that happens again?

I shake away the invading thoughts. He wouldn't do that. We're going to make this work, and we'll find a way to stay together.

We have to.

41

ASHER

"I do have one surprise left for you," I say with a smile after we finish lunch at the resort's Mexican restaurant. The warm breeze blows her blonde hair around as we walk back to our villa.

"Asher, I love you, but my vag is waving the white flag. I am quite literally tapped out, which I didn't even know was possible. So, congratulations, but I decline."

I roll my eyes. "Not that. We're going somewhere special."

"Oh, where are we going?" she squeals, clapping her hands together. "What is it?"

"You'll see." I shoot her a wink. "Get your swimsuit on."

Thirty minutes later, we're on the shuttle bus, Angie somewhat annoyed that I'm still not divulging where we're going. I can't wait to see the look on her face when we get there.

"Patience, Sunshine," I say after she lets out another audible sigh. "I promise it will be worth the wait."

"Ugh, fine," she says, opening her beach bag. "Then I'm gonna read my book. Tell me when we're there."

I put my arm around her shoulders, pulling her close for the fifteen-minute ride. My phone buzzes in my pocket, and I have to readjust both of us to get it out.

WES

Let's talk about the trip when you get home tomorrow

I've got some questions

My heart starts pounding. What kind of questions? He must know about Angie and me by now, and what we're doing at his resort. At least the fake marriage part. Hopefully not...all the other stuff. With my free hand, I type back:

ME

Would love to talk!

I'll let you know when we're back

I try to keep it vague in case he somehow doesn't know.

But...

Does it really matter if he does? I mean, if Angie and I are doing this for real and are going to keep seeing each other, then we're going to tell him eventually. Wes and I just made up again after so many years apart. I don't want to lie to him anymore.

ME

I'll call you

WES

👍

I attempt to rest my eyes, but I'm still buzzing by the time we pull up to a large sign that says "Shoreline Marina."

The bus stops in front of the main entrance, and Angie looks around. "A marina? What are we doing here? Not more snorkeling."

"You'll see," I reply in a sing-song tone.

She swats my arm. "Oh my god, we're here, just tell me already!"

"You are an impatient little thing, aren't you." I kiss the top of her head.

"And you're a giant obnoxious tease. You can't say you have a surprise and then string me along for forty-five minutes. So rude."

I take her hand as we exit the bus and approach the front doors, where we meet our guide for the afternoon and six other guests. Once we're inside, the group heads toward the cove, and Angie finally puts it all together. Her hand clasps over her mouth as she looks to me with wide eyes, tears brimming.

"*No.* Are you serious? Is this real?" She covers her nose and mouth with both hands like she's praying. "You brought me to swim with dolphins?"

"Well, yeah." I swipe away a tear that has escaped the corner of her eye. "No trip to the Caribbean is complete without dolphins."

"Oh my god. You know I love dolphins. Like...an obsessive amount."

"I know. It's adorable."

"Thank you," she says before launching into my arms. "This is perfect."

I squeeze her tight before realizing that we've fallen behind the rest of the group. We meet up with the others at a lounge space where they hand out free drinks while explaining the safety rules. Angie and I sip on Blue Antiguans as they run through the briefing and how we will interact with the dolphin. All the while, her face is split into a wide grin as she bounces from foot to foot between sips of her drink.

After putting our stuff in lockers and securing our life vests, we finally ease ourselves into the warm water. The group is instructed to stay by the rock wall of the cove while they finish setting everything up. And then...we finally get our first glimpse of the dolphin as it suddenly swims past us.

Angie squeals, and my heart bursts at the sight of her pure joy. I know in this moment we're going to be okay. Because I will do anything if it means I can make her smile like this every day.

We reach our hands out to pet the dolphin—whose name is Sebastian—as he swims back and forth in front of us. His slick body glides beneath our fingers as the marina photographer takes pictures nearby. I made sure to purchase the best photo package beforehand. I want to capture every expression on her face today.

After a while, the guide splits us up into groups of two for the first activity.

"Each pair will get their turn riding our friend, Sebastian," the guide calls out.

Angie gasps. "We get to ride him? Oh my god, I'm going to pass out. This is the best day of my life."

And I made that happen. I pull her to my side, my smile rivaling hers as the man with the headset microphone continues speaking.

When it's finally our turn, Sebastian flips on his back, exposing his white belly, and holds his flippers up. Angie grabs hold as instructed and is jolted forward through the water, screaming and laughing hysterically. I swear I've never seen anyone happier in my entire life.

They swim around the cove together for a few minutes

before I get my chance to go. I had been so focused on Angie's happiness that I never stopped to realize what I was actually about to do, and now I'm nervous.

Sebastian pulls me faster than I expect, and my face gets partially submerged. I gasp for air whenever I manage to breach the surface, halfway panicking that I'm not getting enough oxygen. When we finish our laps around the pool, Angie tips her head back, cackling. I try to catch my breath as I push my hair back and wipe the water from my face.

"What's so funny?" I pinch her side, making her double over. She reaches for my arm to steady herself.

"I thought he was going to drown you!"

I press a hand to my chest. "And you think that's funny?"

"Oh god, I hope the photographer got some good shots of that. Your face was priceless."

I take her chin between my thumb and index finger, tilting her head up to mine. "Funny, I was thinking the same thing about yours." Unable to resist any longer, I kiss her right there in front of everyone.

After the rest of the group gets a turn being violently pulled around the water, and another segment of watching Sebastian do some flashy tricks, the guide finishes out the session by letting the dolphin come to each individual person, holding himself upright in the water and letting each of us gently shake his fin.

"Aah!" she cries out as soon as she lets go of him. "I can't believe this is real!"

My smile is wide as I look at her. Just her. "Me neither."

We arrive back at the resort as the sun is beginning to set. It's the perfect backdrop for our last night here. Walking along the beach hand in hand, she rests her head on my arm, holding it tight. I kiss the top of her head and make a silent wish we could stay in this moment forever.

We end up near the jewelry stand where I bought her the sunshine ring, but today there's a man next to it holding a sign that says "Surfing."

Angie's head whips up. "Hey, you owe me a surfing lesson. I taught you pickleball, and you said if we ever got the chance, you'd teach me to surf."

"I did say that, didn't I?" It feels like so long ago we talked about that. I never thought we'd actually get the chance. "Do you want to right now?"

She shrugs. "Not really. I'm pretty wiped out. And I'm enjoying the quiet with you." She presses up on her toes to kiss my cheek.

"Me too. Have you enjoyed this vacation with me? Overall, what would you rate it?"

She makes a show of contemplating. "Hmm, are we talking five-star or ten-star rating? Or is this like a trophy-slash-medal situation?"

I pinch her side. "You're ridiculous."

She holds her hand out. "Wait. I just thought of something. We need to add a tournament to the itinerary."

"A tournament?"

"People booking a big pickleball vacation are going to want some kind of championship game or something at the end. The last full day could be a round-robin tournament, and you would give out medals or trophies to the winners." She spins to face me, her arms sliding up my back and pulling me close. "We could even do a farewell brunch where we present the awards and make a big show of it. What do you think?"

"I think...you are the most amazing person I've ever met. And I'm so lucky to have you in my life."

I lean down to kiss her. What did I do to deserve her?

"Raincheck on the surfing, then," I say. "We'll just have to do another beach vacation someday."

"It's okay. We've got time."

I bury my face in her neck and hold her tight, breathing in her sweet scent. "Yes, we do."

42

ANGIE

August 1

I can't stop crying. Asher left for college today. I knew this day was coming, but it still felt so sudden. I guess I thought I would be over him by now, or maybe somehow, he would decide to stay. I didn't believe it would really happen. Except I'm still so totally in love with him, and this hurts more than anything I've ever felt before.

Maybe I should've told him? But what would it matter? He was never going to stay here, especially not for me. He's been wanting to leave this town and move out to California his whole life. I wouldn't have been enough for him to stay.

Wesley is leaving soon too. The house is already too quiet.

I feel so empty, like someone ripped out my heart.

I'll never love anyone again, not as much as I love

Asher. I'll miss his smile, his laugh. The way my stomach would do flips every time he was near. His smell. I still have his hoodie, which smells like him, and he can never have it back. Which is only fair because he took my heart with him.

For the rest of my life, he'll be the one I compare every other guy to. And I already know they'll never measure up.

I feel so alone.

43

ASHER

I wake with a hint of nausea in my stomach. I wish we didn't have to leave today. We have some big decisions to make when we get home. At least it sounds like she and I are on the same page about making this work, but it's not going to be easy.

There's nothing tying me to Indianapolis, so it makes the most sense for me to move closer to her. I've spent too much time away from her already, and I don't think I could survive a long-distance thing. Hopefully, working remotely won't be a problem. I could drive there for important meetings or whatever Bryn might need. Or I guess I'm finding a new job.

We wouldn't move in together right away, but the idea of coming home to Angie, falling asleep with her in my arms, waking up next to her each morning like I have the past few days, is all I've ever wanted.

It's all I need.

I don't even care what Wes says about it at this point. If he doesn't think I'm good enough for his sister then maybe we were never as good of friends as I thought we were. We already have things to work through in our friendship, but it's time to clear the air with him. Tonight.

In truth, I'm not entirely convinced that I am worthy of her, but I will spend every day for the rest of my life trying to be better, to be good enough. Whatever it takes.

The sun barely begins to filter into our room as I continue watching Angie sleep. I don't want to wake her just yet; she looks so peaceful.

I decide to check out what she's done with my Instagram. I hope she was serious about wanting to be a travel agent full-time, because she has a natural talent for it. Plus, she's so good at connecting with people.

Maybe we could even work together, if that's not too weird for her.

The idea lights something in me.

Opening my account, I notice I somehow have...*fourteen thousand* followers. Is that real? How is it possible that many people care about what I'm doing? But when I scroll through all the photos, I get it.

Every picture is breathtaking. She has captured the essence of every experience and every place we've been to. White sand beaches with crystal blue water and foamy waves. Exotic cuisine of every color and texture imaginable. Underwater with all different types of fish and sea creatures and bright coral. The lush, green rainforest where we went ziplining.

And sprinkled in are photos of the two of us. The perfect married couple we've been pretending to be, enjoying a romantic getaway. None with our faces in them, but some silhouettes with beautiful scenery behind us, others are of us walking away from the camera or with me in front holding her hand like I'm pulling her forward.

These photos are the perfect encapsulation of our trip

together. Frozen in time, for all to see. I'll never have to forget a single moment of this for the rest of my life.

In the corner of the app, I notice red notifications over the mail icon. Must be all the messages I never check. Clicking through them, I see some from potential clients, which Angie has already responded to and gotten their information for me to contact them when I return. But scrolling further, one name jumps out at me and stops me dead in my tracks.

Charles Hayes.

Dad.

What the hell could he possibly want?

I hover over the unread message for a few moments before finally clicking it.

Hey son, found your account, glad to see you're doing well. Looks like you found yourself a good woman too. We would love to meet her one day. Take care, Pops.

My breathing picks up. Why is he reaching out now all of a sudden? After making my childhood miserable and then barely wanting anything to do with me the rest of my life. Is it because now I've "got a girl" and a job where I can travel around the world? I'm sure he's thrilled at the idea of me finally settling down and getting married so I can become an asshole husband like him.

I'm not surprised he didn't recognize Angie from the photos, considering he never took an interest in my life or my friends. Even his own neighbors. Because he's always been a selfish prick.

Where was he when I was crying myself to sleep from him and Mom screaming at each other? When he would skip town for days on end, leaving Mom alone to deal with everything, only to have her not even speak to me because I reminded her too much of him?

That's not how love works. You can't just show up when it's convenient and everything is already working out. When things are finally looking up for me. Of course he wants to swoop in now and reap the benefits of a thriving, happy son, as if he had anything to do with how I turned out.

I re-read the message, because I can't help myself. My eyes catch on the word "we." Reminding me that they're *still* together, even though they hate each other. Their goddamn twisted belief that divorce is a sin. Like raising a child in a loveless, neglectful home isn't a sin?

Does marriage do this to everyone? Make them so miserable that they have to make the people around them miserable too? Or is it just me and the asshole genes he's passed along?

I suddenly remember why I was never going to be good enough for Angie. She deserves everything in this world, and I'm just a broken man who doesn't even believe "happily ever after" exists. Because of him.

I never want to put Angie in that situation. To turn her into a woman who gives up and can't even love her own child. To dim the light in her soul that makes her who she is. It wouldn't be fair to her.

She stirs beside me, and I quickly click off my phone, wishing I had never read that message.

I suppose if this is all the time I have left with her before reality tears us apart, I'm going to try and enjoy every last second. Savor this last moment of our pretend marriage, wishing with every breath that this is how marriage could actually be. So simple. So right.

Draping my arm around her and pulling her into my front, I breathe her in as strands of her long hair tickle my cheek, committing this all to memory.

"Morning, Sunshine," I whisper in her ear, barely hiding the quiver in my voice. "Time to go home."

44

ANGIE

It's not until we arrive at V.C. Bird International Airport that we find out our flight to Chicago is delayed due to snow. Apparently, a winter storm passed through yesterday and everything has been pushed back for hours. We're going to be stuck here for a while, and probably won't land until late tonight.

Luckily, we ate a big breakfast at the resort, so we should be good for a while. We weren't expecting to have lunch here, and it's a fairly small airport with only a few food options.

"Not looking forward to leaving here for a snowstorm," I say as we head toward customs.

"Okay, let's just stay. I'll grab a cab." He turns and half-heartedly pretends to walk toward the exit.

I catch his arm and reel him back, pressing my lips to his knuckles. His smile is warm, but guarded. I know we're thinking the same thing. Worried about what happens to us when our relationship is forced out into the real world.

But I can't think about that right now or I might burst into tears. We'll just have to take it one day at a time.

We get into the long line, passports in hand and ready to have our bags screened. Asher had insisted we pack only a carry-on for this trip because he knows how often airlines lose bags. It was a little tricky fitting ten days' worth of stuff in this luggage, but since it's the Caribbean, it was all summer clothes and swimsuits.

When we finally get to the front of the line, the agent looks at our customs cards and sternly asks to open our suitcases. After a moment of searching, the man unwraps the conch shell Asher had put inside one of his shirts and holds it up.

"Sir, is this a queen conch?"

Asher's eyebrows pinch together as his eyes dart between me and the customs agent. "I, uh...I don't know. The guy on the boat just handed it to us."

"Queen conchs are endangered and are not permitted."

We both stand there in silence like kids getting a lecture from our angry school teacher. Is he not going to let us take it home? I don't want to give it up, it's my favorite souvenir from this trip.

The man places the shell back in his suitcase before stamping something on our cards, a little more forceful than necessary. "Please follow the yellow line and hand the agents these cards. They'll know what to do." He points to a line on the floor between a green and red line, effectively dismissing us.

We awkwardly grab our stuff and do as we're told by the guy with a stick up his ass, following a mysterious yellow line to god-knows-where. When we finally arrive at the designated area, we're instructed to put our bags on an X-ray machine and walk through the scanner.

An agent at the end of the line is leaning back in her chair with her feet propped up and arms crossed as she watches the screen, barely sparing us a glance. Three other agents stand behind her, engrossed in their own lively conversation.

When we both make it through the scanner and our bags meet us there as well, Asher shoots me a confused glance. "What do we do? No one here gives a shit."

I grab my bag and look around, announcing to no one in particular, "So I guess we're leaving now?"

Asher follows suit when none of the agents even glance our way, huffing out a harsh breath as he shakes his head. He's definitely getting annoyed, and I'm right there with him.

What was the point of all that? Thirty minutes we're never getting back. I guess it's a good thing our flight is delayed, or we'd be sprinting to the gate right now.

We make our way there, where we sit down and barely speak for the next three hours. I decide to text Willow to help pass the time.

ME

flight is delayed, ugh

why didn't you warn me that you got hit with snow?

WILLOW

you're right, that's not like me not to gloat

it's downright gross here

can't wait for you to join me!!!

ME

bitch

I'm staying now

WILLOW

sorry love, the honeymoon is over

Asher nudges me with his elbow. "Want to find some lunch?"

Right on cue, my stomach lets out a nasty growl, and I shoot him a weak smile. "What if I said no right now?"

He grabs my hand as he stands. "Come on, can't risk you getting hangry before the flight."

I roll my eyes. Like *I'm* the grumpy one here. He's been distant and pissy all morning. "If we ever get out of this place."

"Uh oh, it's starting already." I know he's teasing, but I'm not really in the mood. I just want to get home. I'm tired, I'm achy, and...yes, probably hangry.

Several hours later, we are finally on the plane, buckled into our seats, and cleared for takeoff. I take Asher's hand in mine, but he is still barely talking. He must be frustrated about all the delays and the runaround at the airport.

Thank goodness we were able to bring home the conch shell. I'll cherish this memento for the rest of my life.

After a long, quiet flight, we finally land in Chicago around eleven p.m., completely exhausted and ready for a shower and sleep. As nice as the resort has been these past ten days, my bed is calling my name. There's nothing quite like sleeping in your own bed after a long time away.

The brisk wind is a slap in the face as we step off the small plane directly onto the tarmac. The chill slices all the way to the bone. After ten days of bliss in the sun, I almost forgot how harsh the winters are in the Midwest, especially since we didn't bring coats. I was not emotionally or spiritually prepared for any of this.

"Pretty successful trip," he says with a tired smile, once we're in the warmth of the airport building. They're the first words he's said to me in hours, and something about the way he's been acting today is really rubbing me the wrong way.

Even when we woke up at the resort this morning, he was quieter than normal. What's going on with him?

I force a smile. "Yeah, I'd say so. I still have a ton of photos and content to add to your Instagram. You'll be set for weeks."

He rubs my arm up and down to warm me up when he sees me shiver. "Thanks again for helping me with all that. I really owe you one."

"Nah," I say with a shrug. "I was happy to do it."

"No really. Thanks to you, I have tons of potential clients to get back to, so hopefully I'll be pretty busy getting that all worked out." He takes my hand, and my heart skips a beat when he presses it to his chest.

"Well, thank you for letting me help. I can't wait to learn more."

"You're a natural," he says. "And we make a great team."

"Yeah, we do."

Could this actually work between us outside of our perfect vacation? I know it's been a stressful day for both of us, so I squash those negative feelings about something being off between us.

I want him with me everywhere I go, even the mundane everyday stuff like grabbing lunch or going to the bank. I want his to be the last face I see at night and the first when I wake up.

We walk hand in hand through the airport, my heart a thousand times lighter, when I get the strangest feeling. The hairs on the back of my neck stand up. I roll my shoulder to try and get rid of the overwhelming sensation as my eyes dart around the terminal, but I don't see anything out of the ordinary or anyone looking at me.

"You okay?" he asks, squeezing my hand.

I suck in a breath. "Yeah, just a little out of it, I think. I'll be glad to get back home."

We continue walking until I hear a deep voice call out, "Angie?"

Everything around me goes quiet. Time comes to a standstill when I look over my shoulder and see *him*.

Our eyes meet, and it's like I've been hit by a truck.

Like I'm folding in on myself.

His smile is just as I remember.

Those familiar amber eyes sparkling.

I only realize I've stopped walking right in the middle of the crowd when Asher's hand tugs mine, unaware I am now frozen in place. My hand falls to my side.

"It is you. Wow, it's been a while."

My mouth is open, but no sounds are coming out. Because what do I say to the man I thought I would spend the rest of my life with?

"Hi, John." It comes out as a wobbly whisper, the boulder on my chest making it difficult to breathe.

One thing is for sure: Willow was right. The honeymoon is over.

45

ANGIE

October 2

There's a really cute new guy at school this year. His name is John, and I think he's been flirting with me??? He sits next to me in English, and we make eye contact all the time. I'm trying to play it cool, but I know he's been checking me out. Christina said he moved here from California.

It made me think of Asher. I can't help but wonder how he's doing out there. If he's already dating someone. Probably having the time of his life.

Does he think of me?

God, I really need to move on. It's been two whole months now.

This is beyond pathetic.

Maybe I'll get the courage to talk to John tomorrow and ask if he wants to hang out sometime.

What's the worst that could happen? I've already had my heart smashed into a million pieces.

It can only get better from here, right?

46

ASHER

She pulled her hand out of mine.

She pulled it away, just as this preppy douchebag approached us and started talking to her, barely sparing me a glance. I can hardly process what's happening, but I've managed to glean three pieces of information so far: his name is John, he lives here in Chicago, and based on how he's looking at her, he's one hundred percent in love with her.

Wait.

I know that face.

This is the guy. The one from her social media a few months after I left. They were definitely together and in love. I think I'm going to be sick.

"This just feels like fate," John says with an awe-struck smile. "We both land at the same airport at the same time... what are the chances we'd meet here, after all this time?"

There hasn't been much time for the ex talk and everything that happened in the ten or so years we were apart. It's only been a few days since we even crossed that line and acted on our feelings for each other. I didn't ask about him because I didn't really want to know. What's in the past can stay there for all I care.

But it's not in the past, is it? It's standing right in front of us.

Lord knows I'm not eager to tell her all about Sarah. But I will. I'm ready to divulge everything. I told her I was an open book and I meant it. I just wish I had some time to prepare before coming face-to-face with the guy she fell in love with after me.

I know I've had a short temper all day after the issue at customs and being delayed for hours, but I've tried hard not to take it out on Angie. Especially after my dad's message this morning.

I will not end up like him.

I convinced myself I was willing to try this whole serious relationship thing because it was her. But only for her. And now the love of her life shows up, and he's talking to her. Staring at her—not me, because I'm invisible apparently.

I'm third-wheeling this magical reunion between Angie and her true love.

Reunited and it feels so fucking shitty.

"Sorry, John," she says when he finally shuts his goddamn mouth about his stupid boring job in finance. "This is Asher, my..."

I tilt my head pointedly, daring her to finish that sentence. I'm actually dying to know what I am to her right now, in this moment. Because just this morning I was inside of her. We were husband and wife on our pretend honeymoon, making love as the sunrise painted the sky a purplish-pink hue, and I couldn't help but think it was my new favorite color.

As if we're in slow motion, I watch Angie's upper teeth graze her bottom lip to form an "f" sound, and I can't bear to hear the word I know she's about to say, so I step closer to

John, towering over him as I stick my hand out. "Hey, man. Nice to meet you," I lie.

"Oh, hey. Yeah, nice to meet you too," he says with a wince as I squeeze his hand a little harder than necessary. Like I said, I'm an asshole. And I don't particularly like the way he's been looking at her.

I step back, draping my arm over her shoulder to clearly signal to this slimy shithead how his presence makes me feel right now. Part of me is hoping this is where Angie finally jumps in to tell him in no uncertain terms to take his little wheely bag and get the fuck out of our sight. But she doesn't. We all just stand there, steeped in uncomfortable silence.

Why is she acting so strangely with him? Nervous, maybe? She's picking at her nails and barely saying anything, which is not like her at all. Is she still in love with him? *This guy*?

She was about to call me her goddamn "friend," right after she fucking pulled her hand away. The thought of her with him sends my stomach roiling. But I only have myself to blame. I was the one who left. I never told her how I felt. She had every right to go date someone else and be happy, and there's nothing I can do to change that.

John finally backs away a step and grabs the handle of his luggage. "Well, I'll leave you to it. It's getting pretty late after all. Asher, it was nice to meet you," he says, and I lift my chin, hardly giving him a second look. "Angie. You still have my number?"

My eyes go wide when she nods. She still has his phone number? After all this time? When was the last time they talked or texted?

Or fucked?

Now I might really throw up.

"It was really great seeing you again. Give me a call sometime, I'd love to catch up. Bye, Angie."

"Bye, John," she says, her eyes immediately going to her feet and not to me. Her voice sounds so small and meek too. Nothing like the sunny girl I know and love. The one who is unapologetically loud and adventurous, always smiling brightly. Laughing joyously. Moving through each day like the world is something to discover one moment at a time, to savor and cherish.

No, the person standing in front of me right now is a mere shadow of her. I don't like anything about this.

When John is finally gone, I don't even know what to say to her, and apparently neither does she. She looks...sad. Defeated. Has she been missing him the entire time we've been together this week? Am I "the other guy?" Some rebound as she waited for her real love to become available and show up in her life again?

"Come on, let's get you home." I almost call her Sunshine, but somehow saying it in the vicinity of where John has been feels all wrong.

We start walking together as she shakes her head and puts on a fake smile. "Sorry, that was really awkward. That was—"

"The old boyfriend," I finish for her. "Yeah, I got that part."

"He was the last person I expected to see. Just caught me off guard, you know?"

I hum. "You want to talk about it?" Not that I really want to hear anything more about this douchecanoe, but I still want to prove I can be there for her if she needs me.

"Not really," she says.

I take her hand in mine because it feels wrong not to be touching her. Not after everything we've been through.

We make our way to the car as the sound of our footsteps echoes through the concrete parking garage. We throw our stuff in the trunk and begin the silent drive back to Athens.

47

ANGIE

What the fuck was that?

I can still barely process anything. It all happened so fast. My two pasts colliding into one major fucking shit-storm. And my reaction to it may have ruined things with Asher. What is he thinking right now?

Neither of us has said more than a few words the entire ride back to my house, and I can't stand this silence between us. I was already worried about things changing once the vacation was over, but I never could have anticipated running into John and everything blowing up in my face like that.

This is not how I wanted Asher to learn about him. I should have explained everything the other night when he brought him up.

Fuck.

And John lives in Chicago, only forty-five minutes away from me. That is the last thing I need. I've barely thought about him in years, and it felt like he was finally out of my life and out of my head for good. Why did he have to show up now?

I wonder if he met "the one." That special someone he was

convinced was out there who was better than me in every conceivable way. Someone I could never measure up to in his mind. Someone he could actually see himself settling down with.

As much as I dislike him, I do hope he found that.

Because I think I finally have it with Asher. Or...had.

Why couldn't I have just told John to fuck off the moment I saw him? Claim Asher as mine so he and the whole world could see what we have. He wouldn't be driving me home in silence, questioning how I feel for him, that's for sure. I need to figure out how to fix this.

We pull into my neighborhood at 12:28 a.m., both completely worn out, but I'm not sure I'm going to be able to sleep until we talk about this.

"You're staying with me tonight, right?" I ask as he pulls into my driveway. We hadn't talked about it, but we can't leave things like this.

He puts his car in park, still staring forward, and scratches at his thick beard. "I don't know, is that what *friends* do?"

When he turns to face me, his piercing glare makes my stomach drop.

Shit.

I thought I saw a flash of hurt on his face right before he shook John's hand, but I hoped he was just as confused as I was about what to label what we are.

"Ash, please come inside. We need to talk about this."

He's silent for another moment, but then nods.

We gather our bags from his trunk and walk along the sidewalk to my house without saying another word. I hate this. The silence, the tension. How could we go from non-stop love-making to *this* so quickly?

I unlock my front door, pulling my suitcase into my town-home, Asher following close behind. My living room is cold with the heat set way down. Before I can even let go of my bag and get to the thermostat, he asks, "Do you still love him?"

I whirl around on him, so surprised by the bluntness of his question that I may have pulled a muscle in my neck. "What? No. It's not like that."

"Then what is it like? Am I really just a friend to you? After what just happened between us out there? You're really going to tell me you don't feel what I feel?"

"Please, stop!" I say, choking back a sob. "I panicked, okay? But it's not because I'm still in love with him. I just...I don't know what happened. I wasn't expecting to see him and I froze. I haven't seen him or talked to him in years. This isn't at all how I wanted to tell you about him."

He runs a hand through his disheveled red hair. Standing there, he looks tormented, and it breaks my heart.

"You pulled your hand away," he says quietly.

"What? What do you mean?"

"When you saw him coming over. You pulled your hand away from mine, like you didn't want him to see us holding hands or know we were together. Then you were about to call me a *friend*."

"You are my friend, Asher," I say, trying to keep an even tone.

He scoffs, shaking his head, and I worry he might leave. I squeeze my eyes shut at the memory of seeing him for the last time, right before he left for college. My heart pounds in my chest, and my throat feels tight, like I can't get enough air.

I force myself to continue, "You're also more than that to me, you know that. You've been my friend since I was ten years old! That's over half my life. Our friendship is one of the things I hold most dear to my heart and have truly missed. We can be so much more than that, Ash, but our friendship was there first. That will never change for me. We only crossed that line into something more a few days ago. *Days*. After years of wanting more with you. This is something I never thought would happen between us."

He finally seems to calm down enough to stay. Plopping down on my bright blue couch, he buries his head in his hands. "So what happened back there? That didn't feel like the reaction of someone who's completely over their ex."

I chew on my lip, trying to find the right words. "I am over him, it's just...complicated."

"Okay, so explain it to me," he says softly. "We didn't get a chance to have this talk before, but we agreed we could tell each other anything, right? This is stuff we would need to talk about eventually. Let's get it all out in the open now." He pats the seat next to him.

"Let me turn the thermostat on real quick." I rub my arms as I walk over and push a few buttons, then approach him on shaky legs and sit. He tucks a strand of hair behind my ear so gently, looking at me so reverently, my heart cracks.

I take a deep breath and release it slowly. "John and I were together for three years. It was serious. I thought we would settle down and get married and raise a family together. He was my first real boyfriend, and when it ended, I was...crushed. It was really hard for me to trust people after that, and I never really got too close to anyone again."

He nods. I know it's hard for him to hear this.

"Looking back now, I wish I hadn't jumped into a relationship with him so quickly. But I was devastated when you left, and John was...charming and he said all the right things to make me think it was for real." I shrug.

Asher rests his cheek on his fist, staring at me lovingly. Trying desperately to mask his pain.

"I am so sorry I reacted the way I did. I was blindsided. Seeing him so suddenly brought back all those memories with him, and with you standing there, I just couldn't think straight. It's like I was reliving it. Every moment and every emotion all at once."

He takes my hand, and I lean my head on his shoulder, hot tears stinging the back of my eyes.

"Why did you break up?" he asks softly, no anger left in his voice.

"Turns out he wasn't in love with me nearly as much as I was with him. He didn't want to be quote-unquote 'tied down'"—I half-heartedly make air quotes with my fingers—"while he was so young. He thought he could do better and wanted to see what was out there before settling down. Though I wouldn't be surprised if he already had been sleeping around at that point. He made up his mind and was completely checked out."

While I was secretly reading bridal magazines, he was on to the next girl.

Asher is quiet for a beat. "I'm sorry," he finally says, rubbing circles over the back of my hand with his thumb. "That must've been really hard for you."

I shake my head. "It doesn't even matter anymore. I've barely given him a second thought in years. But you?" I reach up to cup his jaw. "God, I thought about you every day. I was so fucking in love with you, and I still am."

He kisses me softly, pulling me closer. I press my nose into his neck to breathe him in.

"I need to tell you..." he says before swallowing audibly. "About what happened with my ex."

48

ASHER

Angie pulls away and nods, her face is soft and kind. It always is. I rub my thumb over the curve of her cheek, and she blinks sleepily.

"I've been wanting to tell you, but it's just...kind of depressing."

"When is the ex talk not depressing?"

I huff out a laugh. "True, true. But I've never actually told anyone about this."

She pulls her legs to her chest, resting her head on the back of the couch as she reaches for my hand. Giving me the time and space to say what I need to.

"Her name was Sarah. We met shortly after I moved to Indy. She was kind and smart. Things were good between us, and we got along well, enjoyed each other's company." I let out a long breath. "We were together for a year...when she was in a car accident."

Angie gasps as she sits up and puts her free hand over her mouth. "Was she okay?"

I shake my head, unable to look her in the eye. "No, she died."

"Oh my god. Asher, I'm so sorry. I had no idea." She moves in closer, taking our interlaced hands and hugging them to her chest.

I try to find the right words. "There are still a lot of conflicting feelings over what happened."

"What do you mean?" she asks.

"I was the one who asked her to come over. She was driving to see me." That familiar guilt washes through me.

Tears form in Angie's eyes, and she swipes them away before I can. I don't want her shedding tears for me over this. It's not her burden to bear.

"That is not your fault." She squeezes my hand for emphasis.

"I asked her to come over because I was going to break up with her."

Angie goes still.

I can't bear to know what she thinks of me, so I keep going. "I'm pretty sure she thought we were about to get engaged, which just makes everything so much worse. But instead, I was ready to end things." I rub the back of my neck. "And then...she was gone. Just like that. Her family had thought we would eventually get married too, so I ended up playing the part of the grieving, heartbroken boyfriend. For months. I couldn't bear to tell them the truth, that I was going to break it off, that I had checked out of our relationship long before that. That I didn't love her."

"Oh, Asher." A single tear falls down her cheek.

"I still carry a lot of guilt from it, deceiving her family like that. They were kind, decent people. They loved me, and so did she, but I didn't deserve it."

"Hey," she says softly. "You have nothing to feel guilty over.

It doesn't matter that you weren't in love with her when she passed away. You recognized people were hurting, and you stepped in to help them get through it. This is what I mean when I tell you that you are a good man. And you *do* deserve love. Do you really not see that?"

I fight the tears stinging the back of my eyes. "I guess I never really thought of it that way."

"You take care of people. It's what you do best."

My lips twist to the side. "At the time, I felt like such a fraud, keeping the truth from them like that. But...looking back, I do hope it provided them with some comfort. In the end, it wouldn't have done anyone any good to tell them the truth."

"Exactly. And I *know* you helped them. I know it because you did the same thing for us. You were there for me and Wesley and my mom during *our* difficult time. That's who you are, Ash. You're so thoughtful and considerate of others. Just being there for people is enough."

"You think so?"

"I know so. Maybe that's why it hurt so much when you left. Because I could eventually get over us not being together romantically, but I just wanted you *there*."

I pull her in for a crushing hug, inhaling the top of her head. God, I love this woman. More than I've ever loved anyone. "I'm sorry I wasn't there."

"It's okay," she says. "You're here now. We found our way back to each other."

"And I'm not going anywhere." I kiss the top of her head again and squeeze her tight.

"Let's go to bed. It's been a long day." She pulls me off the couch and leads me to her room, both of us too tired to do anything but strip down to our underwear and climb under her soft, peach-colored sheets.

"I know today was stressful," she says once we're snuggled up together, her head tucked into the crook of my neck and her arm draped over my torso. "So tell me one good thing that happened."

I smile. "Well, if we're being technical, it was yesterday that was stressful."

She taps my chest. "You know what I mean. The past twenty-four hours then."

"Hmm, something good. I guess I'd have to say...this. Where we are now. Finally being open and honest about our past. It's like I was waiting to talk about all that before I could let it feel real."

She hums and rubs her hand along my arm.

"What about you?" I ask her.

"Definitely getting to keep that conch shell."

The laugh that bubbles out of her when I pinch her side warms me up, and I pull her closer. We lie there embraced in each other's arms until she finally yawns and mumbles, "Goodnight, Ash."

I've been trying to fall asleep for the past four hours.

At this point, the sun is getting ready to come up, and it's not worth it. Even with how exhausted I've been from the trip, I still couldn't get the image of Angie and John out of my head.

I know she said it wasn't like that, and I believe her when she says she's not still in love with him. But something about that whole situation still bothers me.

He was her high school sweetheart, and she was ready to commit the rest of her life to him, start a family together. That is not something a person gets over easily.

And they started dating right after I left.

What if he hadn't broken it off and they had gone through with it? She'd be married to some idiot in finance who's boring as fuck, and every day she would shrink herself more and more for him. He doesn't deserve her.

Will she call him and catch up like he wanted? What could he possibly have to say except how much he screwed up and wants her back? How could he have had a woman like Angie and let her go? How could anyone think they could do better than her?

It makes me want to punch his stupid fucking face until he can't remember his own name.

God. Why am I letting him get to me like this? Angie says she loves me. She's never given me any reason to doubt that. To doubt her.

I find comfort in the fact that she's still here with me, in my arms. That she chose me. I have everything I've ever wanted.

As I watch the sun come up, delirious and sleep-deprived, I silently pray I don't have to leave this bed anytime soon.

This right here is how it's supposed to be.

John is too late. She's mine.

I'm a selfish asshole and I don't intend on letting her go.

But...

What happens when she wants to get married? Have kids? Am I really up for all that? Could being married to her work out, or would I end up like my father?

The real question is: would she stay with me if we couldn't get married? I'm pretty sure I already know the answer, and that terrifies me more than anything.

So how is it fair to keep her? An honorable man would let her go now before this goes too far and there's no going back.

Except I know it's already too late. There is no going back now that I know what we have together is real.

Fuck it. Forget fair.

I'm keeping her as long as she'll have me. We'll take this one day at a time.

Angie whimpers in her sleep like she's having a bad dream, so I nudge her gently to wake her up. "Hey, it's okay. I'm here. I'm not going anywhere," I promise as I wipe the stray hairs off her forehead.

But *she* might, once she realizes I can't give her everything she wants.

49

ANGIE

I blink my eyes open, completely unrested and groggy. Guess it's going to take a while to get back to my usual self after that trip. Rolling over, I find the bed empty where Asher should be. My heart starts pounding. I know we had some difficult conversations last night, but he wouldn't just leave in the middle of the night, would he? Without even saying goodbye?

A bright pink sticky note catches my eye next to my phone on the nightstand.

Went to grab coffee. Be back soon.

There's a little sunshine doodle on the bottom right corner, and a smile overtakes my face as I curl myself back under my warm satin sheets. It's way too cold out there right now. I squeeze myself tight and allow my mind to drift back into the memories of this past week.

Except of course, now I need to pee.

The moment I stand, I realize I got my period. Ah, that

would explain some of the moodiness yesterday. At least my body had the good sense to wait until our vacation was over and I was back in the comfort of my own home. And by some stroke of luck, I managed to avoid getting any blood on the bedsheets. Yay me.

After finishing up in the bathroom, I hear the front door close. Asher walks into my bedroom holding two tall Starbucks cups. He hands me mine, and I instantly recognize the smell. Caramel Macchiato.

My jaw drops open. "How did you know I wanted this?"

He shrugs. "You mentioned it at the resort."

I did? I don't even remember that.

"Thank you," I say with a smile, taking a deep inhale of my drink. "How did you sleep?"

He shakes his head. "Not great. Still exhausted from the trip, but my brain wouldn't shut off."

No doubt because of John, Sarah, and everything we talked about last night. I don't blame him. I'm surprised I managed to get any sleep after that myself.

My heart breaks for him for everything he went through with Sarah, but I wish he would let go of all that unnecessary guilt.

"Are we okay?" I finally ask, wrapping my cold hands around the cup. "I know last night was a bit intense, and we're kind of doing things out of order here. It's a lot."

"We're okay, I promise," he says, pulling me to sit next to him on the bed and placing his coffee on the side table. "I'm sorry if I've been weird lately. I'm way out of my element here. Now that I have you here...the idea of losing you again sends me into a bit of a spiral. I tend to overthink things, and I just got a little jealous, is all. I understand if you want to call John and see him again. He was a big part of your life, and I would never tell you what to do or who you can spend time with."

I lay my hand over his. "I want to spend time with *you.* I want to figure this out and find out how we can make this work. Don't you?"

"Yes," he says quickly. "Yes, absolutely. I'm going to talk to my boss about going fully remote so I can stay close by. I don't have a lot keeping me out there, so it's an easy decision."

"Are you saying you'd move out here?" Hope fills my chest. Could this really work? Could it be that easy?

"In a heartbeat. I mean, I'd get my own place. I don't think either of us is ready to move in together just yet...right?"

I huff out a laugh. "You're not sick of me after ten days together?"

"The opposite, actually. I don't think I'll ever get enough of you. If anything, we need to make up for lost time." He cups my cheek, and I lean into his palm, savoring the warmth. He adds, "You're not...sick of me?"

His expression is playful, but there's real worry underneath.

"Never. I love you too damn much."

"I love you too, Sunshine." He slides his hand to the back of my neck, pulling me in for a crushing kiss, and I smile around his mouth, grateful I brushed my teeth before he got back.

When we pull apart, I let out a contented sigh. "When do you have to go back?" I'm already dreading it. I don't want him to leave. My hand snakes around his back under his sweatshirt, just to feel him beneath my fingertips.

"Tonight. Gotta be in the office tomorrow bright and early to meet with Bryn. Give her the rundown on the trip and everything."

"What's tomorrow? Thursday? I have no concept of time right now."

He nods. "Also, I have no clothes left, especially nothing winter appropriate." He looks down and gestures at his blue jeans and hoodie. "This was all I had for the Starbucks run, and it's what I wore to the airport that first day."

"I'll trade you for that hoodie," I say. I've been eyeing it since he first picked me up for our trip.

His eyebrow raises. "Trade me for what?"

I set my cup on my nightstand and walk over to my closet, opening one of the drawers in the dresser tucked in the corner. Right where I knew it would be, I grab what's inside and hold it up.

"Stop. Are you kidding me?" He stands to get a closer look at his old gray Indiana Beach sweatshirt. "I drove myself crazy looking for this. And you had it the whole time? You still have it."

I smirk, popping my hip. "So we have a deal?"

He takes off his hoodie in one smooth motion, leaving him bare-chested, and I curse my uterus for choosing today to yeet itself from my body. We trade sweatshirts, and I fling my new one over my head, instantly transporting me back to sixteen years old as I hug myself. God, it's so warm, and it smells like him.

When I look over at him, I can't help but laugh. I guess he's grown a little since high school, and it's also possible the sweatshirt has shrunk in the wash over the years. But he looks adorable. Squeezed into it, he looks like a teenager again, the hem barely coming to his waist and the sleeve cuffs landing above his wrists.

I see the boy I fell in love with all those years ago.

"I think I got the raw end of this deal," he says, lifting his arms so the sleeves and hem creep up even higher.

"Sorry, no take-backs."

This is definitely an upgrade. Softer, fresher, and it's so big it lands at my thighs. I follow his eyesight down to the same spot and know what he must be thinking.

"Well...the timing actually works out for you to head back home for a few days. I just got my period, so I'm the opposite of sexy right now." I plop back down on the bed, bracing myself for his disappointment. John would always get annoyed when I was on my period because it meant he wasn't getting laid.

Asher's face contorts in confusion. "First of all, you're the very definition of sexy, especially in *my* clothes. And second, do you think I'm just in this for the mind-blowing sex? I don't need you to be jumping my bones every second for me to want to spend time with you. Seriously, we've known each other forever and only started having said sex a few days ago."

I smile up at him, grabbing my Caramel Macchiato and picking at the lid. "Jumping your bones?"

"Or whatever the kids call it these days. Besides, you need someone to take care of you today. You're probably feeling terrible and are in serious need of some pampering. Let me do that for you before I go."

I think back to how he took care of me on this trip. Gently rubbing aloe over my sunburn and reading to me until I fell asleep. He's a caretaker at heart.

Asher takes my Starbucks cup and puts it next to his again before sitting on the bed and pulling me into his lap. He squeezes me tight, peppering the top of my head with soft kisses, and I melt into him.

Maybe this really could work. He's willing to relocate and work remotely. He's moving here.

We're really doing this.

We spend the rest of the day relaxing on the couch. Asher dotes on me by bringing me a heating pad and soft, fluffy blankets, rubbing my feet and giving me a scalp massage, and even going to the store in his tiny hoodie to surprise me with my favorite sweets—cookie dough ice cream and Twix bars. I must have told him they were my favorites at some point, but I can't remember when. Come to think of it, he's been doing stuff like this since we were teenagers. How does he always know?

I text Willow because she's been hounding me to hang out since I got home, but I told her I wanted one last day with him.

ME

He's leaving soon 😩

WILLOW

Sorry babe

I'll let you have your goodbye and then I'm coming over

ME

why are you so obsessed with me?

WILLOW

I will kick your ass

love you tho

Asher gathers his stuff just after six o'clock—including the storage bin my mom saved for him, but forgot to take back the first time he showed up here—and loads it all in his car. We hold each other at my door for what feels like an eternity. I don't want to let him go. That hope I felt earlier starts to wither. Blinding sadness strikes me, and I start crying. Those feelings of him leaving all those years ago still live deep down inside, no matter how hard I try to forget.

"Hey, hey," he says, pulling back and wiping a tear away. "I'll be back in a few days."

"I know, this is so stupid. I'm sorry." I wipe my face with the sleeve of his oversized hoodie that I may never take off. "Probably just hormones and stuff, you know?"

He wraps me in another tight hug, threading his hand through my messy hair. "I love you, Sunshine."

"I love you. Let me know when you get home," I say as our hands pull apart.

He climbs into his car, and more tears spill out as I watch him drive away.

I tell myself this isn't like the last time.

It's not forever.

He's coming back.

50

ANGIE

May 11

Yesterday was prom! It was the best night I've had in a long time!!! John and I went with Christina and Ethan to this fancy restaurant in a LIMO! We stayed out until three in the morning. It's really starting to feel real that we're graduating in a few weeks and John and I will be going to the same school! I would've happily done the long-distance thing with him, but I'm sooo glad we don't have to. I love him so much.

There's something about him, I just feel so safe. Like I can fully trust myself with him. I would marry him in a heartbeat. He would make a wonderful husband and father. We really would have the cutest kids. I know I'm getting ahead of myself, but I can't help it.

He came into my life at the perfect time, I just know it was meant to be.

I wonder if he would ask me to take his last name or if he'd consider taking mine. I already tease him about it, and I'm not sure I want to be Angie Bohner... but I would for him. What's in a name, anyway?

~~*Angie Harris-Bohner*~~
~~*Angie Bohner-Harris*~~
~~*Angie Bohnis*~~
~~*Angie Harriner*~~

51

ASHER

When I arrive at my apartment later that night, it really hits me that I have no emotional connection to this place whatsoever. I got this place when I first moved to Indianapolis, thinking it would be temporary while I figured things out and saved up enough money for a house. But I didn't even bother to decorate. Sarah and I would always hang out at her place because mine was so depressing.

Looking around at the bare gray walls, I realize there are no happy memories here.

In fact, there are no happy memories in this entire city.

My friends consist of a few neighbors I'll wave to, or coworkers I'll grab a drink with. Bryn maybe. But no one like Wes or Angie.

Shit. I forgot to call Wes yesterday, and it's the middle of the night in London right now. I need to remember to call him tomorrow, especially after running into John. I need more information on this guy.

I shoot off a quick text to Angie to let her know I made it here, before jumping in the shower and getting ready for bed. I would call her, but I know she's hanging out with her friend, Willow, who I'm not entirely convinced likes me.

The silence is deafening as I climb under my cold sheets.

Angie's absence feels too heavy.

My eye catches on the storage bin sitting in the corner of my bedroom. The one her mom saved for me for all these years. Curiosity gets the best of me, and I climb out of bed to see what's inside. My heart swells when I find old report cards, newspaper clippings from my basketball tournaments, ribbons and medals, some spiral-bound notebooks, and tons of printed photos of me, Wes, and Angie.

In that moment, as I fight back tears, I know I'm making the right decision to move out of here. It's not even a question. I'll find a place somewhere in Athens to be near Angie, and I'll keep working for Bryn remotely, commuting whenever she needs me in the office. After this meeting with her tomorrow, I'll grab some boxes on my way home and put in my notice with the landlord.

I'll pay whatever fine I need to, to break the lease early.

I don't care anymore.

I know exactly where I need to be.

The next morning, after starting a load of laundry and trimming the beard I let grow a little long on vacation, I head out to the office to meet with Bryn. She wants a rundown of the trip, and then I'll break it to her that I'm moving and explain what I'll need going forward.

First, I need coffee, so I hit up the Starbucks drive-thru. My mind drifts to Angie as I sit in the car line, and I imagine always getting her favorite things wherever I go. The Notes app in my phone already contains several of these items, including her Starbucks order, treats, wine, and food orders from most major restaurants. But I need more.

The list started back when we were in high school; I wanted to make sure I knew what she liked so I could surprise her every once in a while and make her smile. Sometimes I would even buy her favorite cookie dough ice cream and sneak it into their freezer so she wouldn't know it was me. I didn't need the credit; I just wanted her to be happy.

When I finally make it to the office, I step into the bright, open space with my hot coffee in hand and drop my laptop and papers off at my desk. Nine o'clock rolls around, and I grab my folder full of notes from the trip and knock on Bryn's door.

"Come in," she calls out from inside her office as I let myself in, inhaling the familiar citrus scent. "Welcome back!"

Bryn stands to shake my hand, which makes me smile. We've known each other for years, but she still acts so formal at the office. She explained it once, something about always projecting an air of confidence and power, even when people don't expect it. I'll take her word for it. She's considered one of the most successful Black women in Indianapolis, and she's earned every bit of praise within the industry.

"Thanks," I say, dropping into one of the leather chairs facing her desk. "Missed you."

"Obviously," she deadpans, waving her hand around. "Tell me everything. Antigua looked amazing. I was watching your Instagram blow up. Much deserved."

A smile tugs at my lips. "That was all Angie. She enjoys doing that kind of stuff, so she offered to help post all the content."

"Well, she did an incredible job. Any new leads?"

"Tons. We've already gotten back to all the potential clients, with more still coming in. It's insane." I realize I used the word "we" right around the same time she does. Luckily, she chooses to ignore it as she takes a sip of her own drink.

"Thank you again for making me go," I continue. "It was by far the best trip I've ever been on."

Leaning forward in her chair, she says, "You look good, Asher. Rested, rejuvenated. I hope you were able to relax and reconnect with why you fell in love with traveling in the first place."

"I did. It was just what I needed. Here," I say as I place the folder on her desk. She puts on her reading glasses, opening the cover as I keep talking. "All my notes about the resort and the activities we did, plus the itinerary options. They should have sent over the contracts by now."

She nods. "Tell me your overall thoughts."

I explain all the things we liked and disliked, what we did each day—leaving out the part about what specifically went down in that honeymoon villa—then explained the pickleball schedule and round-robin tournament on the last day. Angie also included the contact info for three coaches who might be interested.

After about an hour of talking and catching up, she finally asks the question I know she's been dying to ask.

"So, how's this mystery girlfriend, by the way? And when do I get to meet her?"

I can't help but smile as I look down at my hands. "She's good. Incredible. I'm...in love with her. Like stupid in love."

"Yeah, it's written all over your blushing little face." She swirls her finger at me with a smile. "I'm happy for you."

"Thank you." I shift in my chair, clearing my throat. "That actually leads me to the other thing I wanted to talk to you about."

She takes off her reading glasses and places them on the

desk before clasping her hands over the folder of papers. "Okay."

I take a deep breath. "I'm moving."

Her eyes go wide. "Moving? Are you putting in your notice?"

"No, no. I'd still like to work here," I say quickly. "As long as you're okay with me going fully remote."

"Where are you going?" she asks curiously. I can't quite tell yet if she's okay with this.

I wipe my hands on my pants. "Athens. It's just three hours away though, so I can drive back if you need me for client meetings or anything like that. But I wanted to make sure this works for you first."

"Why Athens? What's—" Her grin slowly widens. "Are you two moving in together?"

"I—it's complicated. I'm moving to be closer to her, but we're not going to be living together just yet. We're still trying to figure this all out."

"Wow. Well, I'm happy for you, Asher. Whatever you need, it's yours. I'm happy to accommodate, especially after this trip. I don't want to lose you."

I let out a long breath, my shoulders relaxing. "Thank you, I really appreciate it."

"How soon? You're still coming in tomorrow for the staff meeting, right?"

Ah shit, I forgot all about that. But I missed the one last month, and it would look really bad to miss another one right after I told her I'm moving away. I was hoping to drive back to Angie's tonight, but it is just one more day.

"Of course." I nod stiffly. "Wouldn't miss it."

"We're gonna miss you around here," she says as she stands and walks around her desk. She surprises the hell out of me by opening her arms for a hug.

"Thanks, Bryn."

"I expect an invite to the wedding," she adds, squeezing my arms.

A nervous laugh bubbles out of me as we pull apart. "You bet."

I spend the rest of the work day catching up on emails and client calls, but all I can think about is getting the hell out of here and being with Angie again as soon as humanly possible.

It's just one more day.

52

ANGIE

I'm still in a funk about Asher leaving yesterday, and Willow is having none of it. She dragged me to Dink Shot to play some pickleball after lunch to help get my mind off him, and also probably so she wouldn't have to listen to me whining.

Last night, Willow came over and I caught her up on everything that happened, including running into John at the airport. We stayed up late, talking until two a.m., and now she's definitely ready for me to get my shit together.

Normally, Luca would have joined us for pickleball, but he's been busy putting together a charity match to benefit the local Alzheimer's organization in a couple of weeks. His mother was diagnosed with early-onset Alzheimer's and passed away about four or five years ago, so the cause is important to him. Sadly, his dad passed away from a heart attack shortly after, something the two of us have bonded over.

"Okay, one more match," Willow says from her side of the court. "You may be a mopey bitch, but you're kicking my ass today."

"Probably all the extra playtime I got in Antigua." I flip my ponytail over my shoulder. "All that sun and heat."

"That's it, now I'm really going to kick your ass. Zeros on start!" she calls out before serving it to me. Willow is ultracompetitive and hates losing, so I enjoy riling her up.

We get into a decent rhythm, both of us evenly matched, when we find ourselves up by the net, hitting it rapidly back and forth. It's fast and intense, and she is not letting up.

She yells out, "Keep firing, assholes!"

The *Spaceballs* quote trips me up, and I miss her shot. Standing there frozen, I blink several times, trying to figure out what just happened.

Willow laughs, wiping the sweat off her brow. "What? You've seen that movie, right?"

I can't help but think about watching it with Asher on vacation, high as kites on New Year's Eve. My heart suddenly aches with how much I miss him.

Squeezing my eyes shut, I gain back my composure. When I lob the ball back to her, I plaster on a smile and say, "I knew it, I'm surrounded by assholes!"

After Willow finally gets her win, we head upstairs to the restaurant bar. Dink Shot has an amazing setup, and this particular spot is one of our favorite hangouts.

Sliding into one of the wooden booths with our giant plate of cheese fries, she eyes me cautiously. "You good?"

"I'm good. Aside from the fact that I've cried more this past week than I have in years." I shake my head. "This period is really testing me."

"Why else did you cry?" she asks before popping a gooey fry into her mouth.

"It was just like, random stuff...about my dad. It happened twice on the trip. Asher must think I've turned into some crazy emotional freak."

"Your dad? Huh. That's interesting."

I shrug, taking a sip of my water.

After a moment, her head tilts. "Was Asher with you when you started crying?"

"Yeah, why?" I ask. Seems like a weird question.

She pauses, looking away. "And he never met your dad, right?"

The question catches me off guard, and I nearly drop my French fry. "No, he moved in next door after he died."

"How soon after?"

I shift in my seat. "Like a few months. Why are you asking me this?"

"It's just..." She waves her hand around. "I don't know, *interesting*."

"Interesting, how?" The fry I picked up earlier is still dangling between my fingers, and I ignore the drop of cheese that hits the table.

Willow crosses her arms and places her elbows on the table, leaning in. "Do you really want to hear this right now? Like, are you in the right headspace for me to potentially give you some hard truths?"

I set the fry back on my plate, wiping my hands on the crumpled napkin beside it. "Hard truths? What does that even mean? Tell me."

Willow takes a deep breath, and my heart starts pounding, because I know that look. "Okay. So...you don't really talk about your dad all that much. For as long as I've known you, I've only gleaned a few pieces here and there. And that's fine, but don't you think it's interesting that"—she holds up one finger—"Asher moved in almost immediately after your dad died." A second finger. "You became really good friends and eventually developed feelings for him." Now she's holding up three fingers. "And when he moved away, you were left devastated?"

"I don't see what that has to do with my dad."

"Stay with me." She puts both of her hands up, palms facing me. "Fast forward to present day. You reconnect with Asher and things are great, right? Except that being with Asher is bringing up all these old feelings about your dad."

She pauses, as if waiting for me to jump in and fill in the blanks, but I'm frozen in place. I want to stick my fingers in my ears and flee from this booth, but I can't. Something tells me this is too important to ignore any longer.

"I think in a way," she continues gently, "you've tangled up your feelings for Asher with some unresolved grief you have for your dad. And what makes matters worse, your brain also seems to associate Asher leaving with nearly the same level of pain as your dad passing away. Which was the start of your abandonment issues."

I blink. "I...my what? Wait. But I...*what*?"

This is too much to take in all at once. I grip the table to stop the spinning. I want to tell her she's wrong, that she has it all backward. That she's crazy, I don't have abandonment issues, and that Asher is *not* the one triggering my emotional outbursts.

But...something resonates deep down.

"What are you, some kind of shrink now?" I say, avoiding her stare.

She grabs a fry and points it at me. "I did take that semester of psych if you remember."

I let out a soft chuckle, but I still can't think straight. It feels like the ground is crumbling beneath me, yet...what's underneath is clarity.

Is it true? Have I been crying over my dad this past week because of Asher? Did I cope with his death all those years ago by burying my feelings deep down, pretending everything was okay, and then distracting myself with an obsession with my brother's best friend? Have I been jumping headfirst into new relationships since Asher left, so I'd never have to feel alone?

What the fuck is my life?

And how did I not put any of this together? It seems so obvious now.

I put my head in my hands and fight back more goddamn tears. What do I even do with this information? How do I process it?

Willow's hand wraps around my wrist, pulling it gently away from my face. "Hey. You okay?"

"I...I honestly don't know," I say between choked sobs.

"Come on. I think you need a drink."

I look over at the bar, where an attractive female bartender is mixing some kind of blue cocktail. I guess I could order something.

Willow smirks. "Actually, I've got a better idea."

53

ANGIE

Later that evening at Simon and Faris's house, I'm still reeling from Willow's life-altering psychoanalysis of me. She likely told them not to give me a hard time about my situation with Asher, because they have been unusually sensible. They've remained focused on asking about the resort and all the activities we did on our trip. Not one inappropriate comment about him or our fake marriage.

Highly suspicious.

The four of us are cozied up on their sectional couch with several pillows and fuzzy blankets as a warm fire crackles in the fireplace. Simon cooked us the most amazing dinner—honey garlic glazed salmon with buttered baby potatoes and roasted asparagus—and now we are all sipping on another bottle of wine in the living room as we digest.

I will never understand why he went into finance law instead of becoming a chef.

"I'm still jealous of everything you did on your trip," Simon says. "It sounds amazing. Even though you didn't take us."

"You must have lost your shit swimming with that dolphin," Faris adds.

"Oh my god, Sebastian." I stick my lip out. "I miss him already. I wanted to take him home with me. You think Max has any experience caring for dolphins?"

Faris's eyes go wide.

I look around, and everyone has the same stricken expression. "What?"

"I can't believe we forgot to tell you," Willow says, grabbing my arm and nearly spilling my Chardonnay.

"*What*? What am I missing?"

Her face falls, just a little. "Max and Kayla are separating."

"Wait, what? When? I wasn't gone that long! I didn't even know they were having problems."

"Kayla has been acting weird for a while," Simon chimes in. "She finally told me over lunch this past week, but was scarce on the details." Simon and Kayla work together at the same law firm, and they've known each other longer than anyone else in this friend group.

I finish the rest of my wine in one swig, and Willow takes a sip of hers. "Apparently, they've been fighting a lot lately, but Luca refuses to ask Max about it. He says guys don't pry about stuff like that." She rolls her eyes.

Simon clears his throat. "You mean straight guys."

Willow touches her nose with the tip of her finger.

He continues, "I get the feeling they've just been growing apart and don't share a lot of common interests."

Like pickleball, for one thing. I have heard significant others complain when their spouse spends a lot of time on the court but they have zero interest in playing themselves. But I don't know anything else about what they like or what they do together.

"It's so sad," Faris says. "Especially for the little ones."

My stomach twists in knots. The twins are only six years old. My mind flashes to a teenage Asher coming to our house looking so defeated because his parents would not stop yelling. An innocent kid whose parents couldn't get along. Putting him in the middle of it all and making him just as miserable.

"Yeah, but..." I pick at my nail. "I will say, if they are fighting all the time and truly aren't happy together, it's worse to try and stay together just for the sake of the kids. Everyone in that house deserves to be happy."

The three of them nod solemnly while Willow also shoots me a concerned look. The weight of everything I've learned today about myself and about Max and Kayla's relationship suddenly becomes too much to take. My throat is closing off, and I can't get enough air.

Excusing myself to their back porch, I struggle to take a deep breath. The winter air is like ice in my lungs, but I welcome it in.

I want to call Asher and talk to him about all this. He'll know exactly what to say to calm me down, he always does.

Just then, my phone buzzes with a text. It's...John.

Jesus Christ, what does he want?

JOHN

I need to tell you something I've wanted to say for a long time. So here goes...

What the actual fuck? Like I'm not dealing with enough right now? He's about to confess his undying love for me or something, isn't he? I saw the look in his eyes at the airport. He would've made a move right then and there if Asher wasn't with me.

A long-ass text comes through.

JOHN

Letting you go was the biggest mistake of my entire life, and I've regretted it every day since. I'll do whatever it takes to earn back your trust, because I want us to try again. I'm still madly in love with you Angie, my darling. I'm not sure I ever stopped. I want a life with you, whatever you want. Marriage, kids, a home. Growing old together? Isn't that what we talked about all those years ago? Please give me another chance. Tell me I'm not too late. I love you with all my heart.

And there it is. All the words I longed to hear, just seven years too late. But they don't mean the same as they once would have. Because I don't want any of that from him.

I take several steadying breaths as I work out in my head what to say back.

ME

John, it was nice to see you the other day but I don't think it's appropriate for us to stay in touch. The man I was with is my boyfriend, and I'm very much in love with him. I wish you the best, but this is goodbye.

There. Straight to the point. No room for misinterpretation.

JOHN

So you're not married?

Or engaged?

My heart stutters. Why is he asking me this? I shouldn't reply at all, but I can't stop myself.

ME

No

JOHN

Does he want to get married?

ME

That's none of your business

JOHN

I only ask because I know that's a deal-breaker for you

ME

You're too late. You've missed your chance

Goodbye

JOHN

Tell me he's willing to offer you everything I am and you'll never hear from me again.

I throw my phone down on the patio furniture and press my face into my hands.

What a fucking prick.

I shouldn't let him get a rise out of me. I've moved on, and he has no power over me anymore.

Except...in the span of five minutes, John of all people, voiced out loud my greatest fear of giving my heart to Asher. Is that still a deal-breaker for me? Or could I be okay with us being together and never actually getting married?

I want to be the type of person who doesn't care about a piece of paper. To be a free spirit and not let myself be defined by labels.

But if I'm being honest...I do want it. I don't know why it's so important to me, but it is.

Before I can talk myself out of it, I grab my phone, screenshot the conversation, and send it to Asher. He should know that John and I texted, and I want him to see how I responded.

I also need to know how he'll react to what John said.

It takes fifteen seconds for my phone to ring.

54

ASHER

I called her the moment she sent me that conversation with John. I don't even know what I'm about to say, but I just need to talk to her. Fuck, I wish I was there, and we could do this in person. I'm no good over the phone.

My hands shake as I sink into the couch, forcing my breath to slow down.

She answers, "Hey, you."

"Hey, Sunshine." My voice comes out strangled, and I clear my throat.

I've barely had time to process what she sent me, but I'm terrified she's about to end things with me. She's getting back together with him, because he's willing to offer her everything I can't and we both know it.

This is my worst nightmare.

"I can't believe he texted you that," I say, trying to sound casual. As if I'm totally okay with the conversation we're about to have.

"It's ridiculous, right? He tries to slide in after seven years like he has any right to say any of that to me? He didn't even apologize."

"Exactly, what an asshole."

I'm met with deafening silence. It lasts so long that I have to check if we got disconnected.

"It's just..." She sighs. "I need to know. I need to know if he's right."

Can she hear the thumping in my chest? The blood roaring in my ears?

"Angie—"

"Because from what I remember, you've said on more than one occasion that you'll *never* get married. So...what am I supposed to do with that information, exactly? Is this a hard line for you?"

I'm going to throw up. Marriage. Kids. Of course he would offer that to her. Any normal, sane man would. Why can't that come easily for me? I'm not ready yet, but I could be with time.

"I...I love you, Angie, you know that. I thought we were going to make this work. One day at a time, right?"

She lets out a harsh, shaky breath. "Look, I'm barely holding it together right now. I need to know if we even have a future together. And the truth is, for me, that includes marriage. Not right away, but...someday."

The knife in my chest twists harder when I hear her sniffle.

"Of course we have a future." My voice cracks on that last word. "I love you so much."

"But you don't want to marry me." It comes out as a statement more than a question, and suddenly I can't breathe. My stomach drops to the floor.

"I... We've only been together a few days—" I know immediately that was the absolute wrong thing to say. "I mean... romantically. Fuck. This is all moving so fast. I'm sorry, please just...give me some time to think."

"We've known each other for sixteen years, and you need more *time* to think about whether you want to be with me?" The hurt in her voice has tears pricking my eyes.

"No, of course I want to be with you," I plead.

"You mean now that you get to fuck me."

"What?" I shout, jumping to my feet. My hand rakes through my hair so forcefully it hurts. How could she think that? "No, that's not what I mean! Please, can we not do this over the phone? I'll be there tomorrow night, and we can talk this out. I'll make it right."

"No. You know what, don't bother coming out here," she says. "I'm going to my mom's tomorrow. I need some time alone."

"No, wait—"

"You were right, this is moving too fast. We should take some time apart to figure out what we want out of this."

Oh god, no.

"Angie, please—"

"Goodbye, Asher." She hangs up on me before I can even formulate a response.

"Wait!" I shout to no one as I sink to my knees.

Fuck, what have I done?

I was not prepared for any of that. I thought we would have at least a few months or even years before the pressure of marriage and kids came crashing down on us. I hoped by then I would have somehow gotten over my shit about all that, but thanks to John, we've just fast-tracked our inevitable breakup. Thanks a lot, asshole.

Except...I'm the asshole.

My head presses into the carpet.

John offered her a real future. Something I've never been sure I was capable of. I'm too broken to give her all those things, and maybe I never could. I was never going to be good enough for her.

Wes knew it. It's why he insisted I stay away from her the moment I mentioned my feelings for her all those years ago. He knew I would never be the man she needed me to be.

Though, somehow after being with her these past few weeks, I actually convinced myself I had a chance. That maybe I *could* be good enough for her. That our love was enough.

I guess it was all just wishful thinking.

Maybe she should get back together with John. He can give her the happily ever after she's always dreamed of.

Slowly, I rise to my feet. The silence in this barren apartment is haunting, and I want to scream.

It's that moment of course, that Wes chooses to text me, and I wince. Fuck, I've been avoiding him for far too long. Another person in my life I'm failing.

WES

hey man, I'm gonna be in your neck of the woods Monday to talk with Bryn about our partnership deal for the agency and maybe get started on a few more vacation packages

ME

oh awesome

you can stay with me if you want

WES

sounds good man. can't wait!

A trace of relief rolls through me. Spending time with Wes might be exactly what I need right now. My best and oldest friend. That should help put things in perspective. Maybe he has some insight into what the hell I should do about Angie.

Which means it's time to be completely honest about what

happened with his sister. How we pretended to be married, fell for each other for real, and then I went and fucked it all up like I always do.

Walking to my bedroom, I shut off my phone and bury my face into my pillow until a restless sleep takes me.

55

ANGIE

August 1

My stuff is all packed and I am heading to college soon!!! I can't wait to start this next chapter in my life. I know with John by my side, it will be incredible. I wonder what my new roommate is like? I hope we get along.

Here we go!!!

That was my last journal entry.

I'm sure that if I kept writing, I would see the rapid progression toward becoming an entirely different person. One who prioritized the needs of an undeserving, toxic man over her own. Never talking back or raising her voice. Being so focused on keeping the peace and never causing an argument, she lost herself in the process.

I used to think that was how you showed you cared for someone, by agreeing to keep things civil. Keeping a calm surrounding, being his safe space.

Looking back on my behavior, I am utterly appalled. Who was that girl?

Was I really so desperate to be with someone who only showed me a tiny crumb of attention that I was willing to make myself smaller and quieter?

Unwilling to see John's red flags just to force a childhood fantasy to come true? Using him as a crutch to avoid my unresolved feelings for Asher?

Losing myself to another person because I refused to face reality.

I can *never* let that happen again.

56

ANGIE

The next morning, Willow and I pile in her Jeep with her dog, Henry, so we can finally head up to Mom's house to pick up Cally. I feel a little guilty that I've had her take my dog so much lately so I can go and travel, but I know she loves having her in the house. She would love to get a dog of her own, but she has a fairly active social life and likes to go on spontaneous trips with her friends.

Sounds familiar.

I prop my feet up on the dash, replaying my conversation with Asher in my mind. I probably shouldn't have sprung that on him over the phone after a few drinks, but I couldn't take it anymore. I couldn't go another day wondering if what I had with him was all in my head, and if we were just delaying the inevitable.

Are we really over already? When we've only just begun?

Asher doesn't want to be married, and people don't usually change their minds about something like that. And I shouldn't have to give that up, either.

Maybe it's better for both of us if we walk away now before it goes too far.

"Hey," Willow says sharply, snapping her fingers in front of my face. "Did you hear what I said?"

I sigh and realize I'd been picking my nail so hard it's bleeding, not even paying attention to what she was talking about. "No, I'm sorry. I'm still kinda shook up about yesterday."

"What, the thing I said about Asher and your dad?"

"Well, that and..." I shift in my seat, angling to face her. "Okay, I didn't tell you, but last night I called Asher, and we had a big fight."

Our first fight actually, and maybe our last.

"A fight? Is that why you were acting so weird when you came back inside?"

"Yeah." I shrug, continuing to pick at my thumb and avoid her gaze. "John texted me."

"Wait, what?" she screams, nearly veering us off the road. A horn honks behind us, but she pays it no mind. "What the hell? Why didn't you say anything?"

I drop my hands. "Because I just hit my breaking point! Yesterday was a lot, and after we talked about Max and Kayla, I needed some air, and that's when John confessed his love for me over text and begged me to take him back."

When I finally look over at her, I half expect her to pull the car over and lecture me. She despises John after everything he did back in college.

"Jesus Christ," she growls. Her knuckles are white from gripping the steering wheel.

I scoff. "Men."

"So...what happened? What did you say to him?"

"I basically told him to fuck off, but he insisted he could give me everything Asher wouldn't."

Wouldn't, not couldn't, I remind myself. Big difference.

I continue, "I screenshotted the texts and sent them to Asher. I needed to hear what he had to say about it."

She waves her hand around when I don't elaborate. Exasperated, she says, "And?"

A sob threatens to bubble up, but I hold it back. "He called me and got all flustered and said some crap that just set me off, so I said...I said maybe we should take some time apart to figure out what we really want."

I'm about to burst as I turn and face the window, inhaling sharply, determined not to fall apart again. I'm so tired of crying.

Her hand comes to rest on my leg, and she squeezes. "I'm really sorry, Ang."

"No, I'm sorry. I know you're probably sick of hearing me talk about him. I'll figure it out."

She pulls her hand back, her face suddenly serious. "Hey, don't do that. Don't minimize your feelings for me. You were there for me during all the Luca stuff, and I know that wasn't easy. I am always here if you want to talk." At my prolonged silence, she adds, "Or we can put on a smutty audiobook to distract you. Whatever you want."

I huff a small laugh. "I just...none of this is turning out how I thought it would."

She nods.

"I knew he had hangups on marriage because of his parents, but I guess I thought...I don't know, I thought maybe it would be different with me. Like...if it was really meant to be, he wouldn't be afraid to take that step with me." I hear how naïve it sounds, and I hate it.

"So, this is the point where I ask if you just want to vent, or if you want my advice. Because I can do either."

Squeezing my eyes shut, I say, "I think we're past the point of venting, and I'd like some advice."

She won't sugarcoat it. She never does. And I remind myself it's out of love, because I'm not sure I'm going to like what she's about to say.

"Okay." She clears her throat. "He told you he didn't believe in marriage, and that he never wanted to get married, right?"

I twist my mouth to the side, already knowing where she's going with this. "Yeah."

"And this was before you guys slept together last week, right?" she says, flipping her turn signal to change lanes.

Tears burn the back of my eyes again as I nod. "Yeah."

"So...from my perspective, he technically hasn't done anything wrong. It completely sucks because you do want to get married and have a family and all that. And that's valid too. But..."

"But we want different things," I finish.

She puts her hand over mine just as Henry leans forward and licks the side of my face, like he can sense that I'm about to lose it. Because I am this time.

"Fuck. This is so unfair," I say, swiping at my damp lashes.

"I know. You should talk to him."

"I would've been better off if I had never even known how good it could be with him. Three of the best days of my life, and now...I'm just empty."

"Have you told your mom about any of this?" Her voice is soft, yet pleading.

I shake my head. "No. All she knows is that I went on the trip with him, but I didn't tell her anything else. I was hoping to tell her the good news in person. And now..." My hand splays out, gesturing around at nothing in particular as a sob finally breaks through.

We sit in silence for a while until Willow opens up her audiobook app and starts a rom-com about a female lacrosse player who falls in love with her coach's brother. I rest my head on the cold window, watching the cows and familiar fields of wheat pass by in a blur.

57

ANGIE

We pull into the gravel driveway a few hours later. Henry perks up, knowing exactly what that sound means and where we are. When Willow opens the back of the Jeep, he bolts toward the house like a bat out of hell. The front door of the house opens, and my sweet Cally races out to meet her brother, colliding in a mess of black fur, as if they've been apart for years.

Reunited at last.

They nip and chase each other around the wide-open yard like puppies, and I can't help but smile a little.

Mom holds the front door open for Willow and me, and we leave the dogs to play.

"Hi, Sandy," Willow says as she passes by awkwardly with a stiff hand on her arm. The two of them together makes me laugh, because Willow is not a hugger with most people, and my mom definitely is with *all* people. The tiny flash of disappointment on her face is adorable.

I wrap my mom in a tight hug, refusing to let go. I lean into her comforting embrace, and the smell of home hits me like a ton of bricks. She holds me tighter, stroking my hair as I start to break down like a little kid. She always knows when I need her most.

"Hey...shhh...what's going on?" she asks.

I sniffle as I pull away. "I need to talk to you about something."

Willow makes herself at home in the kitchen, putting on a pot of coffee. On the leather couch in her living room, I fill my mom in on everything that happened with Asher this past week. When I'm finally done, my cheeks are damp as I clutch a tissue I don't remember grabbing.

"Wow," she says. "That is a lot. Though I'm not entirely surprised the two of you *finally* admitted your feelings for one another."

Of course she knew. I wish I had come to her for advice a long time ago.

"What should I do?" I know it sounds childish, like my mom can fix my very real, very adult problems. Problems I've gotten myself into.

She wipes another tear away. "Honey, you know I can't tell you that."

"Okay, but...what do you think? I'm completely lost here."

She puts her arm around my shoulders and pulls me in closer. "I think...you and Asher need to sit down, face to face, and talk this out. You say he doesn't want to get married, and you do, but is it so important to you that it's worth losing him altogether? People can still be together without signing a marriage license. You can still have kids without being married."

"So you think I should be the one to give up what I want?" I ask, trying to squash the disappointment rising in my gut.

"No. What I'm saying is, you need to look deep down and figure out *why* this is so important to you. It sounds like neither of you wants to end the relationship, so this is the one thing keeping you apart. And if it is that important to you, then that's okay too, but he deserves to know why and to have a chance to explain his side. And the only way to do that is to have that conversation with him."

Of course, both she and Willow are the voice of reason. They're right. I can't solve this without actually talking to Asher. I'm so used to dealing with things on my own that I'm not sure I know how to do this. I've never been with someone I considered a true, equal partner, so this is going to take some getting used to.

I pull out of her arms as I wipe my nose on the damp tissue. "I just can't believe we're here. After everything we've been through."

Her face softens, and the way she looks at me tugs at my heartstrings. "You have to remember, hun, you're both different people than you were in high school. You grew up always wanting a traditional wedding like a lot of little girls, but you never really questioned it."

"What do you mean?" I ask, glancing at Willow to see if she is following along.

Mom smiles, picking up her coffee from the table and wrapping her hands around the mug. "You're very nostalgic, like me. But if you hold on to something long enough, you just accept it as how it should be. Sometimes you have to let go of the past if it's not serving you anymore."

"Kind of like how you still have all of Dad's stuff?" I blurt, and she stills. I didn't mean for it to sound so accusatory, but we all heard it.

"You saw the bins then?" she says, avoiding my stare.

I nod. "Why did you tell me you got rid of them?"

She doesn't respond, just finishes off her mug of coffee and places it slowly back on the table, looking around like she's ready to change the subject. And it's what finally sets me off.

"Ugh." I throw my hands in the air. "Why can't anyone in this family ever say what they're really feeling for once?"

A heavy silence falls over the room.

I've never said anything like that to my mom before. I know deep down I'm just as guilty of burying my emotions, but I cannot keep it all in anymore. It's like my body has hit its limit and is finally rejecting the idea of hiding anymore. I'm laying it all out now, and there's no going back.

Willow stands, jabbing her thumb at the back door. "I'm... gonna go check on the kids." She practically sprints around the coffee table and through the kitchen, calling for the dogs.

I'm picking my nail again when Mom finally breaks the uncomfortable silence. "We talk about our feelings all the time."

"Not when it comes to Dad," I shoot back.

"What is that supposed to mean?" she says, hurt flooding her voice.

Suddenly I'm on my feet, arms out wide. "We never talk about him. And I guess that was fine at first when we were just trying to survive, but...god, Mom, it's been sixteen years, and I'm starting to think we never fully grieved him. We just pushed it all away and pretended everything was fine."

Her lips twist to the side with a quiver, and I know she is fighting the urge to run away like we always do. But she must see something in my face, because she steels herself and closes her eyes before saying. "Okay."

I sit back down and take her hands in mine. "Look...the three of us did our best. And without you and Wesley, who knows how I would've ended up. I don't want to forget about him, and I never will, but I don't think I can move forward until

I get some real closure. I'm clinging to some version of the past...and like you said, it's not serving me anymore."

Now it's her turn to cry. I pull her in for a hug. I've hardly ever seen her cry, but that's the problem. She spent so long trying to be strong and brave for us that she inadvertently taught us that was how you dealt with things. We never learned to feel the pain and work through it.

"Okay," she says on a whisper. "What should we do?"

I grab a new tissue and wipe away her tears. "I'd like us to see a grief counselor. You, me, and Wesley, together. He can join on Zoom or whatever."

She nods, a melancholy smile painted on her lips. "I'm in."

We sit there for several minutes, holding each other, allowing ourselves to safely open those old wounds with the intention of finally healing them properly. And for once, I'm not afraid. Because I'm not alone in this feeling, and I know everything will be okay for us.

Mom pulls away and says, "Asher too, you know."

I tilt my head. "What about him?"

"You said the three of us did our best, but he was there too. I'll never forget everything he did for you kids and for me. He's an angel."

My heart cracks. "Yeah. He really is."

58

ANGIE

We stayed way too late at Mom's house yesterday. Now I'm struggling at our weekly Saturday morning pickleball session. I didn't want to leave, not when she and I had such a breakthrough, and I finally felt like we were being open and honest about Dad for once. Like a weight was lifted off my shoulders.

And now I'm back to feeling crappy again. Not only because I'm exhausted, but because I'm forced to watch Willow and Luca and their unbridled PDA, and be reminded that everyone I know is getting their happy ending except for me.

Well, maybe not everyone. I spot Max by the benches, frantically typing something on his phone. His face is scrunched, and he looks like he hasn't slept in weeks.

His separation from Kayla has become an open secret around here, which I'm sure isn't helping matters. Regardless of how a couple got to that point, it can't be easy, especially when kids are involved.

"Hey, Max," I say, approaching him cautiously. "How's it going?"

He looks up from his phone with bloodshot eyes. "Oh hey, Angie. Welcome back. How was your trip?"

"Thanks. It was amazing. Still getting used to this winter weather again."

Awkward silence stretches between us. I know about him and Kayla, but I don't know if he knows I know. But I'm on an honesty kick right now, so I decide to cut right to it.

"I hope I'm not overstepping, but I heard about you and Kayla, and I am so, so sorry."

He shrugs, putting his phone back in his gym bag. "Thank you, I appreciate it."

"I'm here if you ever want to talk," I say. "I know she's friends with Simon, but you're my friend too. If you ever need anything."

"Thanks, Angie. That means a lot, truly." He picks up his paddle, spinning it in his palm. "Just taking it one day at a time, you know?"

I nod solemnly, not wanting to pry any further, until he looks off into the distance and adds, "It happens slowly."

My head tilts to the side as he continues.

"Going from lovers to best friends to...I don't know, roommates? I guess it was so gradual, neither of us really saw what was happening until it was too late."

My heart clenches, and I fight the urge to hug him. "Oh, Max. I'm sorry."

He presses his fingernail into the rubber handle, avoiding my heartbroken stare. "I thought we could make it work if we tried hard enough, but we're just so different. We'll see how the separation goes, but unfortunately, I think our relationship has run its course."

When his eyes meet mine again, it finally hits me like a ton of bricks.

Marriage doesn't guarantee two people will stay together, just like *not* getting married doesn't mean you can't have a family and grow old together. I've been desperately searching for some kind of assurance that whoever I married, we would be together forever. But there are never any guarantees in life. Asher and I both know that all too well.

No one knows what tomorrow will look like; you can only follow your heart and show up each day trying your best.

One day at a time.

Why am I holding on so tightly to this idea that there's only one way to do things? One path with specific milestones that you have to hit in a certain order? Hell, my entire relationship with Asher has been unconventional.

That's just our story, and it can look like whatever we want.

"Anyway," Max finally says, pulling me from another life-altering revelation. "We'll be fine. We're both committed to doing what's best for the kiddos. Whatever happens with us, we're going to show up and be the best coparents we can be for them."

I put a gentle hand on his forearm. "Max, I'm so happy to hear that. They're lucky to have you both."

Max is in his mid-thirties, handsome with short, slightly graying hair, and an all-around great guy. I have no doubt he'll be just fine.

"Thanks, Angie. Come on, let's get a match going before Luca gets Willow pregnant out there."

"God, they're disgusting, aren't they?" I say with a smirk.

"Totally."

I can't help but smile. Max and Kayla are choosing to put their kids' needs first. Putting aside their own differences to give them a good childhood full of love. Their kids won't suffer the same way Asher did.

Asher.

I need to make things right with him, and soon.

"How's the job hunt going?" Max asks as we walk back onto the courts, not knowing how much weight that simple question carries.

I think back to managing Asher's social media during our trip and how much fun it was to travel with him and document all the adventures and special moments. How it felt so easy and surprisingly fulfilling. How I would love to help people plan and book their dream vacations.

And how I'd rather not resort to selling pictures of my feet on the internet again.

"I've got some ideas," I say. "Looking to get into the travel agent business, actually."

His face lights up, a small smile tugging at his lips. "Ah, because of that guy you went on the trip with?"

I narrow my eyes, and he puts his hands up in defense.

"Hey, I'm just glad I'm not the only one they've been talking about this week."

I snort. "Yeah, that's fair."

"When do we all get to meet him, anyway?" He elbows my arm playfully. "I'm pretty sure there's a vetting process around here that you haven't completed."

I don't have the heart to tell him that we didn't even make it through one menstrual cycle before I pushed him away. That I was so terrified of getting my heart broken that I ended up breaking it myself before we even had a chance to begin.

Maybe it's not too late for us, though. Now that I know what I want.

I clap a hand on his shoulder. "One day at a time, Max."

59

ASHER

By Monday morning, I'm convinced it's over.

Angie and I have only texted a few times since our fight on Thursday night. Mostly just quick "good night" or "good morning" texts. I'm trying to respect her wishes to give her space and let her figure out what she wants, but I can't stop the intrusive thoughts of her reconnecting with John and realizing he's the love of her life.

But I can't force her to choose me. All I can do right now is keep loving her, even from afar, and let her know that I'll always be here for her.

I arrive at the Indianapolis airport around ten a.m. to pick up Wes and idle my car in the Arrivals area. When I see him, his face splits into a wide grin, and I open my arms for a hug. At the same time, we both start singing "Reunited," as I ruffle up his dirty blond hair.

"Thanks for picking me up," Wes says, clapping my back.

We pull apart, and I say truthfully, "I'm really glad you're here."

His luggage gets loaded in the trunk, and we climb inside my car before airport security tells me I've been here too long.

Once we're on the interstate, he asks, "How far away is your office?"

"Not far, about fifteen minutes," I reply. "Bryn is excited to finally meet you in person."

"Yeah, she sounds like a cool boss."

I nod, fiddling with the audio console and starting one of my playlists.

"So, how are things going with my sister? Did you two enjoy the honeymoon suite?"

My head whips over to his smirking face, then quickly back to the road, my heart thudding in my chest. "You knew about that?"

He tsks. "Come on, man. You didn't wonder how you got upgraded, or why the staff all thought you were married?"

"Wait...*you* did that? Why?"

I don't understand. Why would he put us in that position? None of this makes any sense.

Wes barks out a laugh. "I saw how you two were looking at each other back in London. Angie was speechless. My sister doesn't do 'speechless.'"

Now I'm the one who's speechless. This is the last thing I expected from him. I've been agonizing about how I would tell him about us, and he already knew.

"So...you told them we were newlyweds? What, to mess with us? I still don't get it."

"To help you out," he says as he swats my shoulder. "To get you both out of your own way. So you're welcome. Based on your stories and posts on Instagram, I'd say my plan was a massive success." He tugs at the lapels of his button-up shirt.

"Your *plan*?" I swallow around a lump in my throat. "I'm not sure what to say, man."

He knows about us, and he's not upset. Not only that, but he came up with a scheme to help us get closer and finally realize our feelings for each other.

All these years, I've held back because I was worried about how he would react. I was sure he would never approve of us being together, and then he does something like this.

"Why?" His giant grin overtakes his face. "Isn't this what you wanted?"

Yes. At least it was, until I ruined everything. Now I have to explain that it's over. Without even really dating in the first place.

What the hell is wrong with me?

"Well..." I rub the back of my damp neck. "So we kinda ended things. I think."

"*What?*" he screams, making me flinch. "The fuck are you talking about?"

Taking a deep breath, I say, "It's complicated. And...a long story."

"Then I guess it's story time, motherfucker. Tell me what happened right now." He jams the button on my console, turning off the music entirely.

I sigh. "I...I think you were right all those years ago, that I'm just not good enough for her."

He rears his head back. "When did I ever say that?"

"Back in high school. You said, and I quote, 'stay the fuck away from her' when I asked about taking her to Homecoming."

He scoffs. "Oh come on, man, we were teenagers just fucking around. Of course I didn't want you messing around with my sister."

"I wasn't fucking around, Wes," I shout. "I really liked her. I wanted to be with her for real."

I meet his gaze, and his eyes are wide, stricken. When I

turn back to the road, he says softly, "I'm sorry, man. I had no idea. But...to be clear, I never said you weren't good enough for her. I would never think that."

"What do you mean?"

"Look, I know things got messed up between us after that night with Stacy."

I shift in my seat, gripping the steering wheel tighter. I guess we're doing this now.

"And I'm really sorry about that," he continues. "I hate that it happened right before you moved away, and we lost touch before we had a chance to make things right."

"Me too," I say. "Look, I want to state for the record, Stacy is the one who came on to me. I had no interest in being with your girlfriend, Wes. Honestly. None."

"I know that now. The truth is, I was really immature back then, and I assumed you were trying to sleep around like I was. I didn't want *anyone* messing with my sister. I was so protective of her, not just because of our dad, but because I knew how guys our age treated girls. How *I* treated girls."

After a beat of silence, I say, "I'm sorry I never reached out."

"I am too. And I want you to know...you were like a brother to me, you still are. But it's different now that we're all grown up. Angie would be lucky to be with someone like you."

"Wow," I say on a sigh. "Thanks, man. That means a lot."

"So what happened? I hope you didn't end things because of me. You guys would be really good for each other."

Fuck. Time really has a way of messing with your memories. I could've sworn he said I wasn't good enough for her. Or did I just project that? Maybe I thought it was implied because of how adamant he was that I stay away from her.

I look over at him, shaking my head. "It wasn't just that. I don't know. Things got kinda weird when we came home from this trip."

"Weird how?" he asks.

"When we landed in Chicago, we ran into her ex. A real piece of work."

"Her ex?" He grabs my arm, and I nearly swerve off the road. "Please don't tell me it was John."

"Yeah, it was. Why?"

"Oh my god!" He smacks the dashboard with his palms. "That guy is such a fucking asshole. I was so glad when they finally broke up."

"What? Why?" I ask, my hands suddenly sweating. "I thought he was like...the love of her life?"

"Ha! John? John the Boner? No fucking way."

"Boner?"

"Dude, his last name is Bohner. I gave Angie so much shit for that, I would've never let her live it down if they got married and she changed her name to Angie Harris Bohner. *Hairy Boner*? Dick jokes like that don't come along very often."

"Oh wow, that is bad," I say. "But...I thought they were madly in love and all that."

Saying the words makes me sick to my stomach.

"Nah. He was always cheating on her. For whatever reason, she was head over heels in love with him, but he didn't give a shit. I know for a fact he was sleeping with her friend Christina the summer before they all went to college together."

I suddenly want to go find him and punch him square in the balls. Fucking John the Boner.

"Are you serious? Did she ever know about that?"

God, I really wish we weren't having this discussion while I'm driving. I just realized my exit is up ahead, and I have to cut across two lanes of traffic without crashing while Wes keeps talking.

"I don't think she knew about Christina, per se, but regardless, it didn't end well. She was pretty messed up about it for a while. That guy is such a prick."

"I certainly got bad vibes from him," I say. "She got all quiet and weird around him. I assumed she still had feelings for him and didn't want him to know there was anything going on between us."

He rubs his clean-shaven chin. "Huh. No, I don't think she still has feelings for him, at least I hope not. He hurt her pretty badly. I'd be surprised if she ever gave him another chance. She should know better by now."

I turn onto the street where my office building is, ready to be done talking about John once and for all. Except there's one more thing Wes needs to know.

"He told her he wants to get back together. Wants to marry her and have babies and all that. Plus, he lives in Chicago now, so he can drive down and see her whenever he wants."

"Oh fuck that!" he says, pounding the dash again. "After this meeting with Bryn, we're gonna go pay my sister a little visit. Make sure she's not entertaining any of this fuckery."

I smile. There's the Wes I remember. The loud, crazy theater kid who is always over the top but also loyal and a damn good best friend.

We park at my office, and I start to unbuckle my seatbelt when Wes says softly, "Did you really believe all this time...I thought that about you?"

I shrug. "Not just you."

"Your parents?" he guesses.

I nod. Growing up in a home where love was never expressed can mess with your head. Makes you feel like you're not worthy of it and that everyone around you considers it a burden to care about you.

Wes and Angie changed everything for me. Being over at their house made me feel loved and appreciated. Cared for without burden. And being apart from them for so long, I had forgotten what that even felt like.

"I hate that you thought that," he says. "You're nothing like them, you never were. You're my family, and I wish we hadn't lost so much time together. Never again."

Tears threaten to fall, and I hold them back with a cough. Wes really is like a brother. More of a family to me than my own flesh and blood.

And I know now he would do anything for me, even conspire to get me together with his sister. All this time, I've projected my own insecurities on him and Angie, assuming the worst and keeping my barriers up to avoid getting hurt.

But it doesn't work like that.

Things always have a way of coming back around.

"You know, I wish you could've known my dad," Wes says, putting his hand on my shoulder and squeezing tight. "He and my mom were perfect for each other. When it's with the right person, it just works."

"I wish I could have met him," I say. "He sounds like a great guy."

"And so are you, man. You're more than good enough for my sister. In fact...I'm not so sure she's good enough for *you* at this point."

I bark out a laugh, and he joins in.

He wants Angie and me to be together. He's seen with his own eyes that marriage can be beautiful and not a disaster, and I trust him enough to finally believe that.

I tap the steering wheel. "Can I tell you something? I didn't hate it. Calling her my wife."

He claps his hands over his mouth dramatically. "Holy shit, dude. Are you...Do you want to marry my sister?"

"Yeah..." I bite my lip. "I really do."

It's the first time I'm actually admitting it, even to myself.

And it doesn't feel scary, it feels right. Like it was always meant to be. I just needed someone to help me get out of my own way.

Then realization sinks in.

I may have fucked this up beyond repair.

I need to get her back.

I only hope I'm not too late.

60

ASHER

The meeting with Bryn went well, even if Wes and I were practically bouncing in our seats, ready to get out of there and drive to Athens. They signed a contract for more vacation packages, shook hands, and we politely declined her offer to go out to lunch. I told her I needed the afternoon off to declare my love for Angie, and she insisted we "get the hell out already."

I pack up my laptop and portfolio bag at my desk, praying I can prove to Angie how I feel about her. How serious I am about making it work with her, no matter what. Knowing now I am capable of offering her anything and everything she could ever want.

How could I have let her doubt my feelings for her?

What if it's too late and I've missed my chance?

I push the thoughts from my mind as I gather the rest of my things and drive Wes to my shitty apartment. I don't know how long I'm staying in Athens, if at all. If she'll even give my sorry ass five minutes to explain.

I hastily shove some shirts and underwear in my overnight bag anyway.

Fuck, what else should I bring? I was not prepared for this.

"You ready? Come on, it's getting late!" Wes shouts from my front door, rapping his knuckles on the frame.

Damn, he really wants me to make up with his sister. This is not how I imagined today going when I picked him up from the airport. Figured we'd just be catching up and ordering a pizza tonight.

"Coming!" I shout. Okay, I can do this.

It's time to get her back. For good.

We drive the three hours straight to Angie's house, no stopping, just vibing to his playlist of mostly classic rock and Broadway musical soundtracks. I almost forgot how often he would make me listen to them in high school, especially when he was preparing for a role in the school musical. I'm not mad about it; they're pretty catchy.

"You Will Be Found" from *Dear Evan Hansen* plays through the speakers as we pull up to her townhouse, and suddenly I might vomit. I've rehearsed everything I want to say to her, but my racing mind empties like water poured from a cup as I stare at her front door. I fear there may be nothing left by the time I get to her. Just a pathetic puddle on the pavement.

"Well? What are you waiting for?" Wes asks, halfway out of the car.

"I can't," I whisper. I'm frozen in place. Barely breathing.

I'm going to fuck this up again.

He places his hand on the door jam, leaning back in. "What do you mean you can't? I thought you wanted to be brothers for real. Are you seriously going to let that polo-wearing fuckboy have the life you want with her?" He narrows his eyes. "You like the idea of Angie *kissing* him, and touching his w—"

"Okay, that's enough. You can stop now," I say as I get out of the car, grabbing my coat and bags out of the trunk.

Wes walks ahead of me and pounds on his sister's front door like a maniac. I have no idea what to expect from all this, but it's too late to turn back now.

Angie's door flies open, but it's not her, it's her friend Willow…and that sweet black Labrador bounding toward me. I lean down to play with Cally, scratching her ears and trying to keep my balance as she circles me. Her tail wags like we're old friends.

"Hey, Willow. Everything okay?" I ask from the yard when she shoots me an assessing glance. Yeah, I really don't think she likes me.

She grabs Wes by the arm, pulling him away. "We'll be down here," she says to me, pointing to a townhouse three doors down. She pats her leg and whistles. "Come on, Cally!"

They all disappear into what I can only assume is Willow's townhouse without another word, leaving me standing there alone.

That was weird.

I step inside Angie's bright, colorful townhouse, but no one is here. Then, from the other room, I hear, "Will, who was at the door, we've gotta get going—" Her arms fall to her sides when she walks into the living room and sees me.

"Hey, Sunshine," I say, dropping my bags and coat to the floor.

Her eyes are wide as saucers. "Hi." It comes out so softly you could mistake it for a sigh. "What, uh…what are you doing here?"

I take a cautious step toward her. "I needed to see you." Then her words from a moment ago finally register. "But it sounds like you were just leaving? I'm sorry, I shouldn't have shown up like this. *Again*."

"No, it's okay—"

I close the space between us in three quick strides. "I understand if you're still mad, but please just give me five minutes. I have a whole presentation planned. If you don't like what I have to say, then I'll go."

Her face contorts in confusion. "Did you say a *presentation*?"

I guide her to the couch before opening my laptop on the coffee table in front of her and pull out my official travel agent binder, placing it gently in her lap as I sit beside her.

"Asher, what the hell is this?" she asks, exasperated.

"Open it." I lift my chin.

She slowly opens the binder. In the side pocket are three envelopes, each with a number 1, 2, or 3 written on the outside. On the metal rings are pages full of notes, divided into color-coded sections.

"Pick one," I say, pointing to the envelopes before wiping my clammy palms on my jeans.

She must think I'm nuts as she pulls out the one with a large "1" on it. She slides her finger under the flap and looks inside. Her head tilts as she says, "What are these?"

She pulls out the folded papers. Printed on the top are the words "Travel Vouchers" in bold letters. Below, it says "Two First Class Tickets to Paris, France."

"You're going to Paris?" Angie asks. God, she's adorable when she's confused.

I smile. "You are." I start the slideshow on my computer. Photos of Paris and the surrounding areas fade in and out on the screen. I know it's probably overkill, but I want her to see how much thought I've put into this. Even if it makes me look pathetic. "Included in the binder are sample itineraries, guided tours, train tickets, you name it."

"So I'm a client of yours now? Just tell me what all this is!"

"Open the next one," I say, nudging her with my elbow.

With a sigh, she opens the second envelope and reads out loud, "Two first-class tickets to Tokyo, Japan?"

The second set of sheets includes itineraries, research, schedules, hotel options, and locations for all upcoming pickleball tournaments in the area, organized by date and city. As well as options to play matches with locals.

She looks over at me, eyes wide. "Wait, these are the places I told you I wanted to go. I thought we were just talking, like shooting off ideas for your travel business."

I scoff. "I don't give a shit about all that. I wanted to know where *you* wanted to go. This is all for you, Angie. You deserve everything you've ever wanted, and more. And I want to be the one to help you get it."

She looks back down at the third envelope. "Does that mean...Is this what I think it is?"

I smile back at her as she excitedly opens the last envelope with tickets to Tromsø, Norway inside, with a list of the best ways to see the Northern Lights. She beams at me, and it warms my heart.

Right here. This is what it's all about. This is what I want for the rest of my life. Every moment of witnessing her awe and wonder. Being with Angie can look like whatever we want, and I know that now.

"Ash, you did all this for me?" She looks back down at the paperwork and frowns. "But...it only has my name on the travel vouchers. Are you not coming too?" Her face falls like I've just crushed her again without even meaning to.

"I...didn't want to assume. Of course I hoped you would take me, but you can also go with Willow or—"

"Don't you dare fucking say 'John' or I will rip your goddamn balls off."

I put my hands up. "Okay, okay. I was going to say Wes,

but...noted." I pause, trying to find the right words. "You know, I wouldn't blame you...if you still had feelings for John. You can tell me." My hands ache to touch her, hold her, but I stop myself.

"Oh my god. Fuck him. I want to take you."

Hope lights up the darkest parts within me. "You do?"

She sniffs and wipes a tear that escapes her long lashes. "Of course I do, but...Ash, I've wanted you for so long. I don't think I can go back to being just friends. I can't keep doing this to myself."

"I don't want to be friends, either," I say quickly.

Shit, that came out wrong. I realize it the minute I see hurt flash across her face.

"No, I mean...I want more too. I want us to be together, for real."

"But—"

"Wait, just...please let me try and get this out," I say on a shaky breath.

She puts the binder and envelopes off to the side, and I take her hands in mine as she turns to face me.

I blow out a steadying breath. "I've been running away my entire life. I would go to your house when we were kids to avoid my parents and all their problems. I left for California when my feelings for you were too big and everything felt hopeless. I've been afraid of getting close to anyone. My job is, quite literally, running away to different countries to avoid sitting still long enough to feel anything real. And I can't do it anymore. Ever since you came back into my life, I've been ripped apart with the urge to run so I don't get hurt, but also a need to be closer to you."

"Ash..."

"What we have is special. It's rare." I cup her cheek, pressing my forehead to hers. "I know I have things I need to work on, but I'm not afraid anymore. I'm not afraid to imagine my future anymore—our future—because you're here with me. I promise you, there is nothing John can offer you that I can't."

"Asher, stop," she says forcefully, and my heart drops. I'm too late. It's not enough.

"Angie—"

"Asher, please let me talk now."

My hand drops from her face as I reluctantly pull away. "Okay."

"I've done a lot of thinking these past few days. And what I've come to realize is that I have some serious work to do on myself, too. With my family."

I nod, but my heart is in my throat. What does that mean?

"Look, you came into my life right after my dad died, and I'm so grateful for that, but I don't think I ever fully processed his death." She takes a breath before saying, "I'm going to start seeing a therapist to help deal with all this unresolved trauma, and I may need some time to sort things out."

"Oh," I say, my shoulders relaxing. "Of course, whatever you need. As long as it takes, I'll be here." I kiss the back of her hand.

This isn't the end for us; it's just the beginning.

"Thank you." She pulls our hands to her chest and squeezes.

"Is that why you were crying on the trip? Because I was bringing up all these old feelings?"

She nods sadly, and something clicks for me.

"So...when I left for college...god, that must have felt so lonely. I never really thought about how hard that would have been for you. I didn't think you'd even care." I place a hand behind her neck, pulling her in to kiss her temple. "I'm so sorry. I should have stayed."

She wraps her hand around my wrist. "No. This is what I'm trying to tell you. That was all *my* stuff. It was not your responsibility to manage my grief. You couldn't stay in that town any longer; it would have destroyed you."

I squeeze my eyes shut. She's right. I had to get away from my parents, from that house and everything that happened there.

"I wish you had told me all this before," I say, tucking her blonde hair gently behind her ear. "Don't know if you know this about me, but I have a habit of assuming the worst, so when you don't tell me what you're thinking—"

"You're right, I'm sorry. I am not good at being honest about my feelings. Something else I'm working on." She starts to pick her nail, but I pull her hand away, interlacing our fingers.

"We'll work through this, there's no rush."

Angie nods and says, "We have time. We found our way back to each other, and that's all that matters. And...I don't need all"—she waves her hand around—"that stuff. We don't have to get married, because all I really want is you. A life with you, Asher. Whatever that looks like. That's what I want."

I bite back a smile. "Well, I'm sorry, but that's not enough for me."

Her face falls as she looks down at her lap. I lift her chin with my finger and add, "Because being fake married to you was the happiest I've ever been in my life, and I don't want to pretend anymore. I want the real thing."

61

ANGIE

My head rears back. "*What?*"

Did he just...

Maybe I really do have a hearing problem.

"I'm not saying we have to do it right now," he adds quickly. "But...is that...something you'd still like some day? With me?"

"Wh—Is that something *you* would like?" I jump to my feet. "I thought you said you would never get married. That you don't believe in marriage!" My voice is high and squeaky. I need to calm down.

He shrugs, as if we're talking about sports or the weather, then infuriatingly crosses his ankle over his knee, casual as can be, while I have a full-blown meltdown.

"That was before I thought you and I were ever a possibility. Things change, Sunshine. I wouldn't want to be married to anyone else but you," he says, like it's the most obvious thing in the world. "Plus, I really enjoyed calling you my wife. More than I ever thought I would."

I stand there, unable to form words. Is he actually asking me to marry him, or are we just talking in hypotheticals here? My mouth hangs open, and he stands tall in front of me, cradling my elbows.

"You're cute when you're flustered, you know that?" He leans in to kiss the tip of my nose. "Look, the only future I'm afraid of is one where you're not in it. I want to wake up next to you every day. I want to travel the world with you. I want to keep getting lost with you, because we always find our way back to each other. You can take all the time you need to sort things out, and I'll be right here, ready to start our next adventure."

My breath whooshes out of me as I look up at him. "How do you do that? Always knowing what I need?"

"Because I know you better than I know myself."

I pull away with a smirk. "Oh yeah? Prove it."

Without hesitation, he says, "Your favorite wine is La Chablisienne Chablis La Pierrelee Chardonnay."

"Is that all?" I raise an eyebrow, but he shakes his head.

"You love the smell of lavender, but firmly believe it should never be a flavor you eat or drink."

A laugh bubbles out of me as I cover my mouth.

He continues, "You have thirty-nine freckles on your face; four more than you had at the start of our trip. You cry over videos of babies getting glasses or hearing aids. Your tongue comes to rest in your left cheek when you're concentrating. You love Valentine's Day even though you pretend it's cheesy. Your grandmother gave you that sapphire ring because it reminded her of your eyes."

I mindlessly twist the ring over my finger as tears spring to my eyes.

"Your favorite flowers are lilies, and your favorite cupcakes are the red velvet from Gina's back home." Asher frames my face with his hands. "You see the good in everyone, and you are aggressively loyal and protective of the people you care about. You love out loud. You leave a mark wherever you go. And your smile brightens every room. Angie...You are the *light* of my life."

I crash into him, my head coming to rest on his chest as he wraps his arms around me.

He sees me. He knows me.

This is true love.

My eye catches on the binder and his laptop and everything he put together for me. Planning dream vacations to the places I want to go, always paying attention.

"When did you even plan these trips?" I mumble into his shirt.

He kisses the top of my head. "As soon as we got home from Antigua."

After he met John, and everything went to shit.

"Even though you thought I still might have feelings for my shitty, cheating ex?" I ask, still trying to process the fact that he said he wants us to get married someday.

He pulls back, his arms still draped over my shoulders. "I wanted you to go on these trips because I want you to be happy. With or without me." He looks away and then back to me, eyebrows scrunched. "Wait, you knew about the cheating?"

I shrug. "He wasn't exactly discreet. I was more disappointed in my friend, Christina." That should've been the nail in the coffin for me, but I just pretended it never happened and convinced myself he would change. "Deep down, I think I knew John wasn't the one for me, but he was...there, and you weren't. And I couldn't cope, so I thought that could be enough for me. That...eventually it would be enough."

A stray tear streaks down my cheek, and he catches it with his thumb.

"But then you showed up in my life again, and I knew no one else would ever be enough. You have always been a part of me, and there's no one I would rather get lost with. I choose you, Asher Hayes. I want you by my side forever, because I love you so fucking much."

"I love you too, Sunshine. Always have."

"Then kiss me already," I say before he captures my lips with his. A hungry, frenzied kiss. Magic. I want to stay in this moment forever. His hands brace the back of my thighs and he hikes me up, my legs crossing behind him.

Warmth pools in my lower belly as I deepen our kiss, and suddenly all I want is his hands everywhere and for the neighbors to hear how skilled he is with his tongue.

It could be like this every day.

He pulls away panting. "Weren't you going somewhere when I got here?"

I smile against his lips. "Actually, I had a whole plan to drive out to Indy to surprise you."

His head rears back as he sets me on my feet. "You were coming to see me?" Those green eyes hold so much hope and wonder.

"How many times do I have to tell you I'm in love with you before you believe it?" I scoff as I reach down for the travel binder, flipping through the pages. "I can't believe you thought I would actually take Wesley on these vacations."

"I guess it's a good thing I didn't tell him on the way here," he says.

At my confusion, he smiles innocently. "Oh, did I not mention? We drove out here together. He wanted to make sure I didn't screw this up."

"Wait, Wesley is *here*, here?" The binder lands on the floor with a thud, and I grab his arms. "And he knows about us? That we were really...together on our trip?"

He nods, still smiling.

"And he's *okay* with it? I thought you said he would never approve of us being together."

How is he being so casual about this? What am I going to tell him?

"Wes is the one who told the resort we were married and upgraded us to the honeymoon villa, so we should probably thank him."

What?

Why would he do that? He had to know what was going to happen there. But then it hits me, and I shake my head, unable to control the laughter bubbling out. "He was always a notoriously good wingman."

"That is accurate," Asher says. "After this, maybe the best."

"So, he's what, just hanging out next door with Willow and Luca right now?"

"I honestly don't care." He leans in and starts kissing my neck.

"Well, let's go, he's my brother. I hardly ever get to see him. I can't remember the last time he came out to visit me."

He pulls back with a smirk. "Technically, he came out to the States to visit *me*. He signed the papers with the agency for the pickleball vacation package with more plans for his other hotel properties."

"Oh, that's cool." I start walking toward the front door, but he stops me with a hand on my wrist, pulling me back to him. Pressed against him, I lean into his warmth. The proof of his desire digging into my belly.

"What's your hurry? They can wait." He twists a strand of my hair between his fingers.

"Wait for what?" I tease.

He kisses me deeply. Slow, methodical. Loving.

It holds all the promises of tomorrow. Of our future together.

He takes his time undressing me. Touching, kissing, savoring every inch of my body like we have all the time in the world.

And I guess now we do.

62

ASHER

June 5

Met the new neighbors today and made a new best friend. Wes is my age, and we'll be in the same school in the fall. I hope we get the same teacher! He has a sister named Angie who's just a grade below us, and she's the nicest and funniest person I've ever met. Her bright blonde hair reminds me of the sun, and she always seems to be smiling, despite losing their dad to a heart attack a few months ago. I feel terrible they've been through so much.

Their mom, Sandy, welcomed me right in and invited me to stay for dinner too. It's been a long time since anyone has been so kind to me. The Harrises are my new favorite people.

I noticed when I left their house tonight that their outside lamplight was broken, so I grabbed some of Dad's tools and a new bulb and replaced it real quick.

I bet with their dad gone it's harder to find time to fix things around the house. I'll be on the lookout for more things I can help out with. It's the least I can do for them.

I can't wait to go back over there tomorrow. I can tell that Wes, Angie, and I are going to be spending a lot of time together.

Maybe this move won't be so bad after all.

EPILOGUE
ANGIE

13 months later (Valentine's Day)

The ocean waves crash in the distance as the descending sun warms my face, the sand hot beneath my bare feet. A violin plays up ahead, Willow's cue to start walking out. She gives me one last look in her long, flowy, golden yellow dress, her brown hair braided into a crown atop her head as she holds a bouquet of white lilies.

Taking my hand, she says, "You ready?"

My smile is wide. "I've been ready for this my whole life."

She squeezes once and nods before turning around and walking out onto the beach.

I take a deep, steadying breath, looking down at the canary diamond ring sitting on my finger, small white diamonds circling the silver band. On my other hand is the golden spiral ring we picked out the first time we came to Antigua, stacked on top of my grandmother's sapphire ring. I told Asher I didn't need a diamond, but he insisted we do it right.

"We started here," he had said, down on one knee under-

neath the Eiffel Tower, tapping the large yellow diamond and running his finger along the band, circling it all the way back around to the top. *"And ended up here again. We always find our way back to each other. Je t'aime, mon rayon de soleil."*

And now I'm about to get my happily ever after with him. The love of my life. The man who has been with me through so many ups and downs. Who knows me better than anyone in this world.

We chose to get married at Wesley's Antigua resort, because it's where everything changed for us. Though on paper, it's listed as a vow renewal, because we already stayed in the honeymoon villa as newlyweds last year. We opted for the "deluxe suite" this time to keep up the ruse.

Simon and Faris jokingly accused me of copying them by having a beach wedding two and a half years after their lavish beach wedding in the Bahamas. I told them to suck a clown dick.

Without an ounce of hesitation, I step forward when the music changes to a rendition of "Canon in D," holding my bouquet of yellow and white lilies as Wesley offers his arm. Without Dad here, it was only right to have him walk me down the aisle, even though he is Asher's Best Man.

Asher stands beneath a simple white arch, dressed in a fitted midnight blue tuxedo. His auburn red hair is styled back, matching perfectly with the orange-and-red sky behind him. If I'm his sunshine, then he's my sunset.

My calm in the storm, always able to bring me back down to earth.

My peace.

When he sees me, his face splits into the widest, most heart-stopping grin. Like I'm the only person in the world. His chest rises and falls, and he swipes quickly under his eye as we walk toward him.

He is so unbelievably handsome.

Willow stands to the left of the archway, the officiant standing behind Asher. As we walk past our guests, I give a small wave to my mom, who is standing next to Luca, Faris, and Simon, and behind them, Wesley's secretary, Nelle—clearly, they are sleeping together still—and Bryn and her husband. We wanted to keep it small, and as I look around now, I realize these people right here are all I will ever need.

My friends. My family.

All that's missing is our dogs, who would not have done well on a plane. Max offered to watch them back home, even though he and his wife, Kayla, are in the middle of finalizing their divorce. We were all stunned when we found out she had actually been having an affair, usually while Max was out playing pickleball.

I shake the thoughts from my head. I can't be thinking about affairs and divorce as I walk down the aisle.

Coming to a stop in front of the archway, Wesley kisses my cheek as he unlinks our arms and goes to stand next to Asher, clapping him on both shoulders. I hand my bouquet to Willow before stepping up to Asher and placing my hands in his, fighting back my own tears. A wavy strand of hair comes loose from my long, elegant braid before Asher lovingly swipes it away from my face and tucks it behind my ear.

My heart overflows as I wonder, what did I do to deserve this man?

The officiant begins by welcoming everyone and sharing a few words about love and life. Then we finally get to the vows, which we agreed to write ourselves.

My hands shake as I look up at him and recite from memory, "Asher. We've known each other for so long. We've been apart, we've been together, and I know now that being together is the only option for me. Life with you is so much more exciting and full of joy and adventure. Laughter and love. And the fact that we found each other again just proves we belong together. You are the Lone Star to my Princess Vespa."

A few laughs erupt from the guests as I continue, "I love you so much, and I promise to love you every day for the rest of my life. My friend. My husband. My love."

Behind me, Willow sniffles. I turn to her, eyes wide. Is she actually crying? My cynical, hard-ass best friend, crying tears of joy? Now I know I must be dreaming. My lip sticks out in a pout as I turn back to face Asher.

"Angie. My Sunshine. My one true love. You already own my heart, and you will always be a part of me. We've been through so much together, and I promise to be there for you until my last breath, spending every moment caring for you and trying to make you happier than the day before. Until we're old and wrinkly, watching sunsets together just like this. In every country, in every language, I love you so much. My friend. My love. My wife."

Asher and I kiss, and just like that, we're married. For real, this time. My heart is about to burst out of my chest. When we break the kiss, his arms wrap around me and squeeze tight, and I hear him inhale at the top of my head before kissing it. Willow hands me my flowers, and Asher and I walk down the sandy aisle hand in hand as the violinist plays "Reunited."

After the ceremony, and some pictures on the beach with the photographer, we all head to a private area on the resort property. Strings of market lights hang over two round tables covered in yellow rose petals, and an open space that will soon be the dance floor.

Next to a table filled with giant cupcakes from Gina's bakery, a DJ plays upbeat pop music as we grab drinks from the outside bar, and everyone stands around talking.

My heart swells when I see Asher and my mom laughing together. We're all truly a family now.

Simon approaches Willow and me mid-conversation. "Okay, two for two," he says, draping his arms over my shoulder and around her waist. "What beach are *you* getting married at, Willow?"

She levels him with a death glare as I burst out laughing.

"She doesn't strike me as a beach bride," I say. "Can you imagine?"

"Luca won't let us elope, so I'm angling for City Hall." She takes a long swig of her drink as Simon and I gasp.

"Dear god," he says.

Willow and Luca got engaged four months ago after winning the annual pickleball tournament, beating Max and me in the final round.

Asher proposed a few weeks later on our trip to Paris, but unlike Willow, I did not want a long engagement. We had already lost so much time together. We were more than ready.

I started working with him on the travel agent business soon after our first trip, and Bryn offered me a freelance position with the company to help manage their social media accounts until I was fully trained.

So far, the Antigua Pickleball vacation has been our best seller.

Family therapy has been incredibly healing and has brought us all together in a way I never thought possible. I can feel my dad here with us now, and it brings me nothing but joy.

We arrived in Antigua a few days ago with most of the other guests, where we've all been keeping busy playing pickleball and relaxing on the beach. Asher even taught us how to surf.

When we take our seats for dinner, Asher and I are seated alone at the smaller table as waiters serve us all chicken piccata, garlic mashed potatoes, roasted asparagus, and warm buttered rolls.

Laughter and conversation float around us like a melody. I can't remember a time I've been happier.

He leans in to kiss my cheek and says, "Tell me one good thing that happened today...and you can't say getting married. That's too easy."

"Hmm..." I tap my finger to my chin. "I guess...it would have to be when I found out I'm pregnant," I say evenly, grabbing a roll off my plate.

He nods as he starts cutting a piece of his chicken. "I—" He freezes, whipping his head toward me. "Wait. Are you serious right now? You're not kidding?"

I shake my head, unable to stop the smile overtaking my face. "Not kidding. Took a test this morning. It's still early, so we have to keep it quiet for now."

His mouth drops open in shock, and I tip my head back laughing as his fork and knife clatter onto the plate. He runs a hand through his styled hair, messing it up slightly before pulling me in for a crushing kiss. Smiling against my lips, he says, "Looks like there's a new trio in town."

"You're not scared?" I ask softly.

His hand comes to rest on my stomach below the table, where the others can't see. I'm nowhere near showing yet, but my heart flutters at the thought of my belly swelling with our child inside.

"Scared? Not with you by my side, Sunshine. Too many good days ahead to be afraid."

Stay tuned for Max's story...

In the meantime, please consider subscribing to my newsletter for bonus content, ramblings, and other things that totally normal authors do.

ACKNOWLEDGMENTS

This book would not be possible without the support of my incredible family, who always believe in me and cheer me on. My husband, for putting up with my moods. My kids, who think I'm a best-selling author (maybe one day I can prove you right).

My amazing friends in our own version of West Brook. I love you and cherish our friendships. I will never take for granted how lucky I am to have this community.

My fellow authors on Threads and Instagram, I have learned so much from you. Thank you for all your advice and support!

Emilie, my editor, for helping make this story the best it can possibly be. Thank you for the unhinged notes and texts. I hope we meet in person one day!

And to everyone who has taken a chance on me and my stories. As an indie author, it makes a world of difference. THANK YOU!

www.ingramcontent.com/pod-product-compliance
Lightning Source LLC
LaVergne TN
LVHW091250150826
845673LV00006B/1381

* 9 7 9 8 9 9 0 2 8 9 7 4 1 *